Scenarios:

A "Nameless Detective" Casebook

Other Five Star Titles
by Bill Pronzini:

Step to the Graveyard Easy
The Gallows Land

Scenarios:

A "Nameless Detective" Casebook

BILL PRONZINI

Five Star • Waterville, Maine

Scenarios:

A "Nameless Detective" Casebook

Contents

Preface

In terms of life on the printed page, the "Nameless Detective" celebrates his thirty-fifth birthday in 2003. During his three and a half decades, he has appeared in twenty-eight novels and more than forty shorter works, and has undergone professional and personal highs and lows too numerous to mention here. Those various changes, for the most part chronicled in his novel-length adventures, are the reason for the seeming lack of connective tissue among some of the stories which appear in the following pages. New readers are invited—I might even say encouraged—to seek out such novels as *Hoodwink*, *Shackles*, *Illusions*, *Crazybone*, and *Bleeders* in order to fill in the gaps.

The fourteen selections here span the entire thirty-five years of "Nameless's" existence. The opening story, "It's a Lousy World," is his first recorded case, having been published originally in *Alfred Hitchcock's Mystery Magazine* in 1968. The final entry, "Wrong Place, Wrong Time," is his most recent outing in the short form.

A few of the dozen tales sandwiched between invite comment. "The Ghosts of Ragged-Ass Gulch" was written late in 1981, one of four longish novelettes commissioned by a Japanese publisher for a "Nameless" volume published only in that country. Its publication here is the first English language appearance in its original form. (I confess to having expanded and substantially revised the story into the novel *Nightshades*. One of the other novelettes was likewise cannibalized, into

Quicksilver; the remaining two, "Who's Calling?" and "Booktaker," appear in the first collection of "Nameless" shorts, *Casefile*.)

"*La Bellezza delle Bellezze*" and "The Big Bite" are also cannibalized stories, the former incorporated into *Epitaphs*, the latter expanded into the opening three chapters of *Bleeders*. As is the case with "The Ghosts of Ragged-Ass Gulch," these two stories are self-contained and substantially different in form and content from their novelized versions. For that reason it seems fair and reasonable to offer them here in the form in which they were initially written.

"Season of Sharing" was written on commission for Crippen & Landru, for publication as their 2001 Christmas gift pamphlet. It is the third collaboration between my wife Marcia Muller's San Francisco-based sleuth, Sharon McCone, and "Nameless" on a common case; the previous two were a novel, *Double*, and a short story, "Cache and Carry."

As the body of work about "Nameless" attests, he has been a major player in my life and career. In many ways he is my alter ego; he is also a friend, and has sometimes even been (I hope he won't take offense) a much-needed cash cow. He's far from perfect, God knows, but he is hardworking, caring, honest, and pretty good at his job. I like to believe he's also a relatively nice guy, the sort others would enjoy having a beer with or inviting over for dinner. If he comes across that way to you, then I've been pretty good at my job, too.

Bill Pronzini
Petaluma, California

It's a Lousy World

Colly Babcock was shot to death on the night of September 9, in an alley between Twenty-Ninth and Valley streets in the Glen Park District of San Francisco. Two police officers, cruising, spotted him coming out the rear door of Budget Liquors there, carrying a metal box. Colly ran when he saw them. The officers gave chase, calling out for him to halt, but he just kept running; one of the cops fired a warning shot, and when Colly didn't heed it the officer pulled up and fired again. He was aiming low, trying for the legs, but in the half-light of the alley it was a blind shot. The bullet hit Colly in the small of the back and killed him instantly.

I read about it the following morning over coffee and undercooked eggs in a cafeteria on Taylor Street, a block and a half from my office. The story was on an inside page, concise and dispassionate; they teach that kind of objective writing in the journalism classes. Just the cold facts. A man dies, but he's nothing more than a statistic, a name in black type, a faceless nonentity to be considered and then forgotten along with your breakfast coffee.

Unless you knew him.

Unless he was your friend.

Very carefully I folded the newspaper and put it into my coat pocket. Then I stood up from the table, went out to the street. The wind was up, blowing in off the Bay; rubble swirled and eddied in the Tenderloin gutters. The air smelled

11

of salt and dark rain and human pollution.

I walked into the face of the wind, toward my office.

"How's the job, Colly?"

"Oh, fine, just fine."

"No problems?"

"No, none at all."

"Stick with it, Colly."

"Sure. I'm a new man."

"Straight all the way?"

"Straight all the way."

Inside the lobby of my building, I found an out-of-order sign taped to the closed elevator doors. Yeah, that figured. I went around to the stairs, up to the second floor, and along the hallway to my office.

The door was unlocked, standing open a few inches. I tensed when I saw it like that, and reached out with the tips of my fingers and pushed it all the way open. But there was no trouble. The woman sitting in the chair in front of my desk had never been trouble for anyone.

Colly Babcock's widow.

I moved inside, shut the door behind me.

"Hello, Lucille."

Her hands were clasped tightly in the lap of a plain black dress. She said, "The man down the hall, the CPA—he let me in. He said you wouldn't mind."

"I don't mind."

"You heard, I guess? About Colly?"

"Yes," I said. "What can I say, Lucille?"

"You were his friend. You helped him."

"Maybe I didn't help him enough."

"He didn't do it," Lucille said. "He didn't steal that money. He didn't do all those robberies like they're saying."

I stayed silent.

12

"Colly and I were married thirty-one years," she said. "Don't you think I would have known?"

I still didn't say anything.

"I always knew," she said.

I sat down, looking at her. She was a big woman, handsome—a strong woman. There was strength in the line of her mouth, and in her eyes, round and gray, tinged with red now from the crying. She had stuck by Colly through two prison terms and twenty-odd years of running, and hiding, and looking over her shoulder. Yes, I thought, she would always have known.

But I said, "The papers said Colly was coming out the back door of the liquor store carrying a metal box. The police found a hundred and six dollars in the box, and the door jimmied open."

"I know what the papers said, and I know what the police are saying. But they're wrong. Wrong."

"He was there, Lucille."

"I know that," she said. "Colly liked to walk in the evenings. A long walk and then a drink when he came home; it helped him to relax. That was how he came to be there."

I shifted position on my chair, not speaking.

Lucille said, "Colly was always nervous when he was doing burglaries. That was one of the ways I could tell. He'd get irritable, and he couldn't sleep."

"He wasn't like that lately?"

"You saw him a few weeks ago," she said. "Did he look that way to you?"

"No," I said, "he didn't."

"We were happy," Lucille said. "No more running. And no more waiting. We were *happy*."

My mouth felt dry. "What about his job?"

"They gave Colly a raise last week. A fifteen-dollar raise.

13

We went to dinner to celebrate, down on the Wharf."

"You were getting along all right on what he made?" I said. "Nothing came up?"

"Nothing. We even had a little bank account started." She bit her lower lip. "We were going to Hawaii next year, or the year after. Colly always wanted to go to Hawaii."

I looked at my hands. They seemed big and awkward resting on the desk top; I took them away and put them in my lap. "These Glen Park robberies started a month and a half ago," I said. "The police estimate the total amount taken at close to ten thousand dollars. You could get to Hawaii pretty well on that kind of money."

"Colly didn't do those robberies," she said.

What could I say? God knew, and Lucille knew, that Colly had never been a saint; but this time she was convinced he'd been innocent. Nothing, it seemed, was going to change that in her eyes.

I got a cigarette from my pocket and made a thing of lighting it. The smoke added more dryness to my mouth. Without looking at her, I said, "What do you want me to do, Lucille?"

"I want you to prove Colly didn't do what they're saying he did."

"I'd like nothing better, you know that. But how can I do it? The evidence—"

"Damn the evidence!" Her wide mouth trembled with the sudden emotion. "Colly was innocent, I tell you! I won't have him buried with this last mark against his name. I won't have it."

"Lucille, listen to me . . ."

"I won't listen," she said. "Colly was your friend. You stood up for him with the parole board. You helped him find his job. You talked to him, gave him guidance. He was a different man, a new man, and you helped make him that way. Will you sit here and tell me you believe he threw it all away for a few thousand dollars?"

I didn't say anything; I still could not meet her eyes. I stared down at the burning cigarette in my fingers, watching the smoke rise, curling, a gray spiral in the cold air of the office.

"Or don't you care whether he was innocent or not?" she said.

"I care."

"Then help me. Find out the truth."

"All right," I said. Her anger and grief, and her absolute certainty that Colly had been innocent, had finally got through to me; I could not have turned her down now if there had been ten times the evidence against him. "All right, Lucille, I'll see what I can do."

It was drizzling when I got to the Hall of Justice. Some of the chill had gone out of the air, but the wind was stronger now. The clouds overhead looked black and swollen, ready to burst.

I parked my car on Bryant Street, went past the sycamores on the narrow front lawn, up the concrete steps, and inside. The plainclothes detective division, General Works, was on the fourth floor; I took the elevator. Eberhardt had been promoted to lieutenant not too long ago and had his own private office now, but I caught myself glancing over toward his old desk. Force of habit; it had been a while since I'd visited him at the Hall.

He was in and willing to see me. When I entered his office he was shuffling through some reports and scowling. He was my age, pushing fifty, and he seemed to have been fashioned of an odd contrast of sharp angles and smooth, blunt planes: square forehead, sharp nose and chin, thick and blocky upper body, long legs, and angular hands. Today he was wearing a brown suit that hadn't been pressed in a month; his tie was crooked; there was a collar button missing from his shirt. And he had a fat, purplish bruise over his left eye.

"All right," he said, "make it quick."

"What happened to your eye?"

"I bumped into a doorknob."

"Sure you did."

"Yeah," he said. "You come here to pass the time of day, or was there something?"

"I'd like a favor, Eb."

"Sure. And I'd like three weeks' vacation."

"I want to look at an Officer's Felony Report."

"Are you nuts? Get the hell out of here."

The words didn't mean anything. He was always gruff and grumbly while he was working; and we'd been friends for more years than either of us cared to remember, ever since we went through the Police Academy together after World War II and then joined the force here in the city.

I said, "There was a shooting last night. Two squad-car cops killed a man running away from the scene of a burglary in Glen Park."

"So?"

"The victim was a friend of mine."

He gave me a look. "Since when do you have burglars for friends?"

"His name was Colly Babcock," I said. "He did two stretches in San Quentin, both for burglary; I helped send him up the first time. I also helped get him out on parole the second time and into a decent job."

"Uh-huh. I remember the name. I also heard about the

shooting last night. Too bad this pal of yours turned bad again, but then a lot of them do—as if you didn't know."

I was silent.

"I get it," Eberhardt said. "You don't think so. That's why you're here."

"Colly's wife doesn't think so. I guess maybe I don't either."

"I can't let you look at any reports. And even if I could, it's not my department. Robbery'll be handling it. Internal Affairs, too."

"You could pull some strings."

"I could," he said, "but I won't. I'm up to my ass in work. I just don't have the time."

I got to my feet. "Well, thanks, Eb." I went to the door, put my hand on the knob, but before I rotated it he made a noise behind me. I turned.

"If things go all right," he said, scowling at me, "I'll be off duty in a couple of hours. If I happen to get down by Robbery on the way out, maybe I'll stop in. Maybe."

"I'd appreciate it if you would."

"Give me a call later on. At home."

"Thanks, Eb."

"Yeah," he said. "So what are you standing there for? Get the hell out of here and let me work."

I found Tommy Belknap in a bar called Luigi's, out in the Mission District.

He was drinking whiskey at the long bar, leaning his head on his arms and staring at the wall. Two men in work clothes were drinking beer and eating sandwiches from lunch pails at the other end, and in the middle an old lady in a black shawl sipped red wine from a glass held with arthritic fingers. I sat on a stool next to Tommy and said hello.

He turned his head slowly, his eyes moving upward. His face was an anemic white, and his bald head shone with beaded perspiration. He had trouble focusing his eyes; he swiped at them with the back of one veined hand. He was pretty drunk. And I was pretty sure I knew why.

"Hey," he said when he recognized me, "have a drink, will you?"

"Not just now."

He got his glass to his lips with shaky fingers, managed to drink without spilling any of the whiskey. "Colly's dead," he said.

"Yeah. I know."

"They killed him last night," Tommy said. "They shot him in the back."

"Take it easy, Tommy."

"He was my friend."

"He was my friend, too."

"Colly was a nice guy. Lousy goddamn cops had no right to shoot him like that."

"He was robbing a liquor store," I said.

"Hell he was!" Tommy said. He swiveled on the stool and pushed a finger at my chest. "Colly was straight, you hear that? Just like me. Ever since we both got out of Q."

"You sure about that?"

"Damn right I am."

"Then who did those burglaries in Glen Park?"

"How should I know?"

"Come on, you get around. You know people, you hear things. There must be something on the earie."

"Nothing," he said. "Don't know."

"Kids?" I said. "Street punks?"

"Don't know."

"But it wasn't Colly? You'd know if it was Colly?"

"Colly was straight," Tommy said. "And now he's dead."

He put his head down on his arms again. The bartender came over; he was a fat man with a reddish handlebar mustache. "You can't sleep in here, Tommy," he said. "You ain't even supposed to be in here while you're on parole."

"Colly's dead," Tommy said, and there were tears in his eyes.

"Let him alone," I said to the bartender.

"I can't have him sleeping in here."

I took out my wallet and put a ten-dollar bill on the bar. "Give him another drink," I said, "and then let him sleep it off in the back room. The rest of the money is for you."

The bartender looked at me, looked at the sawbuck, looked at Tommy "All right," he said. "What the hell."

I went out into the rain.

D. E. O'Mira and Company, Wholesale Plumbing Supplies, was a big two-story building that took up three-quarters of a block on Berry Street, out near China Basin. I parked in front and went inside. In the center of a good-sized office was a switchboard walled in glass, with a card taped to the front that said Information. A dark-haired girl wearing a set of headphones was sitting inside, and when I asked her if Mr. Templeton was in she said he was at a meeting uptown and wouldn't be back all day. Mr. Templeton was the office manager, the man I had spoken to about giving Colly Babcock a job when he was paroled from San Quentin.

Colly had worked in the warehouse, and his immediate supervisor was a man I had never met named Harlin. I went through a set of swing doors opposite the main entrance, down a narrow, dark passage screened on both sides. On my left when I emerged into the warehouse was a long service counter; behind it were display shelves, and behind them long rows of bins that stretched the length and width of the building. Straight ahead, through an open doorway, I could see the loading dock and a yard cluttered with soil pipe and other supplies. On my right was a windowed office with two desks, neither occupied; an old man in a pair of baggy brown slacks, a brown vest, and a battered slouch hat stood before a side counter under the windows.

The old man didn't look I up when I came into the office. A foul-smelling cigar danced in his thin mouth as he shuffled papers. I cleared my throat and said, "Excuse me."

He looked at me then, grudgingly. "What is it?"

"Are you Mr. Harlin?"

"That's right."

I told him who I was and what I did. I was about to ask him about Colly when a couple of guys came into the office and one of them plunked himself down at the nearest desk. I said to Harlin, "Could we talk someplace private?"

"Why? What're you here about?"

"Colly Babcock," I said.

He made a grunting sound, scribbled on one of his papers with a pencil stub, and then led me out onto the dock. We walked along there, past a warehouseman loading crated cast-iron sinks from a pallet into a pickup truck, and up to the wide, double-door entrance to an adjoining warehouse.

The old man stopped and turned to me. "We can talk here."

"Fine. You were Colly's supervisor, is that right?"

"I was."

"Tell me how you felt about him."

"You won't hear anything bad, if that's what you're looking for."

"That's not what I'm looking for."

He considered that for a moment, then shrugged and said,

"Colly was a good worker. Did what you told him, no fuss. Quiet sort, kept to himself mostly."

"You knew about his prison record?"

"I knew. All of us here did. Nothing was ever said to Colly about it, though. I saw to that."

"Did he seem happy with the job?"

"Happy enough," Harlin said. "Never complained, if that's what you mean."

"No friction with any of the other men?"

"No. He got along fine with everybody."

A horn sounded from inside the adjoining warehouse and a yellow forklift carrying a pallet of lavatories came out. We stepped out of the way as the thing clanked and belched past.

I asked Harlin, "When you heard about what happened to Colly last night—what was your reaction?"

"Didn't believe it," he answered. "Still don't. None of us do."

I nodded. "Did Colly have any particular friend here? Somebody he ate lunch with regularly—like that?"

"Kept to himself for the most part, like I said. But he stopped with Sam Biehler for a beer a time or two after work; Sam mentioned it."

"I'd like to talk to Biehler, if it's all right."

"Is with me," the old man said. He paused, chewing on his cigar. "Listen, there any chance Colly didn't do what the papers say he did?"

"There might be. That's what I'm trying to find out."

"Anything I can do," he said, "you let me know."

"I'll do that."

We went back inside and I spoke to Sam Biehler, a tall, slender guy with a mane of silver hair that gave him, despite his work clothes, a rather distinguished appearance.

"I don't mind telling you," he said, "I don't believe a damned word of it. I'd have had to be there to see it with my own eyes before I'd believe it, and maybe not even then."

"I understand you and Colly stopped for a beer occasionally?"

"Once a week maybe, after work. Not in a bar; Colly couldn't go to a bar because of his parole. At my place. Then afterward I'd give him a ride home."

"What did you talk about?"

"The job, mostly," Biehler said. "What the company could do to improve things out here in the warehouse. I guess you know the way fellows talk."

"Uh-huh. Anything else?"

"About Colly's past, that what you're getting at?"

"Yes."

"Just once," Biehler said. "Colly told me a few things. But I never pressed him on it. I don't like to pry."

"What was it he told you?"

"That he was never going back to prison. That he was through with the kind of life he'd led before." Biehler's eyes sparked, as if challenging me. "And you know something? I been on this earth for fifty-nine years and I've known a lot of men in that time. You get so you can tell."

"Tell what, Mr. Biehler?"

"Colly wasn't lying," he said.

I spent an hour at the main branch of the library in Civic Center, reading through back issues of the *Chronicle* and the *Examiner*. The Glen Park robberies had begun a month and a half ago, and I had paid only passing attention to them at the time.

When I had acquainted myself with the details, I went back to my office and checked in with my answering service.

No calls. Then I called Lucille Babcock.

"The police were here earlier," she said. "They had a search warrant."

"Did they find anything?"

"There was nothing to find."

"What did they say?"

"They asked a lot of questions. They wanted to know about bank accounts and safe-deposit boxes."

"Did you cooperate with them?"

"Of course."

"Good," I said. I told her what I had been doing all day, what the people I'd talked with had said.

"You see?" she said. "Nobody who knew Colly can believe he was guilty."

"Nobody but the police."

"Damn the police," she said.

I sat holding the phone. There were things I wanted to say, but they all seemed trite and meaningless. Pretty soon I told her I would be in touch, leaving it at that, and put the receiver back in its cradle.

It was almost five o'clock. I locked up the office, drove home to my flat in Pacific Heights, drank a beer and ate a pastrami sandwich, and then lit a cigarette and dialed Eberhardt's home number. It was his gruff voice that answered.

"Did you stop by Robbery before you left the Hall?" I asked.

"Yeah. I don't know why."

"We're friends, that's why."

"That doesn't stop you from being a pain in the ass sometimes."

"Can I come over, Eb?"

"You can if you get here before eight o'clock," he said.

"I'm going to bed then, and Dana has orders to bar all the doors and windows and take the telephone off the hook. I plan to get a good night's sleep for a change."

"I'll be there in twenty minutes," I said.

Eberhardt lived in Noe Valley, up at the back end near Twin Peaks. The house was big and painted white, a two-story frame job with a trimmed lawn and lots of flowers in front. If you knew Eberhardt, the house was sort of symbolic; it typified everything the honest, hardworking cop was dedicated to protecting. I had a hunch he knew it, too; and if he did, he got a certain amount of satisfaction from the knowledge. That was the way he was.

I parked in his sloping driveway and went up and rang the bell. His wife Dana, a slender, attractive brunette with a lot of patience, let me in, asked how I was, and showed me into the kitchen, closing the door behind her as she left.

Eberhardt was sitting at the table having a pipe and a cup of coffee. The bruise over his eye had been smeared with some kind of pinkish ointment; it made him look a little silly, but I knew better than to tell him so.

"Have a seat," he said, and I had one. "You want some coffee?"

"Thanks."

He got me a cup, then indicated a manila envelope lying on the table. Without saying anything, sucking at his pipe, he made an elaborate effort to ignore me as I picked up the envelope and opened it.

Inside was the report made by the two patrolmen, Avinisi and Carstairs, who had shot and killed Colly Babcock in the act of robbing the Budget Liquor Store. I read it over carefully, and my eye caught on one part, a couple of sentences, under "Effects." When I was through I put the report back in the envelope and returned it to the table.

Eberhardt looked at me then. "Well?"

"One item," I said, "that wasn't in the papers."

"What's that?"

"They found a pint of Kesslers in a paper bag in Colly's coat pocket."

He shrugged. "It was a liquor store, wasn't it? Maybe he slipped it into his pocket on the way out."

"And put it into a paper bag first?"

"People do funny things," he said.

"Yeah," I said. I drank some of the coffee and then got on my feet. "I'll let you get to bed, Eb. Thanks again."

He grunted. "You owe me a favor. Just remember that."

"I won't forget."

"You and the elephants," he said.

It was still raining the next morning, another dismal day. I drove over to Chenery Street and wedged my car into a downhill parking slot a half-block from the three-room apartment Lucille and Colly Babcock had called home for the past year. I hurried through the rain, feeling the chill of it on my face, and mounted sagging wooden steps to the door.

Lucille answered immediately. She wore the same black dress she'd had on yesterday, and the same controlled mask of grief; it would be a long time before that grief faded and she was able to get on with her life. Maybe never, unless somebody proved her right about Colly's innocence.

I sat in the old, stuffed leather chair by the window: Colly's chair. Lucille said, "Can I get you something?"

I shook my head. "What about you? Have you eaten anything today? Or yesterday?"

"No," she answered.

"You have to eat, Lucille."

"Maybe later. Don't worry, I'm not suicidal. I won't starve myself to death."

I managed a small smile. "All right," I said.

"Why are you here?" she asked. "Do you have any news?"

"No, not yet." I had an idea, but it was only that, and too early. I did not want to instill any false hopes. "I just wanted to ask you a few more questions."

"Oh. What questions?"

"You mentioned yesterday that Colly liked to take walks in the evening. Was he in the habit of walking to any particular place, or in any particular direction?"

"No," Lucille said. "He just liked to walk. He was gone for a couple of hours sometimes."

"He never told you where he'd been?"

"Just here and there in the neighborhood."

Here and there in the neighborhood, I thought. The alley where Colly had been shot was eleven blocks from this apartment. He could have walked in a straight line, or he could have gone roundabout in any direction.

I asked, "Colly liked to have a nightcap when he came back from these walks, didn't he?"

"He did, yes."

"He kept liquor here, then?"

"One bottle of bourbon. That's all."

I rotated my hat in my hands. "I wonder if I could have a small drink, Lucille. I know it's early, but . . ."

She nodded and got up and went to a squat cabinet near the kitchen door. She slid the panel open in front, looked inside. Then she straightened. "I'm sorry," she said. "We . . . I seem to be out."

I stood. "It's okay. I should be going anyway."

"Where will you go now?"

"To see some people." I paused. "Would you happen to have a photograph of Colly? A snapshot, something like that?"

"I think so. Why do you want it?"

"I might need to show it around," I said. "Here in the neighborhood."

She seemed satisfied with that. "I'll see if I can find one for you."

I waited while she went into the bedroom. A couple of minutes later she returned with a black-and-white snap of Colly, head and shoulders, that had been taken in a park somewhere. He was smiling, one eyebrow raised in mock raffishness.

I put the snap into my pocket and thanked Lucille and told her I would be in touch again pretty soon. Then I went to the door and let myself out.

The skies seemed to have parted like the Red Sea. Drops of rain as big as hail pellets lashed the sidewalk. Thunder rumbled in the distance, edging closer. I pulled the collar of my overcoat tight around my neck and made a run for my car.

It was after four o'clock when I came inside a place called Tay's Liquors on Whitney Street and stood dripping water on the floor. There was a heater on a shelf just inside the door, and I allowed myself the luxury of its warmth for a few seconds. Then I crossed to the counter.

A young guy wearing a white shirt and a Hitler mustache got up from a stool near the cash register and walked over to me. He smiled, letting me see crooked teeth that weren't very clean. "Wet enough for you?" he said.

No, I thought, I want it to get a lot wetter so I can

drown. Dumb question, dumb answer. But all I said was, "Maybe you can help me."

"Sure," he said. "Name your poison."

He was brimming with originality. I took the snapshot of Colly Babcock from my pocket, extended it across the counter and asked, "Did you see this man two nights ago, sometime around eleven o'clock?" It was the same thing I had done and the same question I had asked at least twenty times already. I had been driving and walking the streets of Glen Park for four hours now, and I had been to four liquor stores, five corner groceries, two large chain markets, a delicatessen, and half a dozen bars that sold off-sale liquor. So far I had come up with nothing except possibly a head cold.

The young guy gave me a slanted look. "Cop?" he asked, but his voice was still cheerful.

I showed him the photostat of my investigator's license. He shrugged, then studied the photograph. "Yeah," he said finally, "I did see this fellow a couple of nights ago. Nice old duck. We talked a little about the Forty-Niners."

I stopped feeling cold and I stopped feeling frustrated. I said, "About what time did he come in?"

"Let's see. Eleven-thirty or so, I think."

Fifteen minutes before Colly had been shot in an alley three and a half blocks away. "Do you remember what he bought?"

"Bourbon—a pint. Medium price."

"Kesslers?"

"Yeah, I think it was."

"Okay, good. What's your name?"

"My name? Hey, wait a minute, I don't want to get involved in anything . . ."

"Don't worry, it's not what you're thinking."

28

It took a little more convincing, but he gave me his name finally and I wrote it down in my notebook. And thanked him and hurried out of there.

I had something more than an idea now.

Eberhardt said, "I ought to knock you flat on your ass."

He had just come out of his bedroom, eyes foggy with sleep, hair standing straight up, wearing a wine-colored bathrobe. Dana stood beside him looking fretful.

"I'm sorry I woke you up, Eb," I said. "But I didn't think you'd be in bed this early. It's only six o'clock."

He said something I didn't hear, but that Dana heard. She cracked him on the arm to show her disapproval, then turned and left us alone.

Eberhardt went over and sat on the couch and glared at me. "I've had about six hours' sleep in the past forty-eight," he said. "I got called out last night after you left, I didn't get home until three a.m., I was up at seven, I worked all goddamn day and knocked off early so I could get some sleep, and what happens? I'm in bed ten minutes and you show up."

"Eb, it's important."

"What is?"

"Colly Babcock."

"Ah, Christ, you don't give up, do you?"

"Sometimes I do, but not this time. Not now." I told him what I had learned from the guy at Tay's Liquors.

"So Babcock bought a bottle there," Eberhardt said. "So what?"

"If he was planning to burglarize a liquor store, why would he have bothered to buy a bottle fifteen minutes before?"

"Hell, the job might have been spur-of-the-moment."

"Colly didn't work that way. When he was pulling them,

29

they were all carefully planned well in advance. Always."

"He was getting old," Eberhardt said. "People change."

"You didn't know Colly. Besides, there are a few other things."

"Such as?"

"The burglaries themselves. They were all done the same way—back door jimmied, marks on the jamb and lock made with a hand bar or something. " I paused. "They didn't find any tool like that on Colly. Or inside the store either."

"Maybe he got rid of it."

"When did he have time? They caught him coming out the door."

Eberhardt scowled. I had his interest now. "Go ahead," he said.

"The pattern of the burglaries, like I was saying, is doors jimmied, drawers rifled, papers and things strewn about. No fingerprints, but it smacks of amateurism. Or somebody trying to make it look like amateurism."

"And Babcock was a professional."

"He could have done the book," I said. "He used lock picks and glass cutters to get into a place, never anything like a hand bar. He didn't ransack; he always knew exactly what he was after. He never deviated from that, Eb. Not once."

Eberhardt got to his feet and paced around for a time. Then he stopped in front of me and said, "So what do you think, then?"

"You figure it."

"Yeah," he said slowly, "I can figure it, all right. But I don't like it. I don't like it at all."

"And Colly?" I said. "You think he liked it?"

Eberhardt turned abruptly, went to the telephone. He spoke to someone at the Hall of Justice, then someone else. When he hung up, he was already shrugging out of his bathrobe.

He gave me a grim look. "I hope you're wrong, you know that."

"I hope I'm not," I said.

I was sitting in my flat, reading one of the pulps from my collection of several thousand issues, when the telephone rang just before eleven o'clock. It was Eberhardt, and the first thing he said was, "You weren't wrong."

I didn't say anything, waiting.

"Avinisi and Carstairs," he said bitterly. "Each of them on the force a little more than two years. The old story: bills, long hours, not enough pay—and greed. They cooked up the idea one night while they were cruising Glen Park, and it worked just fine until two nights ago. Who'd figure the cops for it?"

"You have any trouble with them?"

"No. I wish they'd given me some so I could have slapped them with a resisting arrest charge, too."

"How did it happen with Colly?"

"It was the other way around," he said. "Babcock was cutting through the alley when he saw them coming out the rear door. He turned to run and they panicked and Avinisi shot him in the back. When they went to check, Carstairs found a note from Babcock's parole officer in one of his pockets, identifying him as an ex-con. That's when they decided to frame him."

"Look, Eb, I—"

"Forget it," he said. "I know what you're going to say."

"You can't help it if a couple of cops turn out that way."

"I said forget it, all right?" And the line went dead.

I listened to the empty buzzing for a couple of seconds. It's a lousy world, I thought. But sometimes, at least, there is justice.

Then I called Lucille Babcock and told her why her husband had died.

They had a nice funeral for Colly.

The services were held in a small nondenominational church on Monterey Boulevard. There were a lot of flowers, carnations mostly; Lucille said they had been Colly's favorites. Quite a few people came. Tommy Belknap was there, and Sam Biehler and old man Harlin and the rest of them from D. E. O'Mira. Eberhardt, too, which might have seemed surprising unless you knew him. I also saw faces I didn't recognize; the whole thing had gotten a big play in the media.

Afterward, there was the funeral procession to the cemetery in Colma, where we listened to the minister's final words and watched them put Colly into the ground. When it was done I offered to drive Lucille home, but she said no, there were some arrangements she wanted to make with the caretaker for upkeep of the plot; one of her neighbors would stay with her and see to it she got home all right. Then she held my hand and kissed me on the cheek and told me again how grateful she was.

I went to where my car was parked. Eberhardt was waiting; he had ridden down with me.

"I don't like funerals," he said.

"No," I said.

We got into the car. "So what're you planning to do when we get back to the city?" Eberhardt asked.

"I hadn't thought about it."

"Come over to my place. Dana's gone off to visit her sister, and I've got a refrigerator full of beer."

"All right."

"Maybe we'll get drunk," he said.

I nodded. "Maybe we will at that."

The Pulp Connection

The address Eberhardt had given me on the phone was a corner lot in St. Francis Wood, halfway up the western slope of Mt. Davidson. The house there looked like a baronial Spanish villa—a massive two-story stucco affair with black iron trimming, flanked on two sides by evergreens and eucalyptus. It sat on a notch in the slope forty feet above street level, and it commanded an impressive view of Lake Merced and the Pacific Ocean beyond. Even by St. Francis Wood standards—the area is one of San Francisco's moneyed residential sections—it was some place, probably worth half a million or more.

At four o'clock on an overcast weekday afternoon this kind of neighborhood is usually quiet and semi-deserted; today it was teeming with people and traffic. Cars were parked bumper-to-bumper on both fronting streets, among them half a dozen police cruisers and unmarked sedans and a television camera truck. Thirty or forty citizens were grouped along the sidewalks, gawking, and I saw four uniformed cops standing watch in front of the gate and on the stairs that led up to the house.

I didn't know what to make of all this as I drove past and tried to find a place to park. Eberhardt had not said much on the phone, just that he wanted to see me immediately on a police matter at this address. The way it looked, a crime of no small consequence had taken place here today—but why summon me to the scene? I had no idea who lived in the

33

house; I had no rich clients, or any clients at all, except for an appliance outfit that had hired me to do a skip-trace on one of its deadbeat customers.

Frowning, I wedged my car between two others a block away and walked back down to the corner. The uniformed cop on the gate gave me a sharp look as I came up to him, but when I told him my name his manner changed and he said, "Oh, right, Lieutenant Eberhardt's expecting you. Go on up."

So I climbed the stairs under a stone arch and past a terraced rock garden to the porch. Another patrolman stationed there took my name and then led me through an archway and inside.

The interior of the house was dark, and quiet except for the muted sound of voices coming from somewhere in the rear. The foyer and the living room and the hallway we went down were each ordinary enough, furnished in a baroque Spanish style, but the large room the cop ushered me into was anything but ordinary for a place like this. It contained an overstuffed leather chair, a reading lamp, an antique trestle desk-and-chair, and no other furniture except for floor-to-ceiling bookshelves that covered every available inch of wall space; there were even library-type stacks along one side. All the shelves were jammed with paperbacks, some new and some which seemed to date back to the 1940s. As far as I could tell, every one of them was genre—mysteries, westerns, science fiction.

Standing in the middle of the room were Eberhardt and an inspector I recognized named Jordan. Eberhardt was puffing away on one of his battered black briars; the air in the room was blue with smoke. Eighteen months ago, when I owned a two-pack-a-day cigarette habit, the smoke would have started me coughing but also made me hungry for a weed. But I'd gone to a doctor about the cough around that time, and he had found what he was afraid might be a malignant lesion on one lung. I'd had a bad scare for a while; if the lesion had turned out to be malignant, which it hadn't, I would probably be dead or dying by now. There's nothing like a cancer scare and facing your own imminent mortality to make you give up cigarettes for good. I hadn't had one in all those eighteen months, and I would never have one again.

Both Eberhardt and Jordan turned when I came in. Eb said something to the inspector, who nodded and started out. He gave me a nod on his way past that conveyed uncertainty about whether or not I ought to be there. Which made two of us.

Eberhardt was wearing a rumpled blue suit and his usual sour look; but the look seemed tempered a little today with something that might have been embarrassment. And that was odd, too, because I had never known him to be embarrassed by anything while he was on the job.

"You took your time getting here, hotshot," he said.

"Come on, Eb, it's only been half an hour since you called. You can't drive out here from downtown in much less than that." I glanced around at the bookshelves again. "What's all this?"

"The Paperback Room," he said.

"How's that?"

"You heard me. The Paperback Room. There's also a Hardcover Room, a Radio and Television Room, a Movie Room, a Pulp Room, a Comic Art Room, and two or three others I can't remember."

I just looked at him.

"This place belongs to Thomas Murray," he said. "Name mean anything to you?"

"Not offhand."

"Media's done features on him in the past—the King of the Popular Culture Collectors."

The name clicked then in my memory; I had read an article on Murray in one of the Sunday supplements about a year ago. He was a retired manufacturer of electronic components, worth a few million dollars, who spent all his time accumulating popular culture—genre books and magazines, prints of television and theatrical films, old radio shows on tape, comic books and strips, original artwork, Sherlockiana, and other such items. He was reputed to be one of the foremost experts in the country on these subjects, and regularly provided material and copies of material to other collectors, students, and historians for nominal fees.

I said, "Okay, I know who he is. But I—"

"Was," Eberhardt said.

"What?"

"Who he *was*. He's dead—murdered."

"So that's it."

"Yeah, that's it." His mouth turned down in a sardonic scowl. "He was found here by his niece shortly before one o'clock. In a locked room."

"Locked room?"

"Something the matter with your hearing today?" Eberhardt said irritably. "Yes, a damn locked room. We had to break down the door because it was locked from the inside, and we found Murray lying in his own blood on the carpet. Stabbed under the breastbone with a razor-sharp piece of thin steel, like a splinter." He paused, watching me. I kept my expression stoic and attentive. "We also found what looks like a kind of dying message, if you want to call it that."

"What sort of message?"

"You'll see for yourself pretty soon."

"Me? Look, Eb, just why did you get me out here?"

"Because I want your help, damn it. And if you say anything cute about this being a big switch, the cops calling in a private eye for help on a murder case, I won't like it much."

So that was the reason he seemed a little embarrassed. I said, "I wasn't going to make any wisecracks; you know me better than that. If I can help you I'll do it gladly—but I don't know how."

"You collect pulp magazines yourself, don't you?"

"Sure. But what does that have to do with—"

"The homicide took place in the Pulp Room," he said. "And the dying message involves pulp magazines. Okay?"

I was surprised, and twice as curious now, but I said only, "Okay." Eberhardt is not a man you can prod.

He said, "Before we go in there, you'd better know a little of the background. Murray lived here alone except for the niece, Paula Thurman, and a housekeeper named Edith Keeler. His wife died a few years ago, and they didn't have any children. Two other people have keys to the house—a cousin, Walter Cox, and Murray's brother David. We managed to round up all four of those people, and we've got them in a room at the rear of the house.

"None of them claims to know anything about the murder. The housekeeper was out all day; this is the day she does her shopping. The niece is a would-be artist, and she was taking a class at San Francisco State. The cousin was having a long lunch with a girlfriend downtown, and the brother was at Tanforan with another horseplayer. In other words, three of them have alibis for the probable time of Murray's death, but none of the alibis is what you could call unshakable.

"And all of them, with the possible exception of the housekeeper, have strong motives. Murray was worth around three million, and he wasn't exactly generous with his money where his relatives are concerned; he doled out allowances to each of them, but he spent most of his ready cash on his popular-culture collection. They're all in his will—they freely admit that—and each of them stands to inherit a potful now that he's dead.

"They also freely admit, all of them, that they could use the inheritance. Paula Thurman is a nice-looking blonde, around twenty-five, and she wants to go to Europe and pursue an art career. David Murray is about the same age as his brother, late fifties; if the broken veins in his nose are any indication, he's a boozer as well as a horseplayer—a literal loser and going downhill fast. Walter Cox is a mousy little guy who wears glasses about six inches thick; he fancies himself an investments expert but doesn't have the cash to make himself rich—he says—in the stock market. Edith Keeler is around sixty, not too bright, and stands to inherit a token five thousand dollars in Murray's will; that's why she's what your pulp detectives call 'the least likely suspect.' "

He paused again. "Lot of details there, but I figured you'd better know as much as possible. You with me so far?"

I nodded.

"Okay. Now, Murray was one of these regimented types—did everything the same way day after day. Or at least he did when he wasn't off on buying trips or attending popular-culture conventions. He spent two hours every day in each of his Rooms, starting with the Paperback Room at eight a.m. His time in the Pulp Room was from noon until two p.m. While he was in each of these Rooms he would read or watch films or listen to tapes, and he would also answer correspondence pertaining to whatever that Room contained—pulps, paperbacks, TV and radio shows, and so on. Did all his own secretarial work—and kept all his correspondence segregated by Rooms."

I remembered these eccentricities of Murray's being mentioned in the article I had read about him. It had seemed to me then, judging from his quoted comments, that they were calculated in order to enhance his image as King of the Popular Culture Collectors. But if so, it no longer mattered; all that mattered now was that he was dead.

Eberhardt went on, "Three days ago Murray started acting a little strange. He seemed worried about something, but he wouldn't discuss it with anybody; he did tell the housekeeper that he was trying to work out 'a problem.' According to both the niece and the housekeeper, he refused to see either his cousin or his brother during that time; and he also took to locking himself into each of his Rooms during the day and in his bedroom at night, something he had never done before.

"You can figure that as well as I can: he suspected that somebody wanted him dead, and he didn't know how to cope with it. He was probably trying to buy time until he could figure out a way to deal with the situation."

"Only time ran out on him," I said.

"Yeah. What happened as far as we know it is this: the niece came home at twelve forty-five, went to talk to Murray about getting an advance on her allowance and didn't get any answer when she knocked on the door to the Pulp Room. She got worried, she says, went outside and around back, looked in through the window and saw him lying on the floor. She called us right away.

"When we got here and broke down the door, we found Murray lying right where she told us. Like I said before, he'd been stabbed with a splinter-like piece of steel several inches long; the outer two inches had been wrapped with adhesive tape—a kind of handle grip, possibly. The weapon was still in the wound, buried some three inches deep."

I said, "That's not much penetration for a fatal wound."

"No, but it was enough in Murray's case. He was a scrawny man with a concave chest; there wasn't any fat to help protect his vital organs. The weapon penetrated at an upward angle, and the point of it pierced his heart."

I nodded and waited for him to go on.

"We didn't find anything useful when we searched the room," Eberhardt said. "There are two windows, but both of them are nailed shut because Murray was afraid somebody would open one of them and the damp air off the ocean would damage the magazines; the windows hadn't been tampered with. The door hadn't been tampered with either. And there aren't any secret panels or fireplaces with big chimneys or crap like that. Just a dead man alone in a locked room."

"I'm beginning to see what you're up against."

"You've got a lot more to see yet," he said. "Come on."

He led me out into the hallway and down to the rear. I could still hear the sound of muted voices; otherwise the house was unnaturally still—or maybe my imagination made it seem that way.

"The coroner's people have already taken the body," Eberhardt said. "And the lab crew finished up half an hour ago. We'll have the room to ourselves."

We turned a corner into another corridor, and I saw a uniformed patrolman standing in front of a door that was a foot or so ajar; he moved aside silently as we approached. The door was a heavy oak job with a large, old-fashioned keyhole lock; the wood on the jamb where the bolt slides into a locking plate was splintered as a result of the forced entry. I let Eberhardt push the door inward and then followed him inside.

The room was large, rectangular—and virtually overflowing with plastic-bagged pulp and digest-sized magazines.

Brightly colored spines filled four walls of floor-to-ceiling bookshelves and two rows of library stacks. I had over six thousand issues of detective and mystery pulps in my Pacific Heights flat, but the collection in this room made mine seem meager in comparison. There must have been at least ten thousand issues here, of every conceivable type of pulp and digest, arranged by category but in no other particular order: detective, mystery, horror, weird menace, adventure, western, science fiction, air-war, hero, love. Then and later I saw what appeared to be complete runs of *Black Mask, Dime Detective, Weird Tales, The Shadow,* and *Western Story;* of *Ellery Queen's Mystery Magazine* and *Alfred Hitchcock's Mystery Magazine* and *Manhunt;* and of titles I had never even heard of.

It was an awesome collection, and for a moment it captured all my attention. A collector like me doesn't often see anything this overwhelming; in spite of the circumstances it presented a certain immediate distraction. Or it did until I focused on the wide stain of dried blood on the carpet near the back-wall shelves, and the chalk outline of a body which enclosed it.

An odd, queasy feeling came into my stomach; rooms where people have died violently have that effect on me. I looked away from the blood and tried to concentrate on the rest of the room. Like the Paperback Room we had been in previously, it contained nothing more in the way of furniture than an overstuffed chair, a reading lamp, a brass-trimmed rolltop desk set beneath one of the two windows, and a desk chair that had been overturned. Between the chalk outline and the back-wall shelves there was a scattering of magazines which had evidently been pulled or knocked loose from three of the shelves; others were askew in place, tilted forward or backward, as if someone had stumbled or fallen against them.

41

And on the opposite side of the chalk outline, in a loosely arranged row, were two pulps and a digest, the digest sandwiched between the larger issues.

Eberhardt said, "Take a look at that row of three magazines over there."

I crossed the room, noticing as I did so that all the scattered and shelved periodicals at the back wall were detective and mystery; the pulps were on the upper shelves and the digests on the lower ones. I stopped to one side of the three laid-out magazines and bent over to peer at them.

The first pulp was a 1930s and 1940s crime monthly called *Clues*. The digest was a short-lived title from the 1960s, *Keyhole Mystery Magazine*. And the second pulp was an issue of one of my particular favorites, *Private Detective*.

"Is this what you meant by a dying message?"

"That's it," he said. "And that's why you're here."

I looked around again at the scattered magazines, the disarrayed shelves, the overturned chair. "How do you figure this part of it, Eb?"

"The same way you're figuring it. Murray was stabbed somewhere on this side of the room. He reeled into that desk chair, knocked it over, then staggered away to those shelves. He must have known he was dying, that he didn't have enough time or strength to get to the phone or to find paper and pencil to write out a message. But he had enough presence of mind to want to point some kind of finger at his killer. So while he was falling, or after he fell, he was able to drag those three magazines off their shelves; and before he died he managed to lay them out the way you see them. The question is, why those three particular magazines?"

"It seems obvious why the copy of *Clues*," I said.

"Sure. But what clues was he trying to leave us with *Keyhole Mystery Magazine* and *Private Detective*? Was he trying to tell us how he was killed or who killed him? Or both? Or something else altogether?"

I sat on my heels, putting my back to the chalk outline and the dried blood, and peered more closely at the magazines. The issue of *Clues* was dated November 1937, featured a Violet McDade story by Cleve F. Adams and had three other, unfamiliar authors' names on the cover. The illustration depicted four people shooting one another.

I looked at *Keyhole Mystery Magazine*. It carried a June 1960 date and headlined stories by Norman Daniels and John Collier; there were several other writers' names in a bottom strip, a couple of which I recognized. Its cover drawing showed a frightened girl in the foreground, fleeing a dark, menacing figure in the background.

The issue of *Private Detective* was dated March, no year, and below the title were the words, "Intimate Revelations of Private Investigators." Yeah, sure. The illustration showed a private eye dragging a half-naked girl into a building. Yeah, sure. Down in the lower right-hand corner in big red letters was the issue's feature story: "Dead Man's Knock," by Roger Torrey.

I thought about it, searching for connections between what I had seen in here and what Eberhardt had told me. Was there anything in any of the illustrations, some sort of parallel situation? No. Did any of the primary suspects have names which matched those of writers listed on any of the three magazine covers? No. Was there any well-known fictional private eye named Murray or Cox or Thurman or Keeler? No.

I decided I was trying too hard, looking for too specific a connection where none existed. The plain fact was, Murray had been dying when he thought to leave these magazine clues; he would not have had time to hunt through dozens of magazines to find particular issues with particular authors or illustrations on the cover. All he had been able to do was to reach for specific copies close at hand; it was the titles of the magazines that carried whatever message he meant to leave.

So assuming *Clues* meant just that, clues, *Keyhole* and *Private Detective* were the sum total of those clues. I tried putting them together. Well, there was the obvious association: the stereotype of a private investigator is that of a snooper, a keyhole peeper. But I could not see how that would have anything to do with Murray's death. If there had been a private detective involved, Eberhardt would have figured the connection immediately and I wouldn't be here.

Take them separately then. *Keyhole Mystery Magazine.* Keyhole. That big old-fashioned keyhole in the door?

Eberhardt said, "Well? You got any ideas?" He had been standing near me, watching me think, but patience had never been his long suit.

I straightened up, explained to him what I had been ruminating about and watched him nod: he had come to the same conclusions long before I got here. Then I said, "Eb, what about the door keyhole? Could there be some connection there, something to explain the locked-room angle?"

"I already thought of that," he said. "But go ahead, have a look for yourself."

I walked over to the door, and when I got there I saw for the first time that there was a key in the latch on the inside. Eberhardt had said the lab crew had come and gone; I caught hold of the key and tugged at it, but it had been turned in the lock and it was firmly in place.

"Was this key in the latch when you broke the door down?" I asked him.

"It was. What were you thinking? That the killer stood out

44

in the hallway and stabbed Murray through the keyhole?"

"Well, it was an idea."

"Not a very good one. It's too fancy, even if it was possible."

"I guess you're right."

"I don't think we're dealing with a mastermind here," he said. "I've talked to the suspects and there's not one of them with an IQ over a hundred and twenty."

I turned away from the door. "Is it all right if I prowl around in here, look things over for myself?"

"I don't care what you do," he said, "if you end up giving me something useful."

I wandered over and looked at one of the two windows. It had been nailed shut, all right, and the nails had been painted over some time ago. The window looked out on an overgrown rear yard—eucalyptus trees, undergrowth, and scrub brush. Wisps of fog had begun to blow in off the ocean; the day had turned dark and misty. And my mood was beginning to match it. I had no particular stake in this case, and yet because Eberhardt had called me into it I felt a certain commitment. For that reason, and because puzzles of any kind prey on my mind until I know the solution, I was feeling a little frustrated.

I went to the desk beneath the second of the windows, glanced through the cubbyholes: correspondence, writing paper, envelopes, a packet of blank checks. The center drawer contained pens and pencils, various-sized paper clips and rubber bands, a tube of glue, a booklet of stamps. The three side drawers were full of letter carbons and folders jammed with facts and figures about pulp magazines and pulp writers.

From there I crossed to the overstuffed chair and the reading lamp and peered at each of them in turn. Then I looked at some of the bookshelves and went down the aisles between the library stacks. And finally I came back to the chalk outline and stood staring down again at the issues of *Clues*, *Keyhole Mystery Magazine*, and *Private Detective*.

Eberhardt said impatiently, "Are you getting anywhere or just stalling?"

"I'm trying to think," I said. "Look, Eb, you told me Murray was stabbed with a splinter-like piece of steel. How thick was it?"

"About the thickness of a pipe cleaner. Most of the 'blade' part had been honed to a fine edge and the point was needle-sharp."

"And the other end was wrapped with adhesive tape?"

"That's right. A grip, maybe."

"Seems an odd sort of weapon, don't you think? I mean, why not just use a knife?"

"People have stabbed other people with weapons a hell of a lot stranger," he said. "You know that."

"Sure. But I'm wondering if the choice of weapon here has anything to do with the locked-room angle."

"If it does, I don't see how."

"Could it have been thrown into Murray's stomach from a distance, instead of driven there at close range?"

"I suppose it could have been. But from where? Not outside this room, not with that door locked on the inside and the windows nailed down."

Musingly I said, "What if the killer wasn't in this room when Murray died?"

Eberhardt's expression turned even more sour. "I know what you're leading up to with that," he said. "The murderer rigged some kind of fancy crossbow arrangement, operated by a tripwire or by remote control. Well, you can forget it. The lab boys searched every inch of this room. Desk, chairs, bookshelves, reading lamp, ceiling fixtures—everything. There's nothing like that here; you've been over the room, you can tell that for yourself. There's nothing at all out of the ordinary or out of place except those magazines."

Sharpening frustration made me get down on one knee and stare once more at the copies of *Keyhole* and *Private Detective*. They had to mean something, separately or in conjunction. But what?

"Lieutenant?"

The voice belonged to Inspector Jordan; when I looked up he was standing in the doorway, gesturing to Eberhardt. I watched Eb go over to him and the two of them held a brief, soft-voiced conference. At length Eberhardt turned to look at me again.

"I'll be back in a minute," he said. "I've got to go talk to the family. Keep working on it."

"Sure. What else?"

He and Jordan went away and left me alone. I kept staring at the magazines, and I kept coming up empty.

Keyhole Mystery Magazine.

Private Detective.

Nothing.

I stood and prowled around some more, looking here and there. That went on for a couple of minutes—until all of a sudden I became aware of something Eberhardt and I should have noticed before, should have considered before. Something that was at once obvious and completely unobtrusive, like the purloined letter in the Poe story.

I came to a standstill, frowning, and my mind began to crank out an idea. I did some careful checking, and the idea took on more weight, and at the end of another couple of minutes I was pretty sure I knew how Thomas Murray had been murdered in a locked room.

47

Once I had that, the rest of it came together pretty quick. My mind works that way; when I have something solid to build on, a kind of chain reaction takes place. I put together things Eberhardt had told me and things I knew about Murray, and there it was in a nice ironic package: the significance of *Private Detective* and the name of Murray's killer.

When Eberhardt came back into the room I was going over it all for the third time, making sure of my logic. He still had the black briar clamped between his teeth and there were more scowl wrinkles in his forehead. He said, "My suspects are getting restless; if we don't come up with an answer pretty soon, I've got to let them go on their way. You, too."

"I may have the answer for you right now," I said.

That brought him up short. "Give."

"All right. What Murray was trying to tell us, as best he could with the magazines close at hand, was how he was stabbed and who his murderer is. I think *Keyhole Mystery Magazine* indicates how and *Private Detective* indicates who. It's hardly conclusive proof in either case, but it might be enough for you to pry loose an admission of guilt."

"You just leave that part of it to me. Get on with your explanation."

"Well, let's take the 'how' first," I said. "The locked-room angle. I doubt if the murderer set out to create that kind of situation; his method was clever enough, but as you pointed out we're not dealing with a mastermind here. He probably didn't even know that Murray had taken to locking himself inside this room every day. I think he must have been as surprised as everyone else when the murder turned into a locked-room thing.

"So it was supposed to be a simple stabbing done by person or persons unknown while Murray was alone in the house. But it wasn't a stabbing at all, in the strict sense of the word; the killer wasn't anywhere near here when Murray died."

"He wasn't, huh?"

"No. That's why the adhesive tape on the murder weapon—misdirection, to make it look like Murray was stabbed with a homemade knife in a close confrontation. I'd say he worked it the way he did for two reasons: one, he didn't have enough courage to kill Murray face to face; and two, he wanted to establish an alibi for himself."

Eberhardt puffed up another great cloud of acrid smoke from his pipe. "So tell me how the hell you put a steel splinter into a man's stomach when you're miles away from the scene."

"You rig up a death trap," I said, "using a keyhole."

"Now, look, we went over all that before. The key was inside the keyhole when we broke in, I told you that, and I won't believe the killer used some kind of tricky gimmick that the lab crew overlooked."

"That's not what happened at all. What hung both of us up is a natural inclination to associate the word 'keyhole' with a keyhole in a door. But the fact is, there are five other keyholes in this room."

"What?"

"The desk, Eb. The rolltop desk over there."

He swung his head around and looked at the desk beneath the window. It contained five keyholes, all right—one in the rolltop, one in the center drawer and one each in the three side drawers. Like those on most antique rolltop desks, they were meant to take large, old-fashioned keys and therefore had good-sized openings. But they were also half-hidden in scrolled brass frames with decorative handle pulls; and no one really notices them anyway, any more than you notice individual cubbyholes or the design of the brass trimming. When you look at a desk you see it as an entity: you see a desk.

Eberhardt put his eyes on me again. "Okay," he said, "I see what you mean. But I searched that desk myself, and so did the lab boys. There's nothing on it or in it that could be used to stab a man through a keyhole."

"Yes, there is." I led him over to the desk. "Only one of these keyholes could have been used, Eb. It isn't the one in the rolltop because the top is pushed all the way up; it isn't any of the ones in the side drawers because of where Murray was stabbed—he would have had to lean over at an awkward angle, on his own initiative, in order to catch that steel splinter in the stomach. It has to be the center drawer, because when a man sits down at a desk like this, that drawer—and that keyhole—are about on a level with the area under his breastbone."

He didn't argue with the logic of that. Instead, he jerked open the center drawer by its handle pull and stared inside at the pens and pencils, paper clips, rubber bands, and other writing paraphernalia.

Then, after a moment, I saw his eyes change and understanding come into them.

"Rubber band," he said.

"Right." I picked up the largest one; it was about a quarter-inch wide, thick and strong—not unlike the kind kids use to make slingshots. "This one, probably."

"Keep talking."

"Take a look at the keyhole frame on the inside of the center drawer. The top doesn't quite fit snug with the wood; there's enough room to slip the edge of this band into the crack. All you'd have to do then is stretch the band out around the steel splinter, ease the point of the weapon through the keyhole and anchor it against the metal on the inside rim of the hole. It would take time to get the balance right and close the drawer without releasing the band, but it could be done by someone with patience and a steady hand. And what you'd have then is a death trap—a cocked and powerful slingshot."

Eberhardt nodded slowly.

"When Murray sat down at the desk," I said, "all it took was for him to pull open the drawer with the jerking motion people always use. The point of the weapon slipped free, the rubber band released like a spring, and the splinter shot through and sliced into Murray's stomach. The shock and impact drove him and the chair backward, and he must have stood up convulsively at the same time, knocking over the chair. That's when he staggered into those bookshelves. And meanwhile the rubber band flopped loose from around the keyhole frame, so that everything looked completely ordinary inside the drawer."

"I'll buy it," Eberhardt said. "It's just simple enough and logical enough to be the answer." He gave me a sidewise look. "You're pretty good at this kind of thing, once you get going."

"Well, the pulp connection started my juices flowing."

"Yeah, the pulp connection. Now what about *Private Detective* and the name of the killer?"

"The clue Murray left us there is a little more roundabout," I said. "But you've got to remember that he was dying and that he only had time to grab those magazines that were handy. He couldn't tell us more directly who he believed was responsible."

"Go on," he said, "I'm listening."

"Murray collected pulp magazines, and he obviously also read them. So he knew that private detectives as a group are known by all sorts of names—shamus, op, eye, snooper." I allowed myself a small, wry smile. "And one more, just as common."

"Which is?"

"Peeper," I said.

He considered that. "So?"

"Eb, Murray also collected every other kind of popular culture. One of those kinds is tapes of old television shows. And one of your suspects is a small, mousy guy who wears thick glasses; you told me that yourself. I'd be willing to bet that some time ago Murray made a certain obvious comparison between this relative of his and an old TV show character from back in the fifties, and that he referred to the relative by that character's name."

"*What* character?"

"Mr. Peepers," I said. "And you remember who played Mr. Peepers, don't you?"

"Well, I'll be damned," he said. "Wally Cox."

"Sure. Mr. Peepers—the cousin, Walter Cox."

At eight o'clock that night, while I was working on a beer and reading a 1935 issue of *Dime Detective*, Eberhardt rang up my flat.

"Just thought you'd like to know," he said. "We got a full confession out of Walter Cox about an hour ago. I hate to admit it—I don't want you to get a swelled head—but you were right all the way down to the Mr. Peepers angle. I checked with the housekeeper and the niece before I talked to Cox, and they both told me Murray called him by that name all the time."

"What was Cox's motive?" I asked.

"Greed, what else? He had a chance to get in on a big investment deal in South America, and Murray wouldn't give him the cash. They argued about it in private for some time, and three days ago Cox threatened to kill him. Murray took the threat seriously, which is why he started locking himself in his Rooms while he tried to figure out what to do about it."

"Where did Cox get the piece of steel?"

"Friend of his has a basement workshop, builds things out of wood and metal. Cox borrowed the workshop on a pretext and used a grinder to hone the weapon. He rigged up the slingshot this morning—let himself into the house with his key while the others were out and Murray was locked in one of the other Rooms."

"Well, I'm glad you got it wrapped up and glad I could help."

"You're going to be even gladder when the niece talks to you tomorrow. She says she wants to give you some kind of reward."

"Hell, that's not necessary."

"Don't look a gift horse in the mouth—to coin a phrase. Listen, I owe you something myself. You want to come over tomorrow night for a home-cooked dinner and some beer?"

"As long as it's Dana who does the home cooking," I said.

After we rang off I thought about the reward from Murray's niece. Well, if she wanted to give me money I was hardly in a financial position to turn it down. But if she left it up to me to name my own reward, I decided I would not ask for money at all; I would ask for something a little more fitting instead.

What I really wanted was Thomas Murray's run of *Private Detective*.

Dead Man's Slough

I was halfway through one of the bends in Dead Man's Slough, on my way back to the Whiskey Island marina with three big Delta catfish in the skiff beside me, when the red-haired man rose up out of the water at an islet fifty yards ahead.

It was the last thing I expected to see and I leaned forward, squinting through the boat's Plexiglas windscreen. The weather was full of early November bluster—high overcast and a raw wind—and the water was too cold and too choppy for pleasure swimming. Besides which, the red-haired guy was fully dressed in khaki trousers and a short-sleeved bush jacket.

He came all the way out of the slough, one hand clapped across the back of his head, and plowed upward through the mud and grass of a tiny natural beach. When he got to its upper edge where the tule grass grew thick and waist-high, he stopped and held a listening pose. Then he whirled around, stood swaying unsteadily as if he were caught in a cross-current of the chill wind. He stared out toward me for two or three seconds; the pale oval of his face might have been pulled into a painful grimace, but I couldn't tell for sure at the distance. And then he whirled again in a dazed, frightened way, stumbled in among the rushes, and disappeared.

I looked upstream past the islet, where Dead Man's Slough widened into a long reach; the waterway was empty, and so were the willow-lined levees that flanked it. Nor was there any sign of another boat or another human being in the wide channel that bounded the islet on the south. That was not surprising, or at least it wouldn't have been five minutes ago.

The California Delta, fifty miles inland from San Francisco where the Sacramento and San Joaquin rivers merge on a course to San Francisco Bay, has a thousand miles of waterways and a network of islands both large and small, inhabited and uninhabited, linked by seventy bridges and a few hundred miles of levee roads. During the summer months the area is jammed with vacationers, water skiers, fishermen, and houseboaters, but in late fall, when the cold winds start to blow, about the only people you'll find are local merchants and farmers and a few late-vacationing anglers like me. I had seen no more than four other people and two other boats in the five hours since I'd left Whiskey Island, and none of those in the half-mile I had just traveled on Dead Man's Slough.

So where had the red-haired man come from?

On impulse I twisted the wheel and took the skiff over toward the islet, cutting back on the throttle as I approached. Wind gusts rustled and bent the carpet of tule grass, but there was no other movement that I could see. Ten yards off the beach, I shut the throttle all the way down to idle; the quick movement of the water carried the skiff the rest of the way in. When the bow scraped up over the soft mud I shut off the engine, pocketed the ignition key and moved aft to tilt the outboard engine out of the water so its propeller blades wouldn't become fouled in the offshore grass. Then I climbed out and dragged half the boat's length onto the beach as a precaution against it backsliding and drifting off without me.

From the upper rim of the beach I could look all across the flat width of the islet—maybe fifty yards in all—and for seventy yards or so of its length, to where the terrain humped up in the middle and a pair of willow trees and several wild black-berry bushes blocked off my view. But I couldn't see anything of the red-haired man, or hear anything of him either; there were no sounds except for the low whistling cry of the wind.

An eerie feeling came over me. It was as if I were alone on the islet, alone on all of Dead Man's Slough, and the red-haired guy had been some sort of hallucination. Or some sort of ghostly manifestation. I thought of the old-timer who had rented me the skiff on Whiskey Island—a local historian well versed on Delta lore and legends dating back to the Gold Rush, when steamboats from San Francisco and Sac-ramento plied these waters with goods and passengers. And I thought of the story he had told me about how the slough got its name.

Back in 1860 an Irish miner named O'Farrell, on his way to San Francisco from the diggings near Sutter's Mill, had disappeared from a sidewheeler at Poker Bend; also missing was a fortune in gold dust and specie he had been carrying with him. Three days later O'Farrell's body was found floating in these waters with his head bashed in and his pockets empty. The murder was never solved. Old-time rivermen swore they had seen the miner's ghost abroad on certain foggy nights, swearing vengeance on the man who had murdered him.

But that wasn't quite all. According to the details of the story, O'Farrell had had red hair—and his ghost was always seen clutching the back of his bloody head with one hand.

Sure, I thought, and nuts to that. Pure coincidence, nothing else. Old-time rivermen were forever seeing ghosts, not only of men but of packets like the *Sagamore* and the *R. K. Page* whose steam boilers had exploded during foolish races in the mid-1800s, killing hundreds of passengers and crewmen. But I did not believe in spooks worth a damn. Nor

57

was I prone to hallucinations or flights of imagination, not at my age and not with my temperament. The red-haired guy was real, all right. Maybe hurt and in trouble, judging from his wobbly condition and his actions.

So where had he gone? If he was hiding somewhere in the rushes I couldn't tell the location by looking from here, or even where he had gone into them; tule grass is pretty resilient and tends to spring back up even after a man plows through it. He could also have gone to the eastern end, beyond the high ground in the middle. The one thing I was sure of was that he was still on the islet: I could see out into the wide channels on the north and south sides, and if he had gone swimming again he would have been visible.

I pulled up the collar on my pea jacket and headed into the rushes on a zigzag course, calling out as I went, offering help if he needed it. Nobody answered me. There was no sign of any red hair as I worked my way along. After a time I stopped, and when I scanned upward toward the higher ground I saw that I was within thirty yards of the line of blackberry bushes.

I also saw a man come hurrying up onto the hump from the opposite side, between the two willow trees.

He saw me, too, and halted abruptly, and we stood staring at each other across the windswept terrain. But he wasn't the red-haired guy. He was dark-looking, heavier, and he wore Levi's, a plaid mackinaw, and a gray fisherman's hat decorated with bright-colored flies. In one hand, held in a vertical position, was a thick-butted fishing rod.

"Hello up there!" I called to him, but he didn't give me any response. Just stood poised, peering down at me like a wary animal scenting for danger. Which left the first move up to me. I took my hands out of my coat pockets and slow-walked toward him over the marshy earth. He stayed where he was, not moving except to slant the fishing rod across the front of his body, weaponlike. When I got past the blackberry bushes I was ten feet from him, on the firmer ground of the hump; I decided that was far enough and stopped there.

We did some more looking at each other. He was about my age, early fifties, with a craggy outdoorsman's face and eyes the color of butterscotch. There was no anxiety in his expression, nor any hostility either; it was just the set, waiting look of a man on his guard.

Past him I could see the rest of the islet—another sixty yards or so of flattish terrain dominated by shrubs and tules, with a mistletoe-festooned pepper tree off to the left and a narrow rock shelf at the far end. Tied up alongside the shelf was what looked to be a fourteen-foot outboard similar to my rented skiff, except that it sported a gleaming green-and-white paint job. There was nothing else to see along there, or in the choppy expanses of water surrounding us.

Pretty soon the craggy guy said, "Who are you?"

"Just another fisherman," I said, which was more relevant and less provocative than telling him I was a private investigator from San Francisco. "Have you been here long?"

"A little while. Why?"

"Alone?"

"That's right. But I heard you shouting to somebody."

"Nobody I know," I said. "A red-haired man I saw drag himself out of the slough a few minutes ago."

He stared at me. "What?"

"Sounds funny, I know, but it's the truth. He was fully dressed and he looked hurt; he disappeared into the tules. I put my boat in and I've been hunting around for him, but no luck so far. You haven't seen him, I take it?"

"No," the craggy guy said. "I haven't seen anybody

since I put in after crayfish an hour ago." He paused. "You say this red-haired man was hurt?"

"Seemed that way."

"Bad?"

"Maybe. He looked dazed."

"You think he could have had a boating accident?"

"Could be. But he also seemed scared."

"Scared? Of what?"

"No idea. You heard me shouting, so he must have heard me, too; but he still hasn't shown himself. That might mean he's hiding because he's afraid to be found."

"Might mean something else, too," the craggy guy said. "He could have gone back into the water and swum across to one of the other islands."

"I don't think so. I would have seen him if he'd done that anywhere off this side; and I guess you'd have seen him if he'd done it anywhere off the other side."

"He could also be dead by now if he was hurt as bad as you seem to think."

"That's a possibility," I said. "Or maybe just unconscious. How about helping me look for him so we can find out?"

The craggy guy hesitated. He was still wary, the way a lot of people are of strangers these days—as if he were not quite convinced I was telling him a straight story and thinking that maybe I had designs on his money or his life. But after a time he said, "All right. If there's a man hurt around here, he'll need all the help he can get. Where did you see him come out of the water?"

I turned a little and pointed behind me. "Back there. You can see part of my boat; that's about where it was."

"So if he's still on the island, he's somewhere between here and your boat."

"Seems that way," I said. "Unless he managed to slip over

where you were without your seeing him."

"I doubt that. I've got pretty sharp eyes."

"Sure." I thought I might as well introduce myself; maybe that would reassure him. So I gave my name, with a by-the-way after it, and waited while he made up his mind whether or not he wanted to reciprocate.

"Jackson," he said finally. "Herb Jackson."

"Nice to know you, Mr. Jackson. How about we each take one side and work back toward my skiff?"

He said that was okay with him and we fanned out away from each other, me into the vegetation on the south side. We each used a switchbacking course from the center out to the edges, where the ground was boggy and the footing a little treacherous. Both of us kept silent, but all you could hear were the keening of the wind and the whispery rustle of the tules as I spread through them with my hands and Jackson probed through them with his fishing rod. I caught him looking over at me a couple of times as if he wanted to make sure I intended to stay on my half of the turf.

Neither of us found anything. The only things hidden among the rushes were occasional rocks and chunks of decaying driftwood; and there was no way anybody could have concealed himself in the sparse offshore grasses. You're always hearing about how people submerge in shallow water and breathe through a hollow reed, and maybe that's a possibility in places like Florida and Louisiana, but not in California. Tule grass isn't hollow and you can't breathe through its stalks; you'd swallow water and probably drown if you tried it.

It took us ten minutes to make our way back down to where my rented boat was. I got there first, and when Jackson came up he halted a good eight feet away and looked down at the empty beach, into the empty skiff, across the empty slough at the empty levee on the far side. Then he put his butterscotch eyes on me.

I said, "He's got to be over where you were somewhere. We've gone over all the ground on this end."

"If he's on the island at all," Jackson said.

"Well, he's got to be." A thought occurred to me. "The outboard on your boat—do you start it with an ignition key or by hand?"

"Key. Why?"

"Did you leave it in the ignition or have you got it with you?"

"In my pocket," he said. "What're you thinking? That he might try to steal my boat?"

"It could happen. But it wouldn't do him much good without power. Unless you keep oars for an emergency."

"No oars." Jackson looked a little worried now, as though he might be imagining his boat adrift and in the hands of a mysterious redheaded stranger. "Damn it, you could be right."

He set off at a soggy run, bulling his way through the rushes and shrubs, slashing at them with whip-like sweeps of the rod. I went after him, off to one side and at a slower pace. He reached the blackberry bushes, cut past them onto the hump, and pulled up near the drooping fan of branches on one willow. Then I saw him relax, take a couple of deep breaths; he turned to wait for me.

When I got up there I could see that his boat was still tied alongside the empty rock shelf. The channels beyond were a couple hundred yards wide at the narrowest point; you could swim that distance easily enough in fifteen minutes—but not on a day like this, with that wind whipping up the water to a froth, and not when you were hurt and so unsteady on your feet you couldn't walk without stumbling.

"So he's still on the island," I said to Jackson. "It shouldn't take us long to find him now."

He had nothing to say to that; he just turned toward the willow, spread the branches, looked in among them and at the ones higher up. I went over and did the same thing at the second tree. The red-haired man was not hiding in either of them—and he wasn't hiding among the blackberry bushes or anywhere else on or near the hump.

We started down toward Jackson's boat, one on each side as before. Rocks, more pieces of driftwood, a rusted coffee can, the carcass of some sort of large bird—nothing else. The pepper tree was on my side; I paused at the bole and peered up through pungent leaves and thick clusters of mistletoe. Nothing. The shoreline on this end was rockier, with shrubs and nettles growing along it instead of tule grass; but there was nobody concealed there, not on my half and not on Jackson's.

Where is he? I thought. He didn't just disappear into thin air. Where is he?

The eerie feeling came back over me as I neared the rock shelf; in spite of myself I thought again of O'Farrell, the murdered Gold Rush miner, and his ghost that was supposed to haunt Dead Man's Slough.

I reached the shelf before Jackson and stopped abaft the boat. She was a sleek little lady, not more than a year old, with bright chrome fittings to go with the green-and-white paint job; the outboard was a thirty-five-horsepower Evinrude. In the stern, I saw then, was a tackle box, a wicker creel, an Olympic spincast outfit, and a nifty Shakespeare graphite-and-fiberglass rod. A heavy sheepskin jacket was draped over the back of the naugahyde seat.

When I heard Jackson come up near me a few seconds later I pivoted around to face him. He said, "I don't like this at all."

Neither did I, not one bit. "Yeah," I said.

He gave me a narrow look. He had that rod slanted across the front of his body again. "You sure you're not just playing games with me, mister?"

"Why would I want to play games with you?"

"I don't know. All I know is we've been over the entire island without finding this redhead of yours. There's nothing here except tule grass and shrubs and three trees; we couldn't have overlooked anything as big as a man."

"I guess not," I said.

"Then where is he—if he exists at all?"

"Dead, maybe."

"Dead?"

"He's not on the island; that means he had to have tried swimming across one of the channels. But you or I would've seen him at some point if he'd got halfway across any of them."

"You think he drowned?"

"I'm afraid so," I said. "He was hurt, probably weak—and that water is turbulent and ice-cold. Unless he was an exceptionally strong swimmer, he couldn't have lasted long."

Jackson thought that over, rubbing fingertips along his craggy jaw. "You might be right, at that," he said. "So what do we do now?"

"There's not much we can do. One of us should notify the county sheriff, but that's about all. The body'll turn up sooner or later."

"Sure," Jackson said. "Tell you what: I'll call the sheriff from the camp in Hogback Slough. I'm heading in there right away."

"Would you do that?"

"Be glad to. No problem."

"Well, thanks. He can reach me on Whiskey Island if he wants to talk to me about it."

"I'll tell him that."

He nodded to me, lowered the rod a little, then moved past me to the boat. I retreated a dozen yards over the rocky ground, watching him as he untied the bowline from a shrub and climbed in under the wheel. Thirty seconds later, when I was halfway up to the willow trees, the outboard made a guttural rumbling noise and its propeller blades began churning the water. Jackson maneuvered backward away from the shelf, waved as he shifted into a forward gear and opened the throttle wide; the boat got away in a hurry, bow lifting under the surge of power. From up on the hump I watched it dwindle as he cut down the center of the southern channel toward the entrance to Hogback Slough.

So much for Herb Jackson. Now I could start worrying about the red-haired man again.

What I had said about being afraid he'd drowned was a lie. He was not a ghost and he had not pulled any magical vanishing act; he was still here, and I was pretty sure he was still alive. It was just that Jackson and I had overlooked something—and it had not occurred to me what it was until Jackson said there was nothing here except tule grass and shrubs and three trees. That was not quite true. There was something else on the islet, and it made one place we had failed to search; that was where the man had to be.

I went straight to it, hurrying, and said my name again in a loud voice and added that I was a detective from San Francisco.

Then I said, "He's gone now; there's nobody around but me. You're safe."

Nothing happened for fifteen seconds. Then there were

65

sounds and struggling movement. I waded in quickly to help him with some careful lifting and pushing.

And there he was, burrowing free of a depression in the soft mud, out from under my rented skiff just above the waterline where I had beached the forward half of it.

When he was clear of the boat I released my grip on the gunwale and eased him up on his feet. He kept trying to talk, but he was in no shape for that yet; most of what he said was gibberish. I got him into the skiff, wrapped him in a square of canvas from the stern—he was shivering so badly you could almost hear his bones clicking together—and cleaned some of the mud off him. The area behind his right ear was pulpy and badly lacerated, but if he was lucky he didn't have anything worse than a concussion.

While I was doing that he calmed down enough to be coherent. The first thing he said was, "He tried to kill me. He tried to *murder* me."

"I figured as much. What happened?"

"We were in his boat; we'd just put in to the island because he said there was something wrong with the ignition. He asked me to take a look, so I pulled off my coat and leaned down under the wheel. Then my head seemed to explode. The next thing I knew, I was floundering in the south-side channel."

"He hit you with that fishing rod of his, probably," I said. "The current carried you along after he dumped you overboard and the cold water brought you around. Why does he want you dead?"

"It must be the insurance. We own a company in Sacramento and we have a partnership policy—double indemnity for accidental death. I knew Frank was in debt, but I never thought he'd go this far."

"Frank? Then his name isn't Herb Jackson?"

"No. It's Saunders, Frank Saunders. Mine's Rusty McGuinn."

Irish, I thought. Like O'Farrell. That figures.

I got out again to slide the skiff off the beach and into the slough. When I clambered back in, McGuinn said, "You knew he was after me? That's why you didn't give me away when the two of you were together?"

"Not exactly." I started the engine and got us under way at a good clip upstream. "I didn't have any idea who you were or where you'd come from until I looked inside Jackson's—or Saunders'—boat. He told me he was alone and he'd put in after crayfish. But he was carrying one rod and there were two more casting outfits in the boat; you don't need all that stuff for crayfish, and no fisherman alone is likely to carry three outfits for any reason. There was a heavy sheepskin jacket there, too, draped over the seat; but he was already wearing a heavy mackinaw, and I remembered you only had on a short-sleeved jacket when you came out of the water. It all began to add up then. I talked him into leaving as soon as I could."

"How did you do that?"

"By telling him what he wanted to hear—that you must be dead."

"But how did you know where I was hiding?"

I explained how Saunders had triggered the answer for me. "I also tried to put myself in your place. You were hurt and scared; your first thought would be to get away as fast as possible. Which meant by boat, not by swimming. So it figured you hid nearby until I was far enough away and then slipped back to the skiff.

"But this boat—like Saunders'—starts with a key, and I had it with me. You could have set yourself adrift, but then Saunders might have seen you and come chasing in his boat.

In your condition it made sense you might burrow under the skiff, with a little space clear at one side so you could breathe."

"Well, I owe you," McGuinn said. "You saved my life."

"Forget it," I said, a little ruefully. Because the truth was I had almost got him killed. I had told Saunders he was on the island and insisted on a two-man search party; and I had failed to tumble to who and what Saunders was until it was almost too late. If McGuinn hadn't been so well hidden, if we'd found him together, Saunders might have jumped me and I might not have been able to handle him; McGuinn and I could both be dead now. I'm not a bad detective, usually. Other times, though, I'm a near bust.

The channel that led to Whiskey Island loomed ahead. Cheer up, I told myself—the important thing is that this time, a hundred and twenty years after the first one, the red-haired Irish bludgeon victim is being brought out alive and the man who assaulted him is sure to wind up in prison. The ghost of O'Farrell, the Gold Rush miner, won't have any company when it goes prowling and swearing vengeance on those foggy nights in Dead Man's Slough.

The Ghosts of Ragged-Ass Gulch

1

The name of the place was Ragged-Ass Gulch.

That was the name the town had been born with anyway, back in the days of the California Gold Rush when gold fever raged up in Trinity County as well as in the Mother Lode and a group of miners discovered nuggets in Musket Creek north of Weaverville. Nobody seemed to know any more why the town that sprang up along the creek's banks had been so colorfully dubbed. But it wasn't unusual for miners, who were themselves a colorful lot, to give their camps unconventional names; Whiskeytown, Lousy Ravine, Rowdy Bar, Bogus Thunder, and Git-Up-And-Git were just a few of their other inventions.

At any rate, Ragged-Ass Gulch had flourished for three or four years, with a population of fifteen hundred at its peak, until the gold in the vicinity petered out and the miners left for other diggings. Then, slowly, it had begun to die. By the mid-1850s, only a hundred or so people remained and the town was renamed Cooperville, after the largest of the families that came to settle there. Those hundred had shrunk to less than thirty by the turn of the century, which made it a virtual ghost town. It was still a virtual ghost town: at last count, exactly sixteen people lived there.

I had my first look at it on a bright morning in mid June. Beside me in the car, Kerry said, "Good Lord, it's beautiful," in a surprised voice. "No wonder the people who live here don't want the place developed."

We had just angled between a couple of high forested cliffs, and down below the mountains had folded back to create a huge parklike meadow carpeted with wild clover, poppies, purple-blue lupine. The town lay sprawled at the back end, where the narrow line of Musket Creek meandered through the high grass and wildflowers. Most of the buildings were tumbledown—and off to the left I could see the blackened skeletons of the four that had burned ten days ago—but at a distance the sunlight and the majestic surroundings softened the look of them, gave them a kind of odd, lonely dignity. Far off to the east, you could see the immense snow-capped peak of Mt. Shasta jutting more than fourteen thousand feet into the dusky blue sky.

"Now why would anybody call a pretty spot like this Ragged-Ass Gulch?" Kerry asked.

"Somebody's idea of a joke, maybe. Miners had strange senses of humor."

"That's for sure."

She put her head out of the open passenger window and sniffed the air like a cat, looking off toward Mt. Shasta. She seemed to have begun to enjoy herself finally, which was a relief. She hadn't wanted to come because she was miffed at me, and I'd had to do some fast talking to convince her. Ordinarily I would not have considered bringing Kerry along on an investigation; my profession being what it was, it was seldom a good idea to mix business and pleasure. But in this instance, there were extenuating circumstances.

When we reached the meadow, the road deteriorated into little more than a pair of ruts with a grassy hump in the middle. It angled off to the right and eventually forked; one branch became the single main street of Cooperville, *nee* Ragged-Ass Gulch, and the other hooked up and disappeared into the flanking slopes to the west, where I had been told some of the townspeople lived.

The first building we came to was on the near side of the fork. It was one of the few occupied ones in the town proper, a combination single-pump gas station, garage and body shop, and general store. The garage and store buildings were weathered and unpainted, but in a decent state of repair; a sign that said Cooperville Mercantile hung over the screen-doored entrance to the latter, and the facing wall was plastered with old metal Coca-Cola and beer signs. Around back, to one side, was a frame cottage with a big native-stone chimney at one end. The folks who lived in the cottage and ran the businesses were the Coleclaws: one husband, one wife, one son.

I pulled in off the road and stopped next to the gas pump. A fat brown-and-white dog came around from behind the store, took one look at the car, and began barking its head off. No one else appeared.

"I'll go see who's here," I said to Kerry. "You wait in the car, okay?"

"Like a nice dutiful little wife?"

Here we go again, I thought. "Come on, babe, you know this is business."

"It wasn't supposed to be business. It wasn't supposed to be Ragged-Ass Gulch either."

"Kerry . . ."

"Oh, all right. Go on, I'll wait here."

I got out of the car, sighing a little, keeping my eye on the dog. It continued to bark, but it didn't make any sudden moves in my direction. I took the fact that its tail was wagging to be a positive sign and started toward the entrance to the store.

Just before I got there, a pudgy young guy in grease-stained overalls appeared in the doorway of the adjacent garage. "Be quiet, Sam," he said to the dog. He didn't say anything to me, or move out of the doorway. And the dog went right on yapping.

I walked over to where the young guy stood. He was in his middle twenties and he had curly brown hair and pink beardless cheeks and big doe eyes that had a remote look in them. The eyes watched me without curiosity as I came up to him.

"Hi," I said. "You're Gary Coleclaw, right?"

"Yeah," he said.

"I'd like to talk to your father, if he's around."

"He's not. He went into Weaverville this morning for supplies."

"How about your mother? Is she here?"

"No. She went to Weaverville too."

"When will they be back?"

He shrugged. "I dunno. This afternoon sometime."

"Well, maybe you can help me. I'm a detective, from San Francisco, and I—"

"Detective?" he said.

"Yes. I'm investigating the death of Allan Randall, over in Redding—"

"The Munroe guy," he said. His face closed up; you could see it happening, like watching a poppy fold its petals at sundown. "The fire. I don't know nothing about that. Except he got what was coming to him."

"Is that what your father says too?"

"That's what everybody says. Listen, you working for them? Them Munroe guys?"

"No."

"Yeah, you are. Them damn Munroe guys."

He wheeled away from me and hurried back inside the garage. I called after him, "Hey, wait," but he didn't stop or turn. An old Chrysler sat on the floor inside, its front end jacked up; there was one of those little wheeled mechanics' carts alongside, and he dropped down onto it on his back and scooted himself under the Chrysler until only his legs were showing. A moment later I heard the sharp, angry sound of some kind of tool whacking against the undercarriage.

The damned dog was still barking. I sidestepped it and went back to the car. When I slid in under the wheel, Kerry asked, "Well?"

"He wouldn't talk to me. And his folks aren't here."

"What now?"

"The Cooperville fire," I said.

2

I drove out along the road again. Just beyond the fork, two more occupied cottages sat side by side; the nearest one had a deserted look, but in the yard of the second, a heavyset woman in her late sixties or early seventies, wearing man's clothing and a straw hat, was wielding a hoe among tall rows of tomato vines. She stopped when she heard the car and stood staring out at the road as we passed by, as if she resented the appearance of strangers in Cooperville.

Kerry said, "None of the natives is very friendly, the way it looks."

"I didn't expect that they would be," I said.

I took the right fork that led through what was left of the town. It amounted to about two blocks' worth of buildings on both sides of the road, although on either end and back into the meadow you could see foundations and other remains of what had once been more buildings and streets. Most of the structures still standing were backed up against the creek. There were about fifteen altogether, all made of logs and whipsawed boards, some with stone foundations, a third with badly decayed frames and collapsed roofs. The largest, two stories, girdled by a sagging verandah at the second level, looked to have been either a hotel or a saloon with upstairs accommodations; it bore no signs, and as was the case with the others we passed, its doors and windows were boarded up. Except for faded lettering over the entrance to one that said *Union Drug Store*, it was impossible to tell what sort of establishments any of them had been.

Kerry seemed impressed. "This is some place," she said. "I've never been in a ghost town before."

"Spooky, huh?"

"No. I'm fascinated. How long have these buildings been here?"

"More than a hundred years, some of them."

"And there've been people living here all that time and nobody ever tried to restore any of them?"

"Not in a good long while."

"Well, why not? I mean, you'd think somebody would want to preserve a historic place like this."

"Somebody does," I said. "The Munroe Corporation."

"I don't mean that kind of preservation. You know what I mean."

"Uh-huh. It's a good question, but I don't know the answer."

She frowned a little, thoughtfully. "What kind of people live here, anyway?"

I had no answer for her. Half of the sixteen residents had been born in Cooperville; the other half had gravitated to it because they liked its isolation. It was up near the Oregon border, three hundred miles from San Francisco, and to get to it you had to take an unpaved road that climbed seven miles off State Highway 3. The tourists hadn't discovered it because it was so far off the beaten track. The residents liked that, too. What they seemed to want more than anything else was to be left alone.

The problem was, they weren't being left alone. Most of the land in the area was government protected—the Shasta Trinity National Recreation Area—but the land on which Cooperville sat was owned by Trinity County. A group of developers, the Munroe Corporation, had begun buying it up during the past year, with the intention of turning Cooperville into a place the tourists would discover: widening and paving the access road, restoring the rundown buildings after the fashion of the Mother Lode towns, adding things like a Frontier Town Amusement Park, stables for horseback rides up into the mountains, and a couple of lodges to accommodate vacationers and overnight guests.

The Cooperville residents were up in arms over this. They didn't want to live in a tourist trap and they didn't want to be forced out of their homes by a bunch of outsiders. So they had banded together and hired a law firm to try to block the sale of the land, to get Cooperville named as a state historical site. Lawsuits were still pending against the Munroe Corporation, but everybody figured it was just a matter of time before the bulldozers and workmen moved in and another little piece of history died and was reincarnated as a chunk of modern commercialism.

One of the residents seemed to have been unwilling to accept that fate, however, and had taken matters into his own hands. Four of the town's abandoned buildings had burned to the ground ten days before, including the remains of a "fandango hall"—a saloon-and-gambling house—that the developers had been particularly interested in restoring. The Munroe people thought it was a blatant case of arson, and put pressure on the county sheriff's office to investigate; but the law had found no evidence that the fire had been deliberately set, and the official report tabbed it as "of unknown origin."

Bad feelings were running high by this time, on both sides. And they got worse—much worse. Two days ago, there had been another fire, not in Cooperville this time but in Redding, some forty miles away, where the Munroe Corporation had its offices. The bachelor home of the president of the Munroe combine, a man named Randall who had been the most outspoken against the citizens of Cooperville, had gone up in flames shortly past midnight. Randall had gone up with it. He was not supposed to be home that night—it was common knowledge that he was going to San Francisco on company business—but he'd put off the trip at the last minute. He had evidently been asleep when the blaze started, had been overcome by smoke before he could get out of the burning house. There was no evidence of arson; as far as the local cops were concerned, his death was a tragic accident.

But the other Munroe partners thought otherwise. The Great Western Insurance Company, which carried a hundred-thousand-dollar double indemnity partnership policy on Randall's life and on the lives of the three remaining partners, was also skeptical. Insurance companies are always leery when a heavily insured party dies under unusual circumstances, especially when his business partners are the beneficiaries. Great Western wanted Randall's death investigated for that reason. And the Munroe people wanted his death investigated both to exonerate themselves of any wrongdoing and to find out which of the Cooperville residents was responsible for the fires.

That was where I came in. Great Western had called me first, in the person of Barney Rivera, their head claims adjustor in San Francisco; they were a small company and did not maintain an investigative staff, so they farmed out that kind of work to private operatives like me. Then, six hours after I accepted the job, one of the three surviving Munroe partners, Raymond Treacle, showed up at my office. He offered Munroe's full cooperation in my investigation, plus five thousand dollars if I helped bring about the arrest and conviction of the guilty person or persons. There was no conflict of interest in that, as long as the guilty person or persons turned out to be someone other than a member of the Munroe Corporation, so I agreed.

Both Barney Rivera and Raymond Treacle had given me plenty of background information, but neither had been able to provide any concrete leads. From what Treacle had told me, all sixteen Cooperville residents were backwoods cretins capable of anything, but I discounted that opinion as biased. He had a list of their names and what they did to earn a living, and I ran a background check on each of them that netted me nothing much. I also ran a background check on Treacle and Randall and the other two Munroe partners; that got me nothing much either.

The only thing left for me to do was to drive up to Trinity County. And that was where the difficulty with Kerry lay. We had planned a nice quiet vacation for this week, down in Carmel. My financial position was not exactly stable, however, and this job—particularly after Raymond Treacle sweetened the pot with his five-thousand-dollar offer—was one I could not afford to turn down. Kerry understood that, but she was still disappointed. So in a weak moment I'd suggested that she come along to Trinity County; maybe I could wrap up my investigation in a few days, I said, and we could still get in some vacation time—Shasta Lake was real pretty this time of year. She'd agreed, but without much enthusiasm, and she had been grumpy on the drive up yesterday. Last night and this morning, too.

Now, though, she seemed a little more pleased about

things, and I had hopes that the trip would turn out all right after all, on the personal as well as the financial front. Maybe tonight I would get what I hadn't got last night. The thought made me lick my lips like a horny old hound.

The four fire-destroyed buildings had been set apart from the others, on the left-hand side of the road. That was one reason the whole of Cooperville hadn't become an inferno; others were that there'd been no wind on the night of the blaze, the meadow grass was still green thanks to late-spring rains, and Jack Coleclaw and some of his fellow residents had spotted the fire immediately and rushed to do battle with it. Even so, there was nothing left of the four structures except a jumble of blackened timbers, with a wide swatch of scorched earth and a hastily dug firebreak ringing them.

I stopped the car at the edge of the firebreak. Kerry said as I fumbled around in back for the old trenchcoat I'd brought along, "I suppose you're going to go poke around over there."

"Yup. You can come along if you want to."

"In all that soot and debris? No thanks. I'll go back and look at the ghosts that are still standing."

We got out into the hot sunshine. It was quiet there, peaceful except for the distant raucous screeching of a jay, and the air was heavy with the scent of evergreens. Kerry wandered off along the road; I put the trenchcoat on and belted it, to protect my shirt and trousers, and then went across the firebreak to the burned-out buildings.

The county sheriff's investigators had been over the area without finding anything; I didn't expect to find anything either. But then, I'd had some training in arson investigation myself, back when I was on the San Francisco cops, and I read the updated handbooks and manuals put out by police associations and by the insurance companies. I had also had a handful of jobs over the years involving arson. So there was a chance that I might stumble onto something that had been overlooked.

The first thing you do on an inspection of a fire scene is to determine the point of origin. Once you've got that, you look for something to indicate how the fire started, whether it was accidental or a case of arson. If it was arson, what you're after is the *corpus delicti*—evidence of the method or device used by the arsonist.

One of the ways to locate point of origin is to check the "alligatoring," or charring, of the surface of the burned wood. This can tell you in which direction the fire spread, where it was the hottest, and if you're lucky you can trace it straight to the origin. I was lucky, as it turned out. And not just once— twice. I not only found the point of origin, I found the *corpus delicti* as well.

It was arson, all right. The fire had been set at the rear of the building farthest to the north, whatever that one might once have been; and what had been used to ignite it was a candle. I found the residue of it, a wax deposit inside a small cup-shaped piece of stone that was hidden under a pile of rubble. It took me ten minutes of sifting around and getting my hands and the trenchcoat leopard-spotted with soot to dredge up the stone. Which was probably why the county sheriff's people hadn't been as thorough as they should have been; not everybody is willing to turn himself into the likeness of a chimney-sweep, even in the name of the law.

As near as I could tell, the candle had been made of purple-colored tallow. Which told me nothing much; purple candles were not uncommon. It had probably been anchored inside the cup-shaped stone to keep it from toppling over and starting the fire before it was intended to.

I was peering at the stone, and it wasn't telling me much, when I heard and then saw the jeep come up. It rattled to a stop behind my car, and a guy about six-four unfolded from behind the wheel and plunked himself down on the road.

He stared over at me for a couple of seconds, shading his eyes against the sun; then he yelled, "Hey! You there! What do you think you're doing?"

I saw no point in yelling back at him. Instead I put the stone into my trenchcoat pocket, swatted some of the soot off my hands, and then made my way through the rubble and across to where the guy stood alongside his jeep. He was in his forties, beanpole thin, with a shock of fiery red hair and a belligerent expression. Behind him in the jeep I could see a folded easel, a couple of blank three-foot-square canvases, and a box that would probably contain oil paints.

When I stopped in front of him he scowled down at me and said, "What's the idea of messing around in that debris? You a scavenger or something?"

"No," I said, "I'm a detective."

"A what?"

"A detective." I told him who I was and where I was from and that I had been hired to investigate the death of Allan Randall.

He didn't like hearing it. His expression got even more belligerent; his eyes were flat and shiny-black, like pieces of onyx. "Who hired you? Those Munroe bastards?"

"No. The insurance company that carries the policy on Randall's life."

"So what the hell are you doing here? Randall died in a fire in Redding."

"You had a fire here too," I said.

"Coincidence."

"Maybe not, Mr. Thatcher."

"How do you know my name?"

"I know the names of everybody who lives here. The

Munroe people supplied them."

"I'll bet they did."

"The list includes one Paul Thatcher, an artist who works primarily in oils." I nodded toward the paraphernalia in the jeep. "I get paid to observe things and to make educated guesses."

Thatcher grunted and screwed up his mouth as if he wanted to spit. He didn't say anything.

I said, "I'd like to ask you a few questions about the fire, if you don't mind."

"Which fire?"

"The one here. Unless you know something about the one in Redding, too."

"I don't know anything about either one. I wasn't in Redding when Randall's place burned. And I wasn't here when those old shacks went up."

"No? That isn't what you told the county sheriff's investigators. According to their report, you were one of the residents who helped dig that firebreak to keep the blaze from spreading."

"Is that so," Thatcher said. "Well, I had to talk to the law. I don't have to talk to you."

"That's right, you don't. But suppose I told you I can prove this fire was deliberately set. Would you want to talk to me then?"

His eyes narrowed down to slits. "How could you prove that? You find something in the debris?"

"Maybe."

"What was it?"

"I have to tell that to the law," I said. "I don't have to tell it to you."

He took a jerky half-step toward me, the menacing kind. I stayed where I was, setting myself; he was not big enough for me to be intimidated. But if he'd had any ideas about mixing it up, he thought better of them. He said something under his breath that sounded like "The hell with you," and turned and stalked around to the driver's side of the jeep. Thirty seconds later he was barreling off down the road, trailing dust, headed toward the pines to the west.

Mr. Thatcher, I thought, the hell with you, too.

3

When I looked back at the ghost town there was still no sign of Kerry. I wondered where she was. Between my search of the burned-out buildings and my conversation with Thatcher, some forty-five minutes had passed since she'd wandered off. I shed my blackened trenchcoat, locked it and the waxy stone cup in the trunk of the car, used a rag to wipe off my hands, and set out looking for her.

It took me another ten minutes to find her. She was at the two-story hotel or saloon building; the back entrance wasn't boarded up the way the front was and the door hung open on one hinge, and when I called her name she answered me from inside. So I went in to see what she was up to.

She was standing in the middle of a big, gloomy, high-ceilinged room. Enough sunlight penetrated through cracks in the outer walls to let me see a balcony on three sides at the second-floor level, with three doorways opening off it on the left side and three more on the right; the balcony sagged badly in places and looked as though it might collapse at any time. So did the crooked staircase leaning in one corner down here. As far as I could tell, the only things the room itself contained were a crudely made hotel reception desk, part of which was hidden by a fallen pigeonhole shelf, and piles of dirt and splintered wood and other detritus on the whipsawed floor.

"What'd you do?" I asked Kerry. "Bust in here?"

"No. The back door was ajar. Isn't this place wonderful?"

"Uh-huh. If you like dust, decay, and rats."

"Rats? There aren't any rats in here."

"Want to bet?"

Rats didn't scare her much, though. She shrugged and said, "Somebody lives in this building."

"What?"

"Well, maybe not lives here, but spends a lot of time here. That's how come the back door isn't boarded up."

"How did you find this out?"

"The same way you find things out," she said. "By snooping around. Come on, I'll show you."

She led me over behind the hotel desk, to where a closed door was half-concealed by the fallen pigeonhole shelf. "The door's got a new latch on it," she said, pointing. "See? That made me curious, so I opened it to see what was inside."

She opened it again as she spoke and let me see what was inside. There wasn't much. It was a room maybe twelve-by-twelve, with a boarded-up window in the far wall. Two of the other three walls were bare; the third one, to the left, had a long, six-foot-high tier of standing shelves, like an unfinished bookcase, leaning against it. The shelves were crammed with all sorts of odds and ends, the bulk of which seemed to be Indian arrowheads, chunks of iron pyrite—fool's gold—and other rocks, and curious-shaped redwood burls. An Army cot with a straw-tick mattress, a Coleman lantern, and an up-ended wooden box supporting several tattered issues of *National Geographic* completed the room's furnishings.

"Packrats," I said. "That's who lives here."

Kerry wrinkled her nose at me.

Bill Pronzini

"Either that, or a small-scale junk dealer."

She said, "Phooey. Where's your sense of mystery and adventure? Why couldn't it be an old prospector with a gold mine somewhere up in the hills?"

"There aren't any more gold mines up in the hills. Besides, if anybody had one, what would he want to come all the way down here for?"

"To forage for food, maybe."

"Uh-huh," I said. "Well, whoever bunks in this place might just get upset if he showed up and found us in his bedroom. Technically we're trespassing. We'd better go; I've got work to do."

This time she made a face at me. "Sometimes," she said, "you're about as much fun as a pimple on the fanny, you know that?"

"Kerry, I'm on a job. The fun can come later."

"Oh, you think so? Maybe not."

"Is that another threat to withhold your sexual favors?"

"Sexual favors," she said. "My, how you talk."

"You didn't answer my question."

"It was a dumb question. I don't answer dumb questions."

"You're still mad at me, right?"

"I'm not sure if I am or not. It could go either way."

She started back across the floor, leaving me to shut the door to the packrat's nest. And to chase after her then like a damned puppy. Outside, we walked in silence to where the car was parked. But once we got inside she pointed over at the burned-out buildings and asked, "Did you find anything?" and she sounded both interested and cheerful again.

Maybe she kept changing moods on purpose, I thought, just to get my goat. Or maybe when it came to women, my head was as full of dusty junk as that room inside the hotel. Which was probable, considering my track record. I could study women for another hundred years and I still wouldn't know what went on inside their heads.

I told Kerry about the melted candle, explaining how I'd found it. She said she thought I was very clever; I decided not to tell her that my methods had been devised by somebody else. I also mentioned my conversation with Thatcher. By the time I was finished with that, I had the car nosing up in front of the second of the two cottages near the fork, the one where the elderly woman was still hoeing among the tomato vines in the front yard.

The woman's name, according to the information I'd been given by Raymond Treacle, was Ella Bloom. She and her husband had moved to Cooperville in the late 1950s, after he sold his plumbing supply company in Eureka in order to pursue a lifelong ambition to pan for gold. He'd never found much of it, but Mrs. Bloom must have liked it here anyway; she'd stayed on after his death eight years ago.

She quit hoeing and glared out at us as she had earlier. She was tall and angular, had a nose like the blade of a paring knife and long straggly black hair. Put a tall-crowned hat on her head and a broomstick instead of a hoe in her hand, I thought, and she could have passed for a witch.

I got out of the car, went over to the gate in the picket fence that enclosed the yard. I put on a smile and called to her, "Mrs. Bloom?"

"Who are you?" she said suspiciously.

I gave her my name. "I'm an investigator working for Great Western Insurance on the death of Allan Randall—"

That was as far as I got. She hoisted up the hoe, waved it over her head, and whacked it down into the ground like an executioner's sword; then she hoisted it again and pointed it at me. "Get away from here!" she said in a thin, reedy voice. "Go on, get away!"

"Look, Mrs. Bloom, I only want to ask you a couple of questions—"

"I got nothing to say to you or anybody else about Munroe. You come into my yard, mister, you'll regret it. I got a shotgun in the house and I keep it loaded."

"There's no need for—"

"You want to see it? By God, I'll show it to you if that's what it takes!"

She threw down the hoe and went flying across the yard, up onto the porch and inside the house. I hesitated for about two seconds and then moved back to the car. There wasn't much sense in waiting there for her to come out with her shotgun; she wasn't going to talk, and for all I knew she was loopy enough to start blasting away at me.

"Christ," I said when I slid in under the wheel. "The woman's a lunatic."

Kerry wasn't even ruffled. "Maybe she's got a right."

"What?"

"If somebody was trying to turn my home into a gold-country Disneyland, I'd be pretty mad about it too."

"Yeah," I said, "but you wouldn't start threatening people for no damn reason."

"I might, if I was her age."

"Bah," I said. But because Mrs. Bloom had reappeared with a bulky twelve-gauge cradled in both hands, I started the car and swung it into a fast U-turn. Kerry might not have been worried, but she'd never been shot at and I had. People with guns make me nervous, no matter who they are.

4

The adjacent cottage was owned by a couple named

Brewster, but with Mrs. Bloom and her shotgun nearby, I decided talking to them could wait. The atmosphere in Cooperville was a lot more hostile than I'd anticipated; I was beginning to regret bringing Kerry with me. I considered calling it quits for the day and heading back to the motel we'd taken in Weaverville. But if I did that, Kerry would never let me hear the end of it; and I couldn't believe that everybody up here was screwy enough to threaten us with guns. I decided to try interviewing one more resident. If that went down as badly as the other attempts had, then the hell with it and I would come back alone tomorrow.

At the fork, I took the branch that led away from town and up onto the wooded slopes to the west. The first dwelling we came to belonged to Paul Thatcher; the second, almost a mile farther along, was a free-form cabin that resembled a somewhat lopsided A-frame, built on sloping ground and bordered on three sides by tall redwoods and Douglas fir. It had been pieced together with salvaged lumber, rough-hewn beams, native stone, redwood thatch, and inexpensive plate glass. A wood butcher's house, wood butchers being people who went off to homestead in the wilds because they didn't like cities, mass-produced housing, or most other people.

When I slowed and eased the car off the road behind a parked Land Rover, Kerry asked, "Who lives here?"

"Man named Hugh Penrose," I said. "He's a writer, so I was told."

"What does he write?"

"Articles and books on natural history. He used to be a professor at Chico State. Treacle says he's an eccentric, to put it mildly."

"He sounds interesting," she said. "How about letting me come with you this time? You don't seem to be doing too well one-on-one."

"I don't think that's a good idea—"

"Phooey," she said, and got out and headed for the cabin.

I caught up with her and we climbed a set of curving limb-and-plank stairs to a platform deck. From inside, I could hear the sound of a typewriter rattling away. I knocked on the door. The typewriter kept on going for half a minute; then it stopped, and there were footsteps, and pretty soon the door opened.

The guy who looked out at us was one of the ugliest men I had ever seen. He was about five and a half feet tall, he was fat, he had a bulbous nose and misshapen ears and cheeks pitted with acne scars, and he was as bald as an egg. His eyes were small and mean, but there was more pain in them than anything else. He was a man who had lived more than fifty years, I thought, and who had suffered through every one of them.

He looked at Kerry, looked away from her as if embarrassed, and fixed his gaze on me. "Yes? What is it?"

"Mr. Penrose?"

"Yes?"

Before I could open my mouth again, Kerry said cheerfully, "We're the Wades, Bill and Kerry. From San Francisco. We're thinking of moving up here—you know, homesteading. I hope you don't mind us calling on you like this."

"How did you know my name?" Penrose asked. He was still looking at me.

"The fellow at the store in town gave it to us," Kerry said. "He told us you were a homesteader and we thought we'd come by and look at your place and see how you liked living here."

I could have kicked her. It was one of those flimsy, spontaneous stories that sound as phony as they are; there were a half dozen ways Penrose could have caught her out on the lie.

But she got away with it, by God, at least for the time being. All Penrose said was, "Which fellow at the store?" and he said it without suspicion.

"Mr. Coleclaw."

"Which Mr. Coleclaw?"

"I didn't know there was more than one. He was in his twenties, I guess, and the only one there." Kerry glanced at me. "Did he give you his first name, dear?"

"Gary," I said. *"Dear."*

"What else did he tell you?" Penrose asked. "Did he say anything about the Munroe Corporation?"

Kerry simulated a blank look that would have got her thrown out of any acting school in the country. But again, Penrose didn't notice; he still wasn't looking at her, except in brief sidelong eye-flicks whenever she spoke. "No," she said, "he didn't. What's the Munroe Corporation?"

"Poor young fool," Penrose said. "Poor lost lad."

"I beg your pardon?"

"He has rocks in his head," Penrose said, and burst out laughing. The laugh went on for maybe three seconds, like the barking of a sea lion, exposing yellowed and badly fitting dentures; then it cut off as if somebody had smacked a hand over his mouth. He looked embarrassed again.

Another fruitcake, I thought. Cooperville was full of them. But Penrose, at least, had my sympathy; the strain of coping with physical deformities like his was enough to unhinge anybody.

"That was a dreadful pun," he said. "Gary can't help it if he's retarded; I don't know what makes me so cruel sometimes. I apologize. No one should make fun of others."

I said, "You mentioned the Munroe Corporation, Mr. Penrose. Is that something we should know about?"

"Yes, definitely. If they have their way, you won't want to

move here." He paused. "But I'm forgetting my manners. I haven't many visitors, you see. Would you like to come in?"

"Yes, thanks," Kerry said. "That would be nice."

So Penrose stepped aside and we went in. The interior of the cabin was a spacious single room, furnished sparsely with mismatched secondhand items. Against the back wall was a big table with a typewriter, a bunch of papers, and an unlit candle on it. The candle caught and held my attention. It was fat, it was stuck inside a wooden bowl, and it was purple—the same color purple as the wax I'd found at the burned-out buildings in town.

I went over to the table for a closer look. When Kerry finished declining Penrose's offer of a cup of coffee I said to him, "That's a nice candle you've got there, Mr. Penrose."

"Candle?" he said blankly.

"I wouldn't mind having one like it." I gave Kerry a look. "We collect candles, don't we, dear?"

"Yes, that's right. We do."

I asked Penrose where he'd bought it.

"From a widow lady who lives in town. Ella Bloom. She makes them; it's her hobby."

"Does she just make purple ones?"

"Yes. Purple is her favorite color."

"Does she also sell them to other residents?"

"I don't know. Why don't you ask her? Gary Coleclaw will tell you which house is hers."

"We'll do that," I said. But I was thinking that with that shotgun of hers and her hostile attitude, it would have to be somebody else in Cooperville that I asked. If she sold her purple candles to others, the arsonist could be anybody who lived here. But if it was only herself and Penrose who used them . . .

I steered Penrose back to the topic of the Munroe Corporation, and this time he managed to stay on it without getting sidetracked. He launched into a two-minute diatribe against the developers and what he called "the warped values of modern society." He didn't seem quite as militant as Thatcher and Mrs. Bloom, but then he didn't know I was a detective.

I said, "Isn't there anything that can be done to stop them, Mr. Penrose?"

"Well, we've hired attorneys, you know—those of us who live here—and they've filed suit to block the sale of the land. But there isn't much hope a judge will rule in our favor once the suit comes to trial."

"Have you tried appealing to the corporation? To get them to modify their development plans?"

"Oh yes. They wouldn't listen to us. Awful people. The head of Munroe was an insensitive swine."

"Was?"

"He died last week," Penrose said, with a hint of relish in his voice. "In a tragic accident."

"What sort of accident?"

"He went to blazes," Penrose said, and did his barking sea-lion number again. This time he did not look quite so embarrassed when the noise stopped. "One shouldn't speak lightly of the dead, should one?" he said.

"You mean he died in a fire?"

"Yes. In Redding."

"That's a coincidence, isn't it."

"Coincidence?"

"You had a fire here recently," I said. "We noticed the burned-out buildings in town."

"Oh, that. It was only four of the ghosts."

"An accident too?"

He didn't answer the question. Instead he said, "I told the

others they should have let the fire spread, let it purge the rest of the ghosts as well, but they wouldn't listen. A pity."

Kerry said, "You wanted the whole town to burn up?"

"No. Just the ghosts."

"But why?"

"Ashes to ashes," he said. "They are long dead; they would be better off cremated."

"Why do you say that?" I asked. "Cooperville was once a Gold Rush camp; shouldn't they be preserved for historical reasons?"

"Definitely not. The past is dead; it should be allowed to rest in peace. Resurrection breeds tourists." He smiled, rubbed his bulbous nose, and repeated the phrase as if he liked the sound of it: "Resurrection breeds tourists."

"Does everybody in Cooperville feel the same way?"

"Yes. Leave the ghosts alone, they say. Leave us alone. Let us live and let us die, all in good time."

"So that's why nobody here ever tried to restore any of the buildings," Kerry said.

"Just so," Penrose agreed. "Natural history is relevant; the history of man is often irrelevant. You see?"

I said, "How do you suppose the fire got started? The one here in Cooperville, I mean."

"Does it matter, Mr. Wade?"

"I'm just curious."

"It was a burning curiosity that laid the ghosts," he said, and cut loose with his laugh again. Listening to it, and to him, was making me a little uncomfortable. I get just as edgy around unarmed oddballs as I do around those with weapons.

"Is it possible somebody set the fire deliberately?" I asked him. "Somebody who feels as you do about cremating the ghosts?"

It was the wrong thing to say. Penrose's mean little eyes

narrowed, and when he spoke again his voice had lost its friendliness. "I think you'd better leave now. I have a great deal of work to do."

Kerry said, "Couldn't we talk a while longer, Mr. Penrose? I really would like to know more about—"

"No," he said. "No. Come back and visit me again if you decide to move here. But I don't think you should; it's probably too late. Goodbye, now."

There was nothing for us to do but to leave. We went out onto the platform deck, and Kerry thanked him for his hospitality, and he said, "Not at all," and banged the door shut behind us.

On the way down the stairs she said to me, "Why do you always have to be so blunt?"

"He was getting on my nerves."

"We could have found out more if you'd been a little more tactful."

"We? Bill and Kerry Wade, from San Francisco. Christ!"

"It got him to talk to us, didn't it?"

"All right, so it got him to talk to us."

"Which is more than you accomplished with your direct approach to Mrs. Bloom," she said. "You probably blurted out that you were a detective to Gary Coleclaw and that artist, Thatcher, too. No wonder they wouldn't tell you anything."

"Listen, don't tell me how to do my job."

"I'm not. I'm only suggesting—"

"Don't suggest. I didn't bring you along to do any suggesting."

"No, I know why you brought me along . Women are only good for one thing, right?"

"Oh, for God's sake—"

"You can be a macho jerk sometimes, you know that? You

think you know everything. Well, why don't you go screw yourself? You've been doing it all day."

She slid into the car and sat there with her arms folded, staring straight ahead. I wanted to say something else to her, but I didn't seem to have any words. The thing was, she was right. I had handled things badly with Penrose, and with Gary Coleclaw and Thatcher and Mrs. Bloom. And with Kerry, too. It was just one of those days when I couldn't seem to get the proper handle on how to deal with anybody. But it galled me to have to admit it. Kerry wasn't the detective here, damn it; I was.

A half-mile farther along there was another homesteader's cabin, this one owned by a family named Butterfield, but I was in no frame of mind for another interview. I drove back into town. When we came to the Coleclaw place I looked it over for some indication that Jack Coleclaw and his wife had returned from Weaverville. There wasn't any—no automobiles, no people, not even any sign of the fat yapping brown-and-white dog. So there was no point in stopping there either; I kept on going up the road and out of town.

Kerry didn't say one word to me all the way back to Weaverville.

5

Thirty seconds after I pulled into the lot of the Pinecrest Motel, Raymond Treacle showed up.

I had forgotten all about him. He lived in Redding, and I had talked to him on the phone last night and arranged to meet him here at five o'clock. It was now two minutes past five. My first thought when I saw him drive in was that it was a good thing I had decided not to stop anywhere else in Cooperville. Failing to show up for a meeting with a man who was willing to pay you five thousand dollars was very poor business. I could not seem to do anything right today, except by accident. Maybe I needed a vacation more than I thought I did.

Kerry and I were already out of the car, and she had finally spoken to me, saying that she was going to go in and take a shower, when Treacle appeared. He was driving a brand new Lincoln Continental, and in spite of the heat—it was a good ten degrees hotter in Weaverville than it had been higher up in the mountains—he was wearing a three-piece suit. But he was one of these people who manage to look cool and comfortable no matter what the temperature might be.

He was a handsome guy in his forties, lean and fit, with close-cropped black hair and a fashionable mustache. Throughout our first meeting in San Francisco, which had lasted about an hour, I had kept trying to dislike him. He was glib, he was materialistic and status-oriented, he didn't seem to care much about the feelings of others—he was everything I wasn't and considered distasteful about the modern businessman. And yet he was also so damned earnest, and tried so hard to be friendly, that I couldn't seem to work up much of an antipathy toward him.

He came over and shook my hand in his earnest way. When I introduced him to Kerry he took her hand, too, and smiled at her approvingly. She seemed to like that; the smile she gave him in return was warmer than any she'd let me have in the past couple of days.

Treacle said to me, "How did it go in Cooperville today?"

"I didn't find out much from the people I talked to," I told him, "but I did find evidence that the fire there was deliberately set."

"Oh?"

"Whoever did it used a candle," I said. I went back and

opened up the trunk and showed him the cup-shaped piece of stone with the wax residue inside. "I found this among the debris."

He used one of the rags in the trunk to pick it up, and peered at it. "Travertine," he said.

"Pardon?"

"That's the kind of mineral this is. Travertine—layered calcium carbonate. Geology is one of my interests."

"An unusual stone?"

"No, not for this part of the country." He rubbed at it with the rag, ridding it of some of the black from the fire. "It's fossilized," he said, and showed me the imprints in the stone. "Bryophytes."

"What are bryophytes?"

"Nonflowering plants. Mosses and liverworts."

"Is that kind of fossil uncommon?"

"Not really. They turn up fairly often around here." Treacle picked at the wax residue with his fingernail. "This is purple, isn't it?"

I nodded. "One of the women in Cooperville makes purple candles as a hobby. Ella Bloom."

"That one," Treacle said wryly. "She's crazy. Did you talk to her?"

"I tried to. She threatened me with a shotgun."

"I'm not surprised. Do you think she . . . ?"

"Maybe. I don't know yet."

I closed the trunk. Kerry was fanning herself with one hand; even as late in the day as it was, the heat out there in the parking lot was intense. Treacle noticed her discomfort and waved a hand toward the motel's restaurant-and-bar. "Why don't we go in where it's cool and have a drink?"

"I could use one," Kerry said.

I said, "I thought you were going to go take a shower?"

"I'd rather have a drink. Do you mind?"

I sighed. I seemed to be doing a lot of sighing today. And the three of us went off together to the bar.

Inside, the air-conditioner was going full-blast and it was nice and cool. We sat in a booth, away from the half-dozen other patrons, and ordered drinks—beer for Kerry and me, a Tom Collins for Treacle. While we were waiting for them I filled him in on how my interviews, or attempted interviews, had gone in Cooperville.

"Didn't I tell you they were a bunch of loonies?" he said.

"Yeah."

Kerry said, "They're not such loonies. They only want to be left alone. And they're frustrated." I gave her a warning look, but she ignored it. "Mr. Treacle, may I ask you a frank question?"

"Go right ahead."

"Don't you or your partners give a damn what happens to those poor people?"

I felt like kicking her under the table. You didn't talk that way to clients, especially not to clients who were willing to part with a nice fat chunk of money for services rendered. At least, I didn't talk to clients that way; if I had I would have ended up unemployed. But she got away with it, just as she'd gotten away with fast-talking Hugh Penrose earlier.

"Of course we care, Ms. Wade," Treacle said. He didn't sound ruffled or defensive, he didn't even sound surprised. Maybe it was a question he'd heard a number of times before. "None of us has a heart of stone, you know."

"Then how can you just waltz into Cooperville and take their land away from them?"

"We're not trying to take their land away from them," Treacle said patiently. He paused while the waitress set our drinks on the table and then moved off again. "They are perfectly welcome to continue living in Cooperville after we've restored it."

"You mean turned it into some kind of tourist-trap Disneyland."

"That's not true. Our plans call for careful, authentic restoration. The Munroe Corporation is a reputable development company, Ms. Wade; we're interested in improvement and preservation of historical landmarks . . ."

I quit listening. Things were going on inside my head, things that had to do with rocks and stones. I picked up my beer and nibbled at it. When I put the bottle down again I had nibbled it dry. And I had an idea. A couple of ideas, maybe.

Kerry was still picking away at Treacle, but there wasn't much heat in her voice; she was being controlled. So was Treacle.

I cleared my throat, loudly, to get their attention. They both looked at me, and I said, "If you don't mind, Mr. Treacle, I'd like to cut this short. There are some things I have to do."

"Oh?" he said.

Kerry said, sounding annoyed, "What do you have to do?"

"Drive back to Cooperville."

"Now? What for?"

"There's something I want to check on."

"I don't feel like going all the way back there."

"That's good, because I'm going alone."

"Are you serious?"

"I'm serious," I said, and to prove it I got out of the booth. "I'll be back in a couple of hours—three at the outside. Then we can have dinner."

"I don't think so," she said, miffed again. She leaned across the table. "Mr. Treacle, do you have any plans for the next few hours?"

"Why no, I don't."

"Fine. How would you like to have dinner with me?"

I blinked at her. A minute ago she'd been haranguing him for being unfeeling and greedy; now she was asking him to have dinner with her. Treacle was just as surprised as I was. He looked at her, looked at me, looked at her again, and said, "Well, I don't know . . ."

"Go ahead," I told him. "Ms. Wade can be pleasant company. Sometimes."

"Well, if you're sure you don't mind . . ."

"I don't mind. I'll call you later with another report." I glanced at Kerry before I started away. "Enjoy your dinner."

She stuck her tongue out at me.

6

It was nearly six-thirty when I came down between the cliffs and back into Cooperville. The sun was dropping behind the wooded slopes to the west; evening shadows had begun to gather among the ghost buildings along the creek. The meadow grass had a warm golden sheen. Cooperville was a nice place to visit, but I wouldn't have wanted to live there—not now and especially not after the Munroe Corporation finished with it.

There was a dark green pickup parked alongside the Cooperville Mercantile, which probably meant that Jack Coleclaw and his wife were back from Weaverville. I wasn't interested in talking to Coleclaw, at least not yet, but when I saw the other cars parked over near the cottage I turned in there on impulse. There were five cars altogether, among them Paul Thatcher's jeep and Hugh Penrose's Land Rover. The way it looked, the residents were having some kind of town meeting.

I stopped where I had that afternoon, alongside the gas pump. When I got out of the car, the door to the mercantile opened and Gary Coleclaw came out with a can of Coke in one hand and a half-eaten sandwich in the other. As soon as he saw me he did an about-face and went right back in again. There was no sign of the fat brown-and-white dog. And nobody else came out of the store.

I was not about to go over to the cottage; facing the entire population of Cooperville was something I had no desire to do. I started to get back inside the car—and a man came hurrying around the far corner of the mercantile, from the direction of the cottage. He was alone, and he was somebody I had never seen before.

He stopped two feet away, put his hands on his hips, and stared at me with eyes as cold as winter frost. He was about my age, mid-fifties; dark-complected, powerfully built, with not much neck and not much chin. Running to fat, though. You couldn't see the belt buckle of his Levi's because of the paunch that hung over it.

"You're the insurance detective," he said.

"More or less. And you?"

"Jack Coleclaw. If you're here to talk to me, you wasted the trip. I've got nothing to say to you."

"Nobody seems to have anything to say to me. Why is that, Mr. Coleclaw?"

"You're trying to make out one of us killed that Munroe man in Redding, that's why. No one here had anything to do with Randall's death, mister; no one here started any fires. Now suppose you just get back in your car and get the hell out of Cooperville. And don't come back, if you know what's good for you."

"Is that a threat, Mr. Coleclaw?"

"Nobody's threatening you."

"Two people this afternoon made a pretty good imitation of it."

"Feelings run high around here where Munroe is con-cerned," he said. "All we want is to be left alone. If we're not . . ." He didn't finish the sentence.

"Suppose I go to the county law and tell them I'm being harassed? Do you want that kind of trouble?"

"You can't prove it. Besides, we cooperated with the county cops when they made their investigation. They didn't find anything; there wasn't anything they could find. The sheriff's department doesn't worry us, mister."

"Then why should I?"

"You don't."

"No? How come the summit meeting, then?"

He scowled. "What?"

"It looks like you're entertaining everybody in town to-night," I said. "I figure that's because of me. Or do you all get together regularly for coffee and cake?"

"What we do of an evening is none of your business," Coleclaw said. "You keep coming around here, you'll get the same you got today—and more of it. Now that's all I got to say. You've been warned."

I watched him stalk off the way he'd come and disappear around the far corner of the store. I did not like the feeling I had now: bad vibes, a sense that there was more to this busi-ness than the idea I had developed back in the motel bar in Weaverville. There was too much hostility here, that was the thing. And it was too intense. But I couldn't seem to get a handle on what lay at the root of it.

I drove away from the pump, out onto the road again. If anybody was watching me from inside Coleclaw's house, the curtained front windows hid them. I couldn't see anybody anywhere now. The whole damned town might have been a ghost, lying still and crumbling in the golden light of an ap-proaching sunset.

When I got to the fork I took the branch that led between the abandoned mining-camp buildings. I parked in front of the hotel, got my flashlight from its clip under the dash, and locked the car. Then I went around to the rear, to where the back door still stood hanging open on one hinge. I stepped inside.

Not much light penetrated now, at this time of day, through the chinks in the outer walls. The place had a murky, eerie look to it, as if there might actually be spooks and specters lying in wait on the shadowed balconies and among the decaying rubble. I switched on the flashlight, crossed the rough whipsawed floor.

The light picked up the collapsed pigeonhole shelf, the door in the wall behind it. I swung the door open. Mica particles and iron pyrites gleamed in the flash beam when I played it across the tier of shelves and their collection of arrowheads and chunks of rock. I moved over there. Some of the rocks had fossils embedded in them, all right. Bryophyte fossils, just like the ones in the stone cup in the trunk of my car.

I picked up one that looked to be the same sort of mineral—travertine, Treacle had called it—as the stone cup, and put it into my pocket. Then I swept the rest of the room with the light, looking for something that might confirm my suspicion as to who it was who spent time here. The Coleman lantern, the stacks of *National Geographic*, the cot with its straw-tick mattress told me nothing. But under the cot I found a small spiral notebook, and the notebook had a name on it, and that was all I needed.

I put the notebook into the same pocket with the fossil rock. As I started out the light, probing ahead, showed me nothing but the edge of the desk and the pigeonhole shelf and dim shadow shapes beyond. I took one step through the doorway—

Something moved to my right, behind the desk.

That was the only warning I had, and it wasn't enough. He came rushing toward me out of the gloom with something upraised in his hand, something that registered on my mind as a length of board. He swung it at me in a flat horizontal arc like a baseball bat. I dropped the flashlight, threw my arm up too late.

The board whacked across the left side of my face and head, and there was a flash of bright pain, and I went down and out.

7

I awoke to pain. And to heat and a whooshing, crackling noise that seemed to come from somewhere close by. And to the acrid smell of smoke.

Fire!

The word surged through my mind even before I was fully conscious. It drove me up onto one knee, a movement that sent shooting pain through my head and neck; I was aware that the whole left side of my face was half numb and felt swollen. I had my eyes open, but I couldn't see anything. It was dark wherever I was—dark and hot and filling up with thin clouds of smoke.

Panic cut away at me; I fought it instinctively, shoved onto my feet, and managed to stay upright even though my knees felt as though they were made of rubber. I still could not see anything except vague outlines in the blackness. But I could hear the thrumming beat of the fire, a frightening sound that seemed to be growing louder, coming closer.

The smoke started me coughing. That led to several seconds of dry-retching before I could get my breathing under control. I took a couple of sliding steps with my hands out in front of me like a blind man; my knee hit something, there was a faint scraping sound as the something yielded, and I almost fell. I bent at the waist, groping with my hands. The cot, the straw-tick mattress: I was still in the room behind the hotel desk.

Coughing again, fighting the panic, I slid my feet around the cot and kept moving until my fingers brushed against wood, touched rock. The shelving, the collection of junk. I went sideways along it to my left, toward where I remembered the door to be. Found it, found the latch.

Locked.

I threw my weight against the door, a little wildly. The wood was old and dry; it gave some, groaning in its frame. I got a grip on myself again and lunged at the door a second time, a third. The wood began to splinter in the middle and around the jamb. The fourth time I slammed into it, the latch gave and so did one of the hinges; the door flew outward and I stumbled through, caught myself against the edge of the hotel desk.

The whole rear wall and part of the side walls and balcony were sheeted with flame.

The smoke was so thick in there that each breath I took seared my lungs, made me dizzy and nauseous. I pushed away from the desk, staggered toward the front entrance; tripped over something and fell skidding on hands and knees, scraping skin off my palms. Flames licked along the front wall, raced over the floor. As old and decayed as it was, the place was a tinderbox. It would be only a matter of minutes before the entire building went up.

In the hellish, pulsing glow I could see the boarded-up door and windows in the front wall. I scrambled to my feet again and ran to the window on the left; a gap was visible between two of the boards nailed across it. I got my fingers in the gap and wrenched one of the boards loose, flung it down, and went after another one. The fire was so close that I could feel the hair on my head starting to singe.

Sparks were falling around me; two of them landed on my shirt, on the back and on one shoulder, but I was only half-conscious of the burns as I tore the second board loose, hammered at a third with my fist where it was already splintered in the middle.

When I broke the two pieces outward, the opening was almost wide enough for me to get through. But not quite—Christ, not quite. I clawed frantically at another board, twisting my head and shoulders through the window and out of the choking billows of smoke. More sparks fell on the legs of my trousers, brought stinging pain in four or five places as if someone was jabbing me with needles. I sucked in heaving lungsful of the night air; I could hear myself making noises that were half gasps and half broken sobs.

The oxygen gave me the strength I needed to yank one end of the board loose, and when I wrenched it out of the way I was able to wiggle my hips up onto the sill and through the opening. In the next second I was toppling over backwards, then jarring into hard earth on my shoulders and upper back—outside, free.

I rolled over twice in the grass, away from the burning building; got up somehow and staggered ten or twelve steps into the middle of the road before I fell down again. Now that I was clear of the fire, I could smell my singed hair, the smoldering cloth of my pants and shirt. The smells made me gag, vomit up the beer I'd drunk earlier in Weaverville.

But I was all right then. My head had cleared, the fear and the wildness were gone; inside me was a thin, sharp rage. I got to my feet again, shakily. Pawed at my smoke-stung eyes and squinted over at the hotel.

My car was gone.

The rage got thinner and sharper. He took it away somewhere, I thought. Took my keys after he slugged me and drove it away and hid it somewhere.

But there was no time now to think about either him or the car. The hotel was coated with flame, like a massive torch, and the fire had spread to the adjacent buildings, was beginning to race across their roofs to the ones beyond. Part of the starlit sky was obscured by dense coagulations of smoke. Soon enough, that whole creekside row would be ablaze.

I ran along the far edge of the road, back toward the fork. Most of my attention was on the fire behind me, so I did not become aware of the cluster of people until I was abreast of the last of the south-side buildings, where the road jogged in that direction.

They were standing in the meadow up there—more than a dozen of them, the whole damned town. Just standing there, watching me run toward them, watching the ghosts of Ragged-Ass Gulch burn as though in some final rite of exorcism.

No one moved even when I stopped within a few feet of them and stood swaying a little, panting. All they did was stare at me. Paul Thatcher, holding a shovel in one hand. Jack Coleclaw, with his arms folded across his fat paunch. Ella Bloom, her mouth twisted into a witch's grimace. Hugh Penrose, shaking his ugly head and making odd little sounds as though he was trying to control a spasm of laughter. Their faces, and those of the others, had an unnatural look in the fireglow, like mummers' masks stained red-orange and sooty black.

"What's the matter with you people?" I yelled at them.

"What're you standing around here for? You can see the whole town's going to go up!"

Jack Coleclaw was the first of them to speak. "Let it burn," he said.

"Ashes to ashes," Penrose said.

"For Christ's sake, it's liable to spread to some of your homes—"

"That won't happen," Ella Bloom said. "There's no wind tonight."

Somebody else said, "Besides, we dug firebreaks."

"You dug firebreaks—that's terrific. Goddamn it, look at me! Can't you see I was in one of those burning buildings? Didn't any of you think of that possibility?"

"We didn't see your car anywhere," Thatcher said. "We thought you'd left town."

"Yeah, sure."

"What were you doing in one of the ghosts? You start the fire, maybe?"

"No, I didn't start it. But somebody sure as hell did."

"Is that so?"

"He was trying to kill me, the same way he killed Allan Randall in Redding. He damned near broke my head with a board and then he locked me in a room he used in the hotel and took my car and hid it somewhere. When he came back he torched the building."

Coleclaw said in a flat, hard voice, "Who you talking about, mister?"

"The only person who isn't here right now, Mr. Coleclaw, that's who I'm talking about. Your son Gary."

The words seemed to have no impact on him. Or on any of the others. They all kept right on staring at me through their mummers' masks. And none of them made a sound until Coleclaw said, "Gary didn't do any of those things. He didn't.'"

"He did them, all right."

"Why? Why would he?"

"You know the answer to that. You all hate the Munroe Corporation, so he hates them too. And he decided to do something about it."

"Gary's slow, mister. You understand that?"

"I understand it. But being retarded doesn't excuse him setting fires and committing murder and attempted murder. Where is he? Why isn't he here with the rest of you?"

He didn't answer me.

"All right," I said, "have it your way. But I'm going to the county sheriff as soon as I find my car. You'll have to turn Gary over to him."

"No," Coleclaw said.

"You don't have a choice—"

"The law won't take him away from me," a thin, harried-looking woman said shrilly. Coleclaw's wife. "I won't let them. None of us will, you hear?"

And that was when I understood the rest of it, the whole truth—the source of the bad vibes I had gotten earlier, the source of all the hostility. It was not any sudden insight, or even what Mrs. Coleclaw had just said; it was something in her face, and in her husband's, and in each of the other faces. Something I had been too distraught to see until now.

"You knew all along," I said to the pack of them. "All of you. You knew Gary set those fires; you knew he killed Randall. A coverup, a conspiracy of silence—that's why none of you would talk to me."

"It was an accident," Mrs. Coleclaw said. "Gary didn't mean to hurt anybody—"

"Hush up, Clara," her husband told her in a sharp voice.

Thatcher said, "No matter what happened to Randall, he

had it coming. That's the way we look at it. The bastard had it coming."

"How about me?" I said. The rage was thick in my throat; I had to struggle to keep from shouting the words. "Did I have it coming too? You don't know me, you don't know anything about me. But you were going to let him kill me the way he killed Randall."

"That's not true," Coleclaw said. "We didn't know you were still here. I told you, we thought you'd left town."

"Even if you didn't know, you could have guessed it. You could have come looking to make sure."

Silence.

"Why?" I asked them. "I can understand the Coleclaws doing it, but why the rest of you?"

"Outsiders like you don't care about us," Ella Bloom said. "But we care about each other; we watch out for our own."

"More than neighbors, more than friends," Penrose said. "Family. No one here lies to me. No one here thinks I'm ugly."

I looked at him, at the rest of them, and the skin along my back began to crawl. Thatcher had lifted his shovel, so that he was holding it in both hands in front of him; one of the men I didn't know had done the same thing. Coleclaw's big hands were knotted into fists. All of their faces were different now in the firelight, and what I felt coming off them was something primitive and deadly, a faint gathering aura of violence.

The same aura a lynch mob generates.

Some of the fear I had known at the hotel came back, diluting my anger. I felt suddenly that if I moved, if I tried to pass through them or around them, they would attack me in the same witless, savage fashion a lynch mob attacks its victims. With shovels, with fists—out of control. If that happened, I could not fight all of them; and by the time they came to their senses and realized what they'd done, I would be a dead man.

I had never run away from anything or anyone in my life, but I had an impulse now to turn and flee. I controlled it, telling myself to stay calm, use reason. Telling myself I was wrong about them, they were just average citizens with misplaced loyalties caught up in a foolish crusade—not criminals, not a mob; that they would not do anything to me as long as I did nothing to provoke them.

Time seemed to grind to a halt. Behind me, I could hear the heavy crackling rhythm of the fire. There was sweat on my body, cold and clammy. But I kept my expression blank, so they wouldn't see my fear, and I groped for words to say to them that would let me get out of this.

I was still groping when headlights appeared on the road to the south, coming down out of the pass between the cliffs.

The tension in me seemed to let go, like a rubber band snapping. I said, "Somebody's coming!" and threw my arm up and pointed. Coleclaw and two or three of the others swiveled their heads. And then the tension in them seemed to break, too; somebody said, "God!" and they all began to move at once. Shuffling their feet, turning their bodies—the mob starting to come apart like something fragile and clotted splitting into fragments.

The headlights probed straight down the road at a good clip. When they neared the bunch of us in the meadow Thatcher threw down his shovel and walked away, jerkily, through the grass. The others went after him, in ragged little groups of two and three. I was the only one standing still when the car slid to a stop twenty feet away on the road.

It was Kerry. And Raymond Treacle. They piled out and came hurrying my way. Her step faltered when she got a good look at me. "My God, are you all right?"

"Yeah," I said. "Yeah, I'm all right."

"What happened here? That fire . . . you look as though you . . ."

"I'm okay. It's over now."

"You didn't come back," she said. "I got worried, I asked Ray to drive me here to find out . . . For heaven's sake, what happened?"

I looked back at the raging fire; then I looked up at the line of people trudging slowly toward Coleclaw's mercantile. "Cooperville just died," I said.

8

Within five minutes, Treacle was driving us back to Weaverville. I did not want to stay there among the ghosts old and new even long enough to hunt for my car.

The burns on my back and legs, the lacerations on my hands, were not serious enough to require medical attention, so we went straight to the sheriff's department. I gave the cop in charge a full account of what had happened on my two visits to Cooperville, of how Gary Coleclaw had tried to kill me and how the whole town had been covering up his guilt in the death of Allan Randall. I also told him what it was that had put me onto Gary: The stone cup with the wax residue inside. The room in the hotel with the pieces of rock on the shelves. Penrose's comments to Kerry and me that Gary was a "poor young fool, poor lost lad" and that he had "rocks in his head." A pun, Penrose had said after the latter remark. He'd meant that Gary had rocks in his head not because he was retarded but because he was a collector of unusual stones—arrowheads and fossils and the like. And Treacle telling me the stone cup contained bryophytes, reminding me of those rocks in the hotel room, making me think that the room might have been outfitted by someone with the mind of a child who used it as a kind of clubhouse where he kept the treasures he'd collected.

Gary Coleclaw was not taken into custody that night. He was gone from what was left of Cooperville when the police got there; so were his father and mother. The cops put out a pick-up order on the family, but it wasn't until three days later that a police officer spotted the three of them at a diner in eastern Oregon, and arrested them without incident.

Kerry and I were long gone from Trinity County by then, comfortably holed up in a private cabin near Shasta Lake. The sheriff's men had found my car hidden in the woods near Paul Thatcher's home and returned it to me, and we were allowed to leave as soon as I signed a formal statement. Raymond Treacle's promise of a Munroe Corporation check in the amount of five thousand dollars had gone with us.

I hadn't told the police—or Kerry or anyone else—of my fear of mob violence. I could not be certain I'd been right about what I felt that night; it could have been my imagination, a product of the darkness and the fire and the brush I'd had with death. And no matter what the residents of Cooperville might have done to me in the heat of their passion, I felt no more anger toward them. When I thought of the Coleclaws and Ella Bloom and Hugh Penrose, I felt only sadness and pity.

Still. Still, I couldn't help wondering: Would they have attacked me, maybe even killed me, if Kerry and Treacle hadn't shown up when they did? It was a question that would trouble my sleep for a long time, because there was no way now that I would ever know the answer.

Cat's-Paw

There are two places that are ordinary enough during the daylight hours but that become downright eerie after dark, particularly if you go wandering around in them by yourself. One is a graveyard; the other is a public zoo. And that goes double for San Francisco's Fleishhacker Zoological Gardens on a blustery winter night, when the fog comes swirling in and makes everything look like capering phantoms or two-dimensional cutouts.

Fleishhacker Zoo was where I was on this foggy winter night—alone, for the most part—and I wished I were somewhere else instead. Anywhere else, as long as it had a heater or a log fire and offered something hot to drink.

I was on my third tour of the grounds, headed past the sea lion tank to make another check of the aviary, when I paused to squint at the luminous dial of my watch. Eleven forty-five. Less than three hours down and better than six left to go. I was already half-frozen, even though I was wearing long johns, two sweaters, two pairs of socks, heavy gloves, a woolen cap, and a long fur-lined overcoat. The ocean was only a thousand yards away, and the icy wind that blew in off it sliced through you to the marrow. If I got through this job without contracting pneumonia, I would consider myself lucky.

Somewhere in the fog, one of the animals made a sudden roaring noise; I couldn't tell what kind of animal or where the noise came from. The first time that sort of thing had happened, two nights ago, I'd jumped a little. Now I was used to it, or as used to it as I would ever get. How guys like Dettlinger and Hammond could work here night after night, month after month, was beyond my comprehension.

I went ahead toward the aviary. The big wind-sculpted cypress trees that grew on my left made looming, swaying shadows, like giant black dancers with rustling headdresses wreathed in mist. Back beyond them, fuzzy yellow blobs of light marked the location of the zoo's cafe. More nightlights burned on the aviary, although the massive fenced-in wing on the near side was dark.

Most of the birds were asleep or nesting or whatever the hell it is birds do at night. But you could hear some of them stirring around, making noise. There were a couple of dozen different varieties in there, including such esoteric types as the crested screamer, the purple gallinule, and the black crake. One esoteric type that used to be in there but wasn't any longer was something called a bunting, a brilliantly colored migratory bird. Three of them had been swiped four days ago, the latest in a rash of thefts the zoological gardens had suffered.

The thief, or thieves, had also got two South American Harris hawks, a bird of prey similar to a falcon; three crab-eating macaques, whatever they were; and half a dozen rare Chiricahua rattlesnakes known as *Crotalus pricei*. He, or they, had picked the locks on buildings and cages, and got away clean each time. Sam Dettlinger, one of the two regular watchmen, had spotted somebody running the night the rattlers were stolen, and given chase, but he hadn't got close enough for much of a description, or even to tell for sure if it was a man or a woman.

The police had been notified, of course, but there was not much they could do. There wasn't much the Zoo Commission could do either, beyond beefing up security—and all that had amounted to was adding one extra night watchman, Al Kirby, on a temporary basis; he was all they could afford. The problem was, Fleishhacker Zoo covers some seventy acres. Long sections of its perimeter fencing are secluded; you couldn't stop somebody determined to climb the fence and sneak in at night if you surrounded the place with a hundred men. Nor could you effectively police the grounds with any less than a hundred men; much of those seventy acres is heavily wooded, and there are dozens of grottoes, brushy fields and slopes, rush-rimmed ponds, and other areas simulating natural habitats for some of the zoo's fourteen hundred animals and birds. Kids, and an occasional grown-up, have gotten lost in there in broad daylight. A thief who knew his way around could hide out on the grounds for weeks without being spotted.

I got involved in the case because I was acquainted with one of the commission members, a guy named Lawrence Factor. He was an attorney, and I had done some investigating for him in the past, and he thought I was the cat's nuts when it came to detective work. So he'd come to see me, not as an official emissary of the commission but on his own; the commission had no money left in its small budget for such as the hiring of a private detective. But Factor had made a million bucks or so in the practice of criminal law, and as a passionate animal lover, he was willing to foot the bill himself. What he wanted me to do was sign on as another night watchman, plus nose around among my contacts to find out if there was any word on the street about the thefts.

It seemed like an odd sort of case, and I told him so. "Why would anybody steal hawks and small animals and rattlesnakes?" I asked. "Doesn't make much sense to me."

"It would if you understood how valuable those creatures are to some people."

"What people?"

"Private collectors, for one," he said. "Unscrupulous individuals who run small independent zoos, for another. They've been known to pay exorbitantly high prices for rare specimens they can't obtain through normal channels—usually because of the state or federal laws protecting endangered species."

"You mean there's a thriving black market in animals?"

"You bet there is. Animals, reptiles, birds—you name it. Take the *pricei,* the southwestern rattler, for instance. Several years ago, the Arizona Game and Fish Department placed it on a special permit list; people who want the snake first have to obtain a permit from the Game and Fish authority before they can go out into the Chiricahua Mountains and hunt one. Legitimate researchers have no trouble getting a permit, but hobbyists and private collectors are turned down. Before the permit list, you could get a *pricei* for twenty-five dollars; now, some snake collectors will pay two hundred and fifty dollars and up for one."

"The same high prices apply on the other stolen specimens?"

"Yes," Factor said. "Much higher, in the case of the Harris hawk."

"How much higher?"

"From three to five thousand dollars, after it has been trained for falconry."

I let out a soft whistle. "You have any idea who might be pulling the thefts?"

"Not specifically, no. It could be anybody with a working knowledge of zoology and the right—or wrong—contacts for disposal of the specimens."

"Someone connected with Fleishhacker, maybe?"

"That's possible. But I damned well hope not."

"So your best guess is what?"

"A professional at this sort of thing," Factor said. "They don't usually rob large zoos like ours—there's too much risk and too much publicity; mostly they hit small zoos or private collectors, and do some poaching on the side. But it has been known to happen when they hook up with buyers who are willing to pay premium prices."

"What makes you think it's a pro in this case? Why not an amateur? Or even kids out on some kind of crazy lark?"

"Well, for one thing, the thief seemed to know exactly what he was after each time. Only expensive and endangered specimens were taken. For another thing, the locks on the building and cage doors were picked by an expert—and that's not my theory, it's the police's."

"You figure he'll try it again."

"Well, he's four-for-four so far, with no hassle except for the minor scare Sam Dettlinger gave him; that has to make him feel pretty secure. And there are dozens more valuable, prohibited specimens in the gardens. I like the odds that he'll push his luck and go for five straight."

But so far the thief hadn't pushed his luck. This was the third night I'd been on the job and nothing had happened. Nothing had happened during my daylight investigation either; I had put out feelers all over the city, but nobody admitted to knowing anything about the zoo thefts. Nor had I been able to find out anything from any of the Fleishhacker employees I'd talked to. All the information I had on the case, in fact, had been furnished by Lawrence Factor in my office three days ago.

If the thief was going to make another hit, I wished he would do it pretty soon and get it over with. Prowling around here in the dark and the fog and that damned icy wind, waiting for something to happen, was starting to get on my nerves. Even if I was being well paid, there were better ways to spend long, cold winter nights. Like curled up in bed with a copy of *Black Mask* or *Detective Tales* or one of the other pulps in my collection. Like curled up in bed with Kerry . . .

I moved ahead to the near doors of the aviary and tried them to make sure they were still locked. They were. But I shone my flash on them anyway, just to be certain that they hadn't been tampered with since the last time one of us had been by. No problem there, either.

There were four of us on the grounds—Dettlinger, Hammond, Kirby, and me—and the way we'd been working it was to spread out to four corners and then start moving counterclockwise in a set but irregular pattern; that way, we could cover the grounds thoroughly without all of us congregating in one area, and without more than fifteen minutes going by from one building check to another. We each had a walkie-talkie clipped to our belts, so one could summon the others if anything went down. We also used the things to radio our positions periodically, so we'd be sure to stay spread out from each other.

I went around the other side of the aviary, to the entrance that faced the long, shallow pond where the bigger tropical birds had their sanctuary. The doors there were also secure. The wind gusted over the pond as I was checking the doors, like a williwaw off the frozen Arctic tundra; it made the cypress trees genuflect, shredded the fog for an instant so that I could see all the way across to the construction site of the new Primate Discovery Center, and cracked my teeth together with a sound like rattling bones. I flexed the cramped fingers of my left hand, the one that had suffered some slight nerve damage in a shooting scrape a few months back; extreme cold aggravated the chronic stiffness. I thought longingly of the hot coffee in my thermos. But the thermos was over at the zoo office behind the carousel, along with my brown-bag supper, and I was not due for a break until one o'clock.

The path that led to Monkey Island was on my left; I took it, hunching forward against the wind. Ahead, I could make out the high dark mass of man-made rocks that comprised the island home of sixty or seventy spider monkeys. But the mist was closing in again, like wind-driven skeins of shiny gray cloth being woven together magically; the building that housed the elephants and pachyderms, only a short distance away, was invisible.

One of the male peacocks that roam the grounds let loose with its weird cry somewhere behind me. The damned things were always doing that, showing off even in the middle of the night. I had never cared for peacocks much, and I liked them even less now. I wondered how one of them would taste roasted with garlic and anchovies. The thought warmed me a little as I moved along the path between the hippo pen and the brown bear grottoes, turned onto the wide concourse that led past the front of the Lion House.

In the middle of the concourse was an extended oblong pond, with a little center island overgrown with yucca trees and pampas grass. The vegetation had an eerie look in the fog, like fantastic creatures waving their append-ages in a low-budget science fiction film. I veered away from them, over toward the glass-and-wire cages that had been built onto the Lion House's stucco facade. The cages were for show: inside was the Zoological Society's current pride and joy, a year-old white tiger named Prince Charles, one of only fifty known white tigers in the world. Young Charley was the zoo's rarest and most valuable possession, but the thief hadn't attempted to steal him.

Nobody in his right mind would try to make off with a frisky, five-hundred-pound tiger in the middle of the night.

Charley was asleep; so was his sister, a normally marked Bengal tiger named Whiskers. I looked at them for a few seconds, decided I wouldn't like to have to pay their food bill, and started to turn away.

Somebody was hurrying toward me, from over where the otter pool was located.

I could barely see him in the mist; he was just a moving black shape. I tensed a little, taking the flashlight out of my pocket, putting my cramped left hand on the walkie-talkie so I could use the thing if it looked like trouble. But it wasn't trouble. The figure called my name in a familiar voice, and when I put my flash on for a couple of seconds I saw that it was Sam Dettlinger.

"What's up?" I said when he got to me. "You're supposed to be over by the gorillas about now."

"Yeah," he said, "but I thought I saw something about fifteen minutes ago, out back by the cat grottoes."

"Saw what?"

"Somebody moving around in the bushes," he said. He tipped back his uniform cap, ran a gloved hand over his face to wipe away the thin film of moisture the fog had put there. He was in his forties, heavyset, owl-eyed, with carrot-colored hair and a mustache that looked like a dead caterpillar draped across his upper lip.

"Why didn't you put out a call?"

"I couldn't be sure I actually saw somebody and I didn't want to sound a false alarm; this damn fog distorts everything, makes you see things that aren't there. Wasn't anybody in the bushes when I went to check. It might have been a squirrel or something. Or just the fog. But I figured I'd better search the area to make sure."

"Anything?"

"No. Zip."

"Well, I'll make another check just in case."

"You want me to come with you?"

"No need. It's about time for your break, isn't it?"

He shot the sleeve of his coat and peered at his watch. "You're right, it's almost midnight—"

Something exploded inside the Lion House—a flat cracking noise that sounded like a gunshot.

Both Dettlinger and I jumped. He said, "What the hell was that?"

"I don't know. Come on!"

We ran the twenty yards or so to the front entrance. The noise had awakened Prince Charles and his sister; they were up and starting to prowl their cage as we rushed past. I caught hold of the door handle and tugged on it, but the lock was secure.

I snapped at Dettlinger, "Have you got a key?"

"Yeah, to all the buildings . . ."

He fumbled his key ring out, and I switched on my flash to help him find the right key. From inside, there was cold dead silence; I couldn't hear anything anywhere else in the vicinity except for faint animal sounds lost in the mist. Dettlinger got the door unlocked, dragged it open. I crowded in ahead of him, across a short foyer and through another door that wasn't locked, into the building's cavernous main room.

A couple of the ceiling lights were on; we hadn't been able to tell from outside because the Lion House had no windows. The interior was a long rectangle with a terra-cotta tile floor, now-empty feeding cages along the entire facing wall and the near side wall, another set of entrance doors in the far side wall, and a kind of indoor garden full of tropical plants flanking the main entrance to the left. You could see all of the enclosure from two steps inside, and there wasn't anybody in it. Except—

"Jesus!" Dettlinger said. "Look!"

I was looking, all right. And having trouble accepting what I saw. A man lay sprawled on his back inside one of the cages diagonally to our right; there was a small glistening stain of blood on the front of his heavy coat and a revolver of some kind in one of his outflung hands. The small access door at the front of the cage was shut, and so was the sliding panel at the rear that let the big cats in and out at feeding time. In the pale light, I could see the man's face clearly: his teeth were bared in the rictus of death.

"It's Kirby," Dettlinger said in a hushed voice. "Sweet Christ, what—?"

I brushed past him and ran over and climbed the brass railing that fronted all the cages. The access door, a four-by-two-foot barred inset, was locked tight. I poked my nose between two of the bars, peering in at the dead man. Kirby, Al Kirby. The temporary night watchman the Zoo Commission had hired a couple of weeks ago. It looked as though he had been shot in the chest at close range; I could see where the upper middle of his coat had been scorched by the powder discharge.

My stomach jumped a little, the way it always does when I come face-to-face with violent death. The faint, gamy, big-cat smell that hung in the air didn't help it any. I turned toward Dettlinger, who had come up beside me.

"You have a key to this access door?" I asked him.

"No. There's never been a reason to carry one. Only the cat handlers have them." He shook his head in an awed way. "How'd Kirby get in there? What happened?"

"I wish I knew. Stay put for a minute."

I left him and ran down to the doors in the far side wall. They were locked. Could somebody have had time to shoot Kirby, get out through these doors, then relock them before Dettlinger and I busted in? It didn't seem likely. We'd been inside less than thirty seconds after we'd heard the shot.

I hustled back to the cage where Kirby's body lay. Dettlinger had backed away from it, around in front of the side-wall cages; he looked a little queasy now himself, as if the implications of violent death had finally registered on him. He had a pack of cigarettes in one hand, getting ready to soothe his nerves with some nicotine. But this wasn't the time or the place for a smoke; I yelled at him to put the things away, and he quickly complied.

When I reached him I said, "What's behind these cages? Some sort of rooms back there, aren't there?"

"Yeah. Where the handlers store equipment and meat for the cats. Chutes, too, that lead out to the grottoes."

"How do you get to them?"

He pointed over at the rear side wall. "That door next to the last cage."

"Any other way in or out of those rooms?"

"No. Except through the grottoes, but the cats are out there."

I went around to the interior door he'd indicated. Like all the others, it was locked. I said to Dettlinger, "You have a key to this door?"

He nodded, got it out, and unlocked the door. I told him to keep watch out here, switched on my flashlight, and went on through. The flash beam showed me where the light switches were; I flicked them on and began a cautious search. The door to one of the meat lockers was open, but nobody was hiding inside. Or anywhere else back there.

When I came out I shook my head in answer to Dettlinger's silent question. Then I asked him, "Where's the nearest phone?"

"Out past the grottoes, by the popcorn stand."

"Hustle out there and call the police. And while you're at it, radio Hammond to get over here on the double—"

"No need for that," a new voice said from the main entrance. "I'm already here."

I glanced in that direction and saw Gene Hammond, the other regular night watchman. You couldn't miss him; he was six-five, weighed in at a good two-fifty, and had a face like the back end of a bus. Disbelief was written on it now as he stared across at Kirby's body.

"Go," I told Dettlinger. "I'll watch things here."

"Right."

He hurried out past Hammond, who was on his way toward where I stood in front of the cage. Hammond said as he came up, "God—what happened?"

"We don't know yet."

"How'd Kirby get in there?"

"We don't know that either." I told him what we did know, which was not much. "When did you last see Kirby?"

"Not since the shift started at nine."

"Any idea why he'd have come in here?"

"No. Unless he heard something and came in to investigate. But he shouldn't have been in this area, should he?"

"Not for another half hour, no."

"Christ, you don't think that he—"

"What?"

"Killed himself," Hammond said.

"It's possible. Was he despondent for some reason?"

"Not that I know about. But it sure looks like suicide. I mean, he's got that gun in his hand, he's all alone in the building, all the doors are locked. What else could it be?"

"Murder," I said.

"How? Where's the person who killed him, then?"

"Got out through one of the grottoes, maybe."

"No way," Hammond said. "Those cats would maul anybody who went out among 'em—and I mean anybody; not even any of the handlers would try a stunt like that. Besides, even if somebody made it down into the moat, how would he scale that twenty-foot back wall to get out of it?"

I didn't say anything.

Hammond said, "And another thing: why would Kirby be locked in this cage if it was murder?"

"Why would he lock himself in to commit suicide?"

He made a bewildered gesture with one of his big hands. "Crazy," he said. "The whole thing's crazy."

He was right. None of it seemed to make any sense at all.

I knew one of the homicide inspectors who responded to Dettlinger's call. His name was Branislaus and he was a pretty decent guy, so the preliminary questions-and-answers went fast and hassle-free. After which he packed Dettlinger and Hammond and me off to the zoo office while he and the lab crew went to work inside the Lion House.

I poured some hot coffee from my thermos, to help me thaw out a little, and then used one of the phones to get Lawrence Factor out of bed. He was paying my fee and I figured he had a right to know what had happened as soon as possible. He made shocked noises when I told him, asked a couple of pertinent questions, said he'd get out to Fleishhacker right away, and rang off.

An hour crept away. Dettlinger sat at one of the desks with a pad of paper and a pencil and challenged himself in a string of tick-tack-toe games. Hammond chain-smoked cigarettes until the air in there was blue with smoke. I paced around for the most part, now and then stepping out into the chill night to get some fresh air: all that cigarette smoke was playing merry hell with my lungs. None of us had much to say. We were all waiting to see what Branislaus and the rest of the cops turned up.

Factor arrived at one-thirty, looking harried and upset. It was the first time I had ever seen him without a tie and with his usually immaculate Robert Redford hairdo in some disarray. A patrolman accompanied him into the office, and judging from the way Factor glared at him, he had had some difficulty getting past the front gate. When the patrolman left, I gave Factor a detailed account of what had taken place as far as I knew it, with embellishments from Dettlinger. I was just finishing when Branislaus came in.

Branny spent a couple of minutes discussing matters with Factor. Then he said he wanted to talk to the rest of us one at a time, picked me to go first, and herded me into another room.

The first thing he said was, "This is the screwiest shooting case I've come up against in twenty years on the force. What in bloody hell is going on here?"

"I was hoping maybe you could tell me."

"Well, I can't—yet. So far it looks like a suicide, but if that's it, it's a candidate for Ripley. Whoever heard of anybody blowing himself away in a lion cage at the zoo?"

"Any indication he locked himself in there?"

"We found a key next to his body that fits the access door in front."

"Just one loose key?"

"That's right."

"So it could have been dropped in there by somebody else after Kirby was dead and after the door was locked. Or thrown in through the bars from outside."

"Granted."

"And suicides don't usually shoot themselves in the chest," I said.

"Also granted, although it's been known to happen."

"What kind of weapon was he shot with? I couldn't see it too well from outside the cage, the way he was lying."

"Thirty-two Iver Johnson."

"Too soon to tell yet if it was his, I guess."

"Uh-huh. Did he come on the job armed?"

"Not that I know about. The rest of us weren't, or weren't supposed to be."

"Well, we'll know more when we finish running a check on the serial number," Branislaus said. "It was intact, so the thirty-two doesn't figure to be a Saturday night special."

"Was there anything in Kirby's pockets?"

"The usual stuff. And no sign of a suicide note. But you don't think it was suicide anyway, right?"

"No, I don't."

"Why not?"

"No specific reason. It's just that a suicide under those circumstances rings false. And so does a suicide on the heels of the thefts the zoo's been having lately."

"So you figure there's a connection between Kirby's death and the thefts?"

"Don't you?"

"The thought crossed my mind," Branislaus said dryly. "Could be the thief slipped back onto the grounds tonight, something happened before he had a chance to steal something, and he did for Kirby—I'll admit the possibility. But what were the two of them doing in the Lion House? Doesn't add up that Kirby caught the guy in there. Why would the thief enter it in the first place? Not because he was trying to steal a lion or a tiger, that's for sure."

"Maybe Kirby stumbled on him somewhere else, somewhere nearby. Maybe there was a struggle; the thief got the drop on Kirby, then forced him to let both of them into the Lion House with his key."

"Why?"

"To get rid of him where it was private."

"I don't buy it," Branny said. "Why wouldn't he just knock Kirby over the head and run for it?"

"Well, it could be he's somebody Kirby knew."

"Okay. But the Lion House angle is still too much trouble for him to go through. It would've been much easier to shove the gun into Kirby's belly and shoot him on the spot. Kirby's clothing would have muffled the sound of the shot; it wouldn't have been audible more than fifty feet away."

"I guess you're right," I said.

"But even supposing it happened the way you suggest, it still doesn't add up. You and Dettlinger were inside the Lion House thirty seconds after the shot, by your own testimony. You checked the side entrance doors almost immediately and they were locked; you looked around behind the cages and nobody was there. So how did the alleged killer get out of the building?"

"The only way he could have got out was through one of the grottoes in back."

"Only he couldn't have, according to what both Dettlinger and Hammond say."

I paced over to one of the windows—nervous energy—and looked out at the fog-wrapped construction site for the new monkey exhibit. Then I turned and said, "I don't suppose your men found anything in the way of evidence inside the Lion House?"

"Not so you could tell it with the naked eye."

"Or anywhere else in the vicinity."

"No."

"Any sign of tampering on any of the doors?"

"None. Kirby used his key to get in, evidently."

I came back to where Branislaus was leaning hipshot against somebody's desk. "Listen, Branny," I said, "this whole thing is too screwball. Somebody's playing games here, trying to muddle our thinking—and that means murder."

"Maybe," he said. "Hell, probably. But how was it done? I can't come up with an answer, not even one that's believably far-fetched. Can you?"

"Not yet."

"Does that mean you've got an idea?"

"Not an idea; just a bunch of little pieces looking for a pattern."

He sighed. "Well, if they find it, let me know."

When I went back into the other room I told Dettlinger that he was next on the grill. Factor wanted to talk some more, but I put him off. Hammond was still polluting the air with his damned cigarettes, and I needed another shot of fresh air; I also needed to be alone for a while.

I put my overcoat on and went out and wandered past the cages where the smaller cats were kept, past the big open fields that the giraffes and rhinos called home. The wind was stronger and colder than it had been earlier; heavy gusts swept dust and twigs along the ground, broke the fog up into scudding wisps. I pulled my cap down over my ears to keep them from numbing.

The path led along to the concourse at the rear of the Lion House, where the open cat-grottoes were. Big, portable electric lights had been set up there and around the front so the police could search the area. A couple of patrolmen glanced at me as I approached, but they must have recognized me because neither of them came over to ask what I was doing there.

I went to the low, shrubberied wall that edged the middle cat-grotto. Whatever was in there, lions or tigers, had no doubt been aroused by all the activity; but they were hidden inside the dens at the rear. These grottoes had been newly renovated—lawns, jungly vegetation, small trees, everything to give the cats the illusion of their native habitat. The side walls separating this grotto from the other two were man-made rocks, high and unscalable. The moat below was fifty feet wide, too far for either a big cat or a man to jump; and the near moat wall was sheer and also unscalable from below, just as Hammond and Dettlinger had said.

No way anybody could have got out of the Lion House through the grottoes, I thought. Just no way.

No way it could have been murder then. Unless . . .

I stood there for a couple of minutes, with my mind beginning, finally, to open up. Then I hurried around to the front of the Lion House and looked at the main entrance for a time, remembering things.

And then I knew.

Branislaus was in the zoo office, saying something to Factor, when I came back inside. He glanced over at me as I shut the door.

"Branny," I said, "those little pieces I told you about finally found their pattern."

He straightened. "Oh? Some of it or all of it?"

"All of it, I think."

Factor said, "What's this about?"

"I figured out what happened at the Lion House tonight," I said. "Al Kirby didn't commit suicide; he was murdered. And I can name the man who killed him."

I expected a reaction, but I didn't get one beyond some widened eyes and opened mouths. Nobody said anything and nobody moved much. But you could feel the sudden tension in the room, as thick in its own intangible way as the layers of smoke from Hammond's cigarettes.

"Name him," Branislaus said.

But I didn't, not just yet. A good portion of what I was going to say was guesswork—built on deduction and logic, but still guesswork—and I wanted to choose my words carefully. I took off my cap, unbuttoned my coat, and moved away from the door, over near where Branny was standing.

He said, "Well? Who do you say killed Kirby?"

"The same person who stole the birds and other specimens. And I don't mean a professional animal thief, as Mr. Factor suggested when he hired me. He isn't an outsider at all; and he didn't climb the fence to get onto the grounds."

"No?"

"No. He was already in here on those nights and on this one, because he works here as a night watchman. The man I'm talking about is Sam Dettlinger."

That got some reaction. Hammond said, "I don't believe it," and Factor said, "My God!" Branislaus looked at me, looked at Dettlinger, looked at me again—moving his head like a spectator at a tennis match.

The only one who didn't move was Dettlinger. He sat still at one of the desks, his hands resting easily on its blotter; his face betrayed nothing.

He said, "You're a liar," in a thin, hard voice.

"Am I? You've been working here for some time; you know the animals and which ones are endangered and valuable. It was easy for you to get into the buildings during your rounds: just use your key and walk right in. When you had the specimens, you took them to some prearranged spot along the outside fence and passed them over to an accomplice."

"What accomplice?" Branislaus asked.

"I don't know. You'll get it out of him, Branny, or you'll find out some other way. But that's how he had to have worked it."

"What about the scratches on the locks?" Hammond asked. "The police told us the locks were picked—"

"Red herring," I said. "Just like Dettlinger's claim that he chased a stranger on the grounds the night the rattlers were stolen. Designed to cover up the fact that it was an inside job." I looked back at Branislaus. "Five'll get you ten Dettlinger's had some sort of locksmithing experience. It shouldn't take much digging to find out."

Dettlinger started to get out of his chair, thought better of it, and sat down again. We were all staring at him, but it did not seem to bother him much; his owl eyes were on my neck, and if they'd been hands I would have been dead of strangulation.

Without shifting his gaze, he said to Factor, "I'm going to sue this son of a bitch for slander. I can do that, can't I, Mr. Factor?"

"If what he says isn't true, you can," Factor said.

"Well, it isn't true. It's all a bunch of lies. I never stole anything. And I sure never killed Al Kirby. How the hell could I? I was with this guy, outside the Lion House, when Al died inside."

"No, you weren't," I said.

"What kind of crap is that? I was standing right next to you, we both heard the shot."

"That's right, we both heard the shot. And that's the first thing that put me onto you, Sam. Because we damned well shouldn't have heard it."

"No? Why not?"

"Kirby was shot with a thirty-two-caliber revolver. A thirty-two is a small gun; it doesn't make much of a bang. Branny, you remember saying to me a little while ago that if somebody had shoved that thirty-two into Kirby's middle, you wouldn't have been able to hear the pop more than fifty feet away? Well, that's right. But Dettlinger and I were a lot more than fifty feet from the cage where we found Kirby—twenty yards from the front entrance, thick stucco walls, a ten-foot foyer, and another forty feet or so of floor space to the cage. Yet we not only heard a shot, we heard it loud and clear."

Branislaus said, "So how is that possible?"

I didn't answer him. Instead I looked at Dettlinger and I said, "Do you smoke?"

That got a reaction out of him. The one I wanted: confusion. "What?"

"Do you smoke?"

"What kind of question is that?"

"Gene must have smoked half a pack since we've been in here, but I haven't seen you light up once. In fact, I haven't seen you light up the whole time I've been working here. So answer me, Sam—do you smoke or not?"

"No, I don't smoke. You satisfied?"

"I'm satisfied," I said. "Now suppose you tell me what it was you had in your hand in the Lion House, when I came back from checking the side doors?"

He got it, then—the way I'd trapped him. But he clamped his lips together and sat still.

"What are you getting at?" Branislaus asked me. "What did he have in his hand?"

"At the time I thought it was a pack of cigarettes; that's what it looked like from a distance. I took him to be a little queasy, a delayed reaction to finding the body, and I figured

133

he wanted some nicotine to calm his nerves. But that wasn't it at all; he wasn't queasy, he was scared—because I'd seen what he had in his hand before he could hide it in his pocket."

"So what was it?"

"A tape recorder," I said. "One of those small battery-operated jobs they make nowadays, a white one that fits in the palm of the hand. He'd just picked it up from wherever he'd stashed it earlier, maybe behind one of the bars in the cage. I didn't notice it because it was so small and because my attention was on Kirby's body."

"You're saying the shot you heard was on tape?"

"Yes. My guess is, he recorded it right after he shot Kirby. Fifteen minutes or so earlier."

"Why did he shoot Kirby? And why in the Lion House?"

"Well, he and Kirby could have been in on the thefts together; they could have had some kind of falling-out, and Dettlinger decided to get rid of him. But I don't like that much. As a premeditated murder, it's too elaborate. No, I think the recorder was a spur-of-the-moment idea. I doubt if it belonged to Dettlinger, in fact. Ditto the thirty-two. He's clever, but he's not a planner, he's an improviser."

"If the recorder and the gun weren't his, whose were they? Kirby's?"

I nodded. "The way I see it, Kirby found out about Dettlinger pulling the thefts; saw him do the last one, maybe. Instead of reporting it, he did some brooding and then decided tonight to try a little shakedown. But Dettlinger's bigger and tougher than he was, so he brought the thirty-two along for protection. He also brought the recorder, the idea probably being to tape his conversation with Dettlinger, without Dettlinger's knowledge, for further blackmail leverage.

"He buttonholed Dettlinger in the vicinity of the Lion

House and the two of them went inside to talk it over in private. Then something happened. Dettlinger tumbled to the recorder, got rough, Kirby pulled the gun, they struggled for it, Kirby got shot dead—that sort of scenario.

"So then Dettlinger had a corpse on his hands. What was he going to do? He could drag it outside, leave it somewhere, make it look like the mythical fence-climbing thief killed him; but if he did that he'd be running the risk of me or Hammond appearing suddenly and spotting him. Instead he got what he thought was a bright idea: he'd create a big mystery and confuse hell out of everybody, plus give himself a dandy alibi for the apparent time of Kirby's death.

"He took the gun and the recorder to the storage area behind the cages. Erased what was on the tape, used the fast-forward and the timer to run off fifteen minutes of tape, then switched to record and fired a second shot to get the sound of it on tape. I don't know for sure what he fired the bullet into; but I found one of the meat locker doors open when I searched back there, so maybe he used a slab of meat for a target. And then piled a bunch of other slabs on top to hide it until he could get rid of it later on. The police wouldn't be looking for a second bullet, he thought, so there wasn't any reason for them to rummage around in the meat.

"His next moves were to rewind the tape, go back out front, and stash the recorder—turned on, with the volume all the way up. That gave him fifteen minutes. He picked up Kirby's body . . . most of the blood from the wound had been absorbed by the heavy coat Kirby was wearing, which was why there wasn't any blood on the floor and why Dettlinger didn't get any on him. And why I didn't notice, fifteen minutes later, that it was starting to coagulate. He carried the body to the cage, put it inside with the thirty-two in Kirby's hand, relocked the access door—he told me he didn't have a key, but that was a lie—and then threw the key in with the body. But putting Kirby in the cage was his big mistake. By doing that he made the whole thing too bizarre. If he'd left the body where it was, he'd have had a better chance of getting away with it.

"Anyhow, he slipped out of the building without being seen and hid over by the otter pool. He knew I was due there at midnight, because of the schedule we'd set up; and he wanted to be with me when that recorded gunshot went off. Make me the cat's-paw, if you don't mind a little grim humor, for what he figured would be his perfect alibi.

"Later on, when I sent him to report Kirby's death, he disposed of the recorder. He couldn't have gone far from the Lion House to get rid of it; he made the call, and he was back within fifteen minutes. With any luck, his fingerprints will be on the recorder when your men turn it up.

"And if you want any more proof I'll swear in court I didn't smell cordite when we entered the Lion House; all I smelled was the gamy odor of jungle cats. I should have smelled cordite if that thirty-two had just been discharged. But it hadn't, and the cordite smell from the earlier discharges had already faded."

That was a pretty long speech and it left me dry-mouthed. But it had made its impression on the others in the room, Branislaus in particular.

He asked Dettlinger, "Well? You have anything to say for yourself?"

"I never did any of those things he said—none of 'em, you hear?"

"I hear."

"And that's all I'm saying until I see a lawyer."

"You've got one of the best sitting next to you. How about it, Mr. Factor? You want to represent Dettlinger?"

"Pass," Factor said thinly. "This is one case where I'll be glad to plead bias."

Dettlinger was still strangling me with his eyes. I wondered if he would keep on proclaiming his innocence even in the face of stronger evidence than what I'd just presented. Or if he'd crack under pressure, as most amateurs do.

I decided he was the kind who'd crack eventually, and I quit looking at him and at the death in his eyes.

"Well, I was wrong about that much," I said to Kerry the following night. We were sitting in front of a log fire in her Diamond Heights apartment, me with a beer and her with a glass of wine, and I had just finished telling her all about it. "Dettlinger hasn't cracked and it doesn't look as if he's going to. The DA'll have to work for his conviction."

"But you were right about most of it?"

"Pretty much. I probably missed a few details; with Kirby dead, and unless Dettlinger talks, we may never know some of them for sure. But for the most part I think I got it straight."

"My hero," she said, and gave me an adoring look.

She does that sometimes—puts me on like that. I don't understand women, so I don't know why. But it doesn't matter. She has auburn hair and green eyes and a fine body; she's also smarter than I am—she works as an advertising copywriter—and she is stimulating to be around. I love her to pieces, as the boys in the back room used to say.

"The police found the tape recorder," I said. "Took them until late this morning, because Dettlinger was clever about hiding it. He'd buried it in some rushes inside the hippo pen, probably with the idea of digging it up again later on and getting rid of it permanently. There was one clear print on the fast-forward button—Dettlinger's."

"Did they also find the second bullet he fired?"

"Yep. Where I guessed it was: in one of the slabs of fresh meat in the open storage locker."

"And did Dettlinger have locksmithing experience?"

"Uh-huh. He worked for a locksmith for a year in his mid-twenties. The case against him, even without a confession, is pretty solid."

"What about his accomplice?"

"Branislaus thinks he's got a line on the guy," I said. "From some things he found in Dettlinger's apartment. Man named Gerber—got a record of animal poaching and theft. I talked to Larry Factor this afternoon and he's heard of Gerber. The way he figures it, Dettlinger and Gerber had a deal for the specimens they stole with some collectors in Florida. That seems to be Gerber's usual pattern of operation anyway."

"I hope they get him too," Kerry said. "I don't like the idea of stealing birds and animals out of the zoo. It's . . . obscene, somehow."

"So is murder."

We didn't say anything for a time, looking into the fire, working on our drinks.

"You know," I said finally, "I have a lot of empathy for animals myself. Take gorillas, for instance."

"Why gorillas?"

"Because of their mating habits."

"What are their mating habits?"

I had no idea, but I made up something interesting. Then I gave her a practical demonstration.

No gorilla ever had it so good.

Skeleton Rattle Your Mouldy Leg

He was one of the oddest people I had ever met. Sixty years old, under five and a half feet tall, slight, with great bony knobs for elbows and knees, with bat-winged ears and a bent nose and eyes that danced left and right, left and right, and had sparkly little lights in them. He wore baggy clothes— sweaters and jeans, mostly, crusted with patches—and a baseball cap turned around so that the bill poked out from the back of his head. In his back pocket he carried a whisk broom, and if he knew you, or wanted to, he would come up and say, "I know you—you've got a speck on your coat," and he would brush it off with the broom. Then he would talk, or maybe re- cite or even sing a little: a gnarled old harlequin cast up from another age.

These things were odd enough, but the oddest of all was his obsession with skeletons.

His name was Nick Damiano and he lived in the building adjacent to the one where Eberhardt and I had our new of- fice—lived in a little room in the basement. Worked there, too, as a janitor and general handyman; the place was a small residence hotel for senior citizens, mostly male, called the Medford. So it didn't take long for our paths to cross. A week or so after Eb and I moved in, I was coming up the street one morning and Nick popped out of the alley that separated our two buildings.

He said, "I know you—you've got a speck on your coat," and out came the whisk broom. Industriously he brushed away the imaginary speck. Then he grinned and said, "Skeleton rattle your mouldy leg."

"Huh?"

"That's poetry," he said. "From archy and mehitabel. You know archy and mehitabel?"

"No," I said, "I don't."

"They're lower case; they don't have capitals like we do. Archy's a cockroach and mehitabel's a cat and they were both poets in another life. A fellow named don marquis created them a long time ago. He's lower case too."

"Uh . . . I see."

"One time mehitabel went to Paris," he said, "and took up with a tom cat named francy, who was once the poet François Villon, and they used to go to the catacombs late at night. They'd dance and sing among those old bones."

And he began to recite:

"prince if you pipe and plead and beg
you may yet be crowned with a grisly kiss
skeleton rattle your mouldy leg
all men's lovers come to this"

That was my first meeting with Nick Damiano; there were others over the next four months, none of which lasted more than five minutes. Skeletons came into all of them, in one way or another. Once he sang half a dozen verses of the old spiritual, "Dry Bones," in a pretty good baritone. Another time he quoted, " 'The Knight's bones are dust/And his good sword rust—/His Soul is with the saints, I trust.' " Later I looked it up and it was a rhyme from an obscure work by Coleridge. On the other days he made sly little comments: "Why, hello there, I knew it was you coming—I heard your bones chattering and clacking all the way down the street." And,

"Cleaned out your closet lately? Might be skeletons hiding in there." And, "Sure is hot today. Sure would be fine to take off our skins and just sit around in our bones."

I asked one of the Medford's other residents, a guy named Irv Feinberg, why Nick seemed to have such a passion for skeletons. Feinberg didn't know; nobody knew, he said, because Nick wouldn't discuss it. He told me that Nick even owned a genuine skeleton, liberated from some medical facility, and that he kept it wired to the wall of his room and burned candles in its skull.

A screwball, this Nick Damiano—sure. But he did his work and did it well, and he was always cheerful and friendly, and he never gave anybody any trouble. Harmless old Nick. A happy whack, marching to the rhythm of dry old bones chattering and clacking together inside his head. Everybody in the neighborhood found him amusing, including me: San Francisco has always been proud of its characters, its kooks. Yeah, everyone liked old Nick.

Except that somebody didn't like him, after all.

Somebody took hold of a blunt instrument one raw November night, in that little basement room with the skeleton leering on from the wall, and beat Nick Damiano to death.

It was four days after the murder that Irv Feinberg came to see me. He was a rotund little guy in his sixties, very energetic, a retired plumber who wore loud sports coats and spent most of his time doping out the races at Golden Gate Fields and a variety of other tracks. He had known Nick as well as anyone could, had called him his friend.

I was alone in the office when Feinberg walked in; Eberhardt was down at the Hall of Justice, trying to coerce some of his former cop pals into giving him background information on a missing-person case he was working. Feinberg said by way of greeting, "Nice office you got here," which was a lie, and came over and plopped himself into one of the clients' chairs. "You busy? Or you got a few minutes we can talk?"

"What can I do for you, Mr. Feinberg?"

"The cops have quit on Nick's murder," he said. "They don't come around anymore, they don't talk to anybody in the hotel. I called down to the Hall of Justice, I wanted to know what's happening; I got the big runaround."

"The police don't quit a homicide investigation—"

"The hell they don't. A guy like Nick Damiano? It's no big deal to them. They figure it was somebody looking for easy money, a drug addict from over in the Tenderloin. On account of Dan Cady, he's the night clerk, found the door to the alley unlocked just after he found Nick's body."

"That sounds like a reasonable theory," I said.

"Reasonable, hell. The door wasn't tampered with or anything; it was just unlocked. So how'd the drug addict get in? Nick wouldn't have left that door unlocked; he was real careful about things like that. And he wouldn't have let a stranger in, not at that time of night."

"Well, maybe the assailant came in through the front entrance and went out through the alley door . . ."

"No way," Feinberg said. "Front door's on a night security lock from eight o'clock on; you got to buzz the desk from outside and Dan Cady'll come see who you are. If he don't know you, you don't get in."

"All right, maybe the assailant wasn't a stranger. Maybe he's somebody Nick knew."

"Sure, that's what I think. But not somebody outside the hotel. Nick never let people in at night, not anybody, not even somebody lives there; you had to go around to the front door and buzz the desk. Besides, he didn't have any outside friends that came to see him. He didn't go out himself either. He had to tend to the heat, for one thing, do other chores, so he stayed put. I know all that because I spent plenty of evenings with him, shooting craps for pennies . . . Nick liked to shoot craps, he called it 'rolling dem bones.' "

Skeletons, I thought. I said, "What do you think then, Mr. Feinberg? That somebody from the hotel killed Nick?"

"That's what I think," he said. "I don't like it, most of those people are my friends, but that's how it looks to me."

"You have anybody specific in mind?"

"No. Whoever it was, he was in there arguing with Nick before he killed him."

"Oh? How do you know that?"

"George Weaver heard them. He's our newest tenant, George is, moved in three weeks ago. Used to be a bricklayer in Chicago, came out here to be with his daughter when he retired, only she had a heart attack and died last month. His other daughter died young and his wife died of cancer; now he's all alone." Feinberg shook his head. "It's a hell of a thing to be old and alone."

I agreed that it must be.

"Anyhow, George was in the basement getting something out of his storage bin and he heard the argument. Told Charley Slattery a while later that it didn't sound violent or he'd have gone over and banged on Nick's door. As it was, he just went back upstairs."

"Who's Charley Slattery?"

"Charley lives at the Medford and works over at Monahan's Gym on Turk Street. Used to be a small-time fighter; now he just hangs around doing odd jobs. Not too bright, but he's okay."

"Weaver didn't recognize the other voice in the argument?"

143

"No. Couldn't make out what it was all about either."

"What time was that?"

"Few minutes before eleven, George says."

"Did anyone else overhear the argument?"

"Nobody else around at the time."

"When was the last anybody saw Nick alive?"

"Eight o'clock. Nick came up to the lobby to fix one of the lamps wasn't working. Dan Cady talked to him a while when he was done."

"Cady found Nick's body around two a.m., wasn't it?"

"Two-fifteen."

"How did he happen to find it? That wasn't in the papers."

"Well, the furnace was still on. Nick always shuts it off by midnight or it gets to be too hot upstairs. So Dan went down to find out why, and there was Nick lying on the floor of his room with his head all beat in."

"What kind of guy is Cady?"

"Quiet, keeps to himself, spends most of his free time reading library books. He was a college history teacher once, up in Oregon. But he got in some kind of trouble with a woman—this was back in the forties, teachers had to watch their morals—and the college fired him and he couldn't get another teaching job. He fell into the booze for a lot of years afterward. But he's all right now. Belongs to AA."

I was silent for a time. Then I asked, "The police didn't find anything that made them suspect one of the other residents?"

"No, but that don't mean much." Feinberg made a disgusted noise through his nose. "Cops. They don't even know what it was bashed in Nick's skull, what kind of weapon. Couldn't find it anywhere. They figure the killer took it away through that unlocked alley door and got rid of it. I figure the killer unlocked the door to make it look like an outside job, then went upstairs and hid the weapon somewhere till next day."

"Let's suppose you're right. Who might have a motive to've killed Nick?"

"Well . . . nobody, far as I know. But somebody's got one, you can bet on that."

"Did Nick get along with everybody at the Medford?"

"Sure," Feinberg said. Then he frowned a little and said, "Except Wesley Thane, I guess. But I can't see Wes beating anybody's head in. He pretends to be tough but he's a wimp. And a goddamn snob."

"Oh?"

"He's an actor. Little theater stuff these days, but once he was a bit player down in Hollywood, made a lot of crappy B movies where he was one of the minor bad guys. Hear him tell it, he was Clark Gable's best friend back in the forties. A windbag who thinks he's better than the rest of us. He treated Nick like a freak."

"Was there ever any trouble between them?"

"Well, he hit Nick once, just after he moved in five years ago and Nick tried to brush off his coat. I was there and I saw it."

"Hit him with what?"

"His hand. A kind of slap. Nick shied away from him after that."

"How about recent trouble?"

"Not that I know about. I didn't even have to noodge him into kicking in twenty bucks to the fund. But hell, everybody in the building kicked in something except old lady Howsam; she's bedridden and can barely make ends meet on her pension, so I didn't even ask her."

I said, "Fund?"

Feinberg reached inside his gaudy sport jacket and produced a bulky envelope. He put the envelope on my desk and pushed it toward me with the tips of his fingers. "There's two hundred bucks in there," he said. "What'll that hire you for? Three-four days?"

I stared at him. "Wait a minute, Mr. Feinberg. Hire me to do what?"

"Find out who killed Nick. What do you think we been talking about here?"

"I thought it was only talk you came for. A private detective can't investigate a homicide in this city, not without police permission . . ."

"So get permission," Feinberg said. "I told you, the cops have quit on it. Why should they try to keep you from investigating?"

"Even if I did get permission, I doubt if there's much I could do that the police haven't already—"

"Listen, don't go modest on me. You're a good detective, I see your name in the papers all the time. I got confidence in you; we all do. Except maybe the guy who killed Nick."

There was no arguing him out of it; his mind was made up, and he'd convinced the others in the Medford to go along with him. So I quit trying finally and said all right, I would call the Hall of Justice and see if I could get clearance to conduct a private investigation. And if I could, then I'd come over later and see him and take a look around and start talking to people. That satisfied him. But when I pushed the envelope back across the desk, he wouldn't take it.

"No," he said, "that's yours, you just go ahead and earn it." And he was on his feet and gone before I could do anything more than make a verbal protest.

I put the money away in the lock-box in my desk and telephoned the Hall. Eberhardt was still hanging around, talking to one of his old cronies in General Works, and I told him about Feinberg and what he wanted. Eb said he'd talk to the homicide inspector in charge of the Nick Damiano case and see what was what; he didn't seem to think there'd be any problem getting clearance. There were problems, he said, only when private eyes tried to horn in on VIP cases, the kind that got heavy media attention.

He used to be a homicide lieutenant so he knew what he was talking about. When he called back a half hour later he said, "You got your clearance. Feinberg had it pegged: the case is already in the Inactive File for lack of leads and evidence. I'll see if I can finagle a copy of the report for you."

Some case, I thought as I hung up. In a way it was ghoulish, like poking around in a fresh grave. And wasn't that an appropriate image; I could almost hear Nick's sly laughter.

Skeleton rattle your mouldy leg.

The basement of the Medford Hotel was dimly lighted and too warm: a big, old-fashioned oil furnace rattled and roared in one corner, giving off shimmers of heat. Much of the floor space was taken up with fifty-gallon trash receptacles, some full and some empty and one each under a pair of garbage chutes from the upper floors. Over against the far wall, and throughout a small connecting room beyond, were rows of narrow storage cubicles made out of wood and heavy wire, with padlocks on each of the doors.

Nick's room was at the rear, opposite the furnace and alongside the room that housed the hot-water heaters. But Feinberg didn't take me there directly; he said something I didn't catch, mopping his face with a big green handkerchief, and detoured over to the furnace and fiddled with the controls and got it shut down.

"Damn thing," he said. "Owner's too cheap to replace it with a modern unit that runs off a thermostat. Now we got some young snot he hired to take Nick's job, don't live here and don't stick around all day and leaves the furnace turned on too long. It's like a goddamn sauna in here."

There had been a police seal on the door to Nick's room, but it had been officially removed. Feinberg had the key; he was a sort of building mayor, by virtue of seniority—he'd lived at the Medford for more than fifteen years—and he had got custody of the key from the owner. He opened the lock, swung the thick metal door open, and clicked on the lights.

The first thing I saw was the skeleton. It hung from several pieces of shiny wire on the wall opposite the door, and it was a grisly damned thing streaked with blobs of red and green and orange candle wax. The top of the skull had been cut off and a fat red candle jutted up from the hollow inside, like some sort of ugly growth. Melted wax rimmed and dribbled from the grinning mouth, giving it a bloody look.

"Cute, ain't it?" Feinberg said. "Nick and his frigging skeletons."

I moved inside. It was just a single room with a bathroom alcove, not more than fifteen feet square. Cluttered, but in a way that suggested everything had been assigned a place. Army cot against one wall, a small table, two chairs, one of those little waist-high refrigerators with a hot plate on top, a standing cupboard full of pots and dishes; stacks of newspapers and magazines, some well-used books—volumes of poetry, an anatomical text, two popular histories about ghouls and grave-robbers, a dozen novels with either "skeleton" or "bones" in the title; a broken wooden wagon, a Victrola without its ear-trumpet amplifier, an ancient Olivetti typewriter, a collection of oddball tools, a scabrous iron-bound steamer trunk, an open box full of assorted pairs of dice, and a lot of other stuff, most of which appeared to be junk.

A thick fiber mat covered the floor. On it, next to the table, was the chalked outline of Nick's body and some dark stains. My stomach kicked a little when I looked at the stains; I had seen corpses of bludgeon victims and I knew what those stains looked like when they were fresh. I went around the table on the other side and took a closer look at the wax-caked skeleton. Feinberg tagged along at my heels.

"Nick used to talk to that thing," he said. "Ask it questions, how it was feeling, could he get it anything to eat or drink. Gave me the willies at first. He even put his arm around it once and kissed it, I swear to God. I can still see him do it."

"He get it from a medical facility?"

"One that was part of some small college he worked at before he came to San Francisco. He mentioned that once."

"Did he say where the college was?"

"No."

"Where did Nick come from? Around here?"

Feinberg shook his head. "Midwest somewhere, that's all I could get out of him."

"How long had he been in San Francisco?"

"Ten years. Worked here the last eight; before that, he helped out at a big apartment house over on Geary."

"Why did he come to the city? He have relatives here or what?"

"No, no relatives, he was all alone. Just him and his bones—he said that once."

I poked around among the clutter of things in the room, but if there had been anything here relevant to the murder, the police would have found it and probably removed it and it would be mentioned in their report. So would anything found among Nick's effects that determined his background. Eberhardt would have a copy of the report for me to look at later; when he said he'd try to do something he usually did it.

When I finished with the room, we went out and Feinberg locked the door. We took the elevator up to the lobby. It was dim up there, too, and a little depressing. There was a lot of plaster and wood and imitation marble, and some antique furniture and dusty potted plants, and it smelled of dust and faintly of decay. A sense of age permeated the place: you felt it and you smelled it and you saw it in the surroundings, in the half-dozen men and one woman sitting on the sagging chairs, reading or staring out through the windows at O'Farrell Street, people with nothing to do and nobody to do it with, waiting like doomed prisoners for the sentence of death to be carried out. Dry witherings and an aura of hopelessness—that was the impression I would carry away with me and that would linger in my mind.

I thought: I'm fifty-four, another few years and I could be stuck in here too. But that wouldn't happen. I had work I could do pretty much to the end and I had Kerry and I had some money in the bank and a collection of six thousand pulp magazines that were worth plenty on the collectors' market. No, this kind of place wouldn't happen to me. In a society that ignored and showed little respect for its elderly, I was one of the lucky ones.

Feinberg led me to the desk and introduced me to the day clerk, a sixtyish barrel of a man named Bert Norris. If there was anything he could do to help, Norris said, he'd be glad to oblige; he sounded eager, as if nobody had needed his help in a long time. The fact that Feinberg had primed everyone here about my investigation made things easier in one respect and more difficult in another. If the person who had killed Nick Damiano was a resident of the Medford, I was not likely to catch him off guard.

When Norris moved away to answer a switchboard call, Feinberg asked me, "Who're you planning to talk to now?"

"Whoever's available," I said.

"Dan Cady? He lives here—two-eighteen. Goes to the library every morning after he gets off, but he's always back by noon. You can probably catch him before he turns in."

"All right, good."

"You want me to come along?"

"That's not necessary, Mr. Feinberg."

"Yeah, I get it. I used to hate that kind of thing too when I was out on a plumbing job."

"What kind of thing?"

"Somebody hanging over my shoulder, watching me work. Who needs crap like that? You want me, I'll be in my room with the scratch sheets for today's races."

Dan Cady was a thin, sandy-haired man in his mid-sixties, with cheeks and nose road-mapped by ruptured blood vessels—the badge of the alcoholic, practicing or reformed. He wore thick glasses, and behind them his eyes had a strained, tired look, as if from too much reading.

"Well, I'll be glad to talk to you," he said, "but I'm afraid I'm not very clear-headed right now. I was just getting ready for bed."

"I won't take up much of your time, Mr. Cady."

He let me in. His room was small and strewn with library books, most of which appeared to deal with American history; a couple of big maps, an old one of the United States and an even older parchment map of Asia, adorned the walls, and there were plaster busts of historical figures I didn't recognize, and a huge globe on a wooden stand. There was only one chair; he let me have that and perched himself on the bed.

I asked him about Sunday night, and his account of how he'd come to find Nick Damiano's body coincided with what Feinberg had told me. "It was a frightening experience," he said. "I'd never seen anyone dead by violence before. His head . . . well, it was awful."

"Were there signs of a struggle in the room?"

"Yes, some things were knocked about. But I'd say it was a brief struggle—there wasn't much damage."

"Is there anything unusual you noticed? Something that should have been there but wasn't, for instance?"

"No. I was too shaken to notice anything like that."

"Was Nick's door open when you got there?"

"Wide open."

"How about the door to the alley?"

"No. Closed."

"How did you happen to check it, then?"

"Well, I'm not sure," Cady said. He seemed faintly embarrassed; his eyes didn't quite meet mine. "I was stunned and frightened; it occurred to me that the murderer might still be around somewhere. I took a quick look around the basement and then opened the alley door and looked out there . . . I wasn't thinking very clearly. It was only when I shut the door again that I realized it had been unlocked."

"Did you see or hear anything inside or out?"

"Nothing. I left the door unlocked and went back to the lobby to call the police."

"When you saw Nick earlier that night, Mr. Cady, how did he seem to you?"

"Seem? Well, he was cheerful; he usually was. He said he'd have come up sooner to fix the lamp but his old bones wouldn't allow it. That was the way he talked . . ."

"Yes, I know. Do you have any idea who he might have argued with that night, who might have killed him?"

"None," Cady said. "He was such a gentle soul . . . I still can't believe a thing like that could happen to him."

Down in the lobby again, I asked Bert Norris if Wesley Thane, George Weaver, and Charley Slattery were on the premises. Thane was, he said, Room 315; Slattery was at Monahan's Gym and would be until six o'clock. He started to tell me that Weaver was out, but then his eyes shifted past me and he said, "No, there he is now just coming in."

I turned. A heavyset, stooped man of about seventy had just entered from the street, walking with the aid of a hickory cane; but he seemed to get along pretty good. He was carrying a grocery sack in his free hand and a folded newspaper under his arm.

I intercepted him halfway to the elevator and told him who I was. He looked me over for about ten seconds, out of alert blue eyes that had gone a little rheumy, before he said, "Irv Feinberg said you'd be around." His voice was surprisingly strong and clear for a man his age. "But I can't help you much. Don't know much."

"Should we talk down here or in your room?"

"Down here's all right with me."

We crossed to a deserted corner of the lobby and took chairs in front of a fireplace that had been boarded up and painted over. Weaver got a stubby little pipe out of his coat pocket and began to load up.

I said, "About Sunday night, Mr. Weaver. I understand you went down to the basement to get something out of your storage locker . . ."

"My old radio," he said. "New one I bought a while back quit playing and I like to listen to the eleven o'clock news before I go to sleep. When I got down there I heard Damiano and some fella arguing."

153

"Just Nick and one other man?"

"Sounded that way."

"Was the voice familiar to you?"

"Didn't sound familiar. But I couldn't hear it too well; I was over by the lockers. Couldn't make out what they were saying either."

"How long were you in the basement?"

"Three or four minutes, is all."

"Did the argument get louder, more violent, while you were there?"

"Didn't seem to. No." He struck a kitchen match and put the flame to the bowl of his pipe. "If it had, I guess I'd've gone over and banged on the door, announced myself. I'm as curious as the next man when it comes to that."

"But as it was you went straight back to your room?"

"That's right. Ran into Charley Slattery when I got out of the elevator; his room's just down from mine on the third floor."

"What was his reaction when you told him what you'd heard?"

"Didn't seem to worry him much," Weaver said. "So I figured it was nothing for me to worry about either."

"Slattery didn't happen to go down to the basement himself, did he?"

"Never said anything about it if he did."

I don't know what I expected Wesley Thane to be like— the Raymond Massey or John Carradine type, maybe, something along those shabbily aristocratic and vaguely sinister lines—but the man who opened the door to Room 315 looked about as much like an actor as I do. He was a smallish guy in his late sixties, he was bald, and he had a nondescript face except for mean little eyes under thick black brows that had no doubt contributed to his career as a B-movie villain. He looked somewhat familiar, but even though I like old movies and watch them whenever I can, I couldn't have named a single film he had appeared in.

He said, "Yes? What is it?" in a gravelly, staccato voice. That was familiar, too, but again I couldn't place it in any particular context.

I identified myself and asked if I could talk to him about Nick Damiano. "That cretin," he said, and for a moment I thought he was going to shut the door in my face. But then he said, "Oh, all right, come in. If I don't talk to you, you'll probably think I had something to do with the poor fool's murder."

He turned and moved off into the room, leaving me to shut the door. The room was larger than Dan Cady's and jammed with stage and screen memorabilia: framed photographs, playbills, film posters, blown-up black-and-white stills; and a variety of salvaged props, among them the plumed helmet off a suit of armor and a Napoleonic uniform displayed on a dressmaker's dummy.

Thane stopped near a lumpy-looking couch and did a theatrical about-face. The scowl he wore had a practiced look, and it occurred to me that under it he might be enjoying himself. "Well?" he said.

I said, "You didn't like Nick Damiano, did you, Mr. Thane," making it a statement instead of a question.

"No, I didn't like him. And no, I didn't kill him, if that's your next question."

"Why didn't you like him?"

"He was a cretin. A gibbering moron. All that nonsense about skeletons—he ought to have been locked up long ago."

"You have any idea who did kill him?"

"No. The police seem to think it was a drug addict."

155

"That's one theory," I said. "Irv Feinberg has another: he thinks the killer is a resident of this hotel."

"I know what Irv Feinberg thinks. He's a damned meddler who doesn't know when to keep his mouth shut."

"You don't agree with him then?"

"I don't care one way or another."

Thane sat down and crossed his legs and adopted a sufferer's pose; now he was playing the martyr. I grinned at him, because it was something he wasn't expecting, and went to look at some of the stuff on the walls. One of the black-and-white stills depicted Thane in Western garb, with a smoking six-gun in his hand. The largest of the photographs was of Clark Gable, with an ink inscription that read, "For my good friend, Wes."

Behind me he said impatiently, "I'm waiting."

I let him wait a while longer. Then I moved back near the couch and grinned at him again and said, "Did you see Nick Damiano the night he was murdered?"

"I did not."

"Talk to him at all that day?"

"No."

"When was the last you had trouble with him?"

"Trouble? What do you mean, trouble?"

"Irv Feinberg told me you hit Nick once, when he tried to brush off your coat."

"My God," Thane said, "that was years ago. And it was only a slap. I had no problems with him after that. He avoided me and I ignored him; we spoke only when necessary." He paused, and his eyes got bright with something that might have been malice. "If you're looking for someone who had trouble with Damiano recently, talk to Charley Slattery."

"What kind of trouble did Slattery have with Nick?"

"Ask him. It's none of my business."

"Why did you bring it up then?"

He didn't say anything. His eyes were still bright.

"All right, I'll ask Slattery," I said. "Tell me, what did you think when you heard about Nick? Were you pleased?"

"Of course not. I was shocked. I've played many violent roles in my career, but violence in real life always shocks me."

"The shock must have worn off pretty fast. You told me a couple of minutes ago you don't care who killed him."

"Why should I, as long as no one else is harmed?"

"So why did you kick in the twenty dollars?"

"What?"

"Feinberg's fund to hire me. Why did you contribute?"

"If I hadn't it would have made me look suspicious to the others. I have to live with these people; I don't need that sort of stigma." He gave me a smug look. "And if you repeat that to anyone, I'll deny it."

"Must be tough on you," I said.

"I beg your pardon?"

"Having to live in a place like this, with a bunch of broken-down old nobodies who don't have your intelligence or compassion or great professional skill."

That got to him; he winced, and for a moment the actor's mask slipped and I had a glimpse of the real Wesley Thane—a defeated old man with faded dreams of glory, a never-was with a small and mediocre talent, clinging to the tattered fringes of a business that couldn't care less. Then he got the mask in place again and said with genuine anger, "Get out of here. I don't have to take abuse from a cheap gumshoe."

"You're dating yourself, Mr. Thane; nobody uses the word 'gumshoe' any more. It's forties B-movie dialogue."

He bounced up off the couch, pinch-faced and glaring. "Get out, I said. Get out!"

157

I got out. And I was on my way to the elevator when I realized why Thane hadn't liked Nick Damiano. It was because Nick had taken attention away from him—upstaged him. Thane was an actor, but there wasn't any act he could put on more compelling than the real-life performance of Nick and his skeletons.

Monahan's Gym was one of those tough, men-only places that catered to ex-pugs and oldtimers in the fight game, the kind of place you used to see a lot of in the forties and fifties but that have become an anachronism in this day of chic health clubs, fancy spas, and dwindling interest in the art of prizefighting. It smelled of sweat and steam and old leather, and it resonated with the grunts of weightlifters, the smack and thud of gloves against leather bags, the profane talk of men at liberty from a more or less polite society.

I found Charley Slattery in the locker room, working there as an attendant. He was a short, beefy guy, probably a light-heavyweight in his boxing days, gone to fat around the middle in his old age; white-haired, with a face as seamed and time-eroded as a chunk of desert sandstone. One of his eyes had a glassy look; his nose and mouth were lumpy with scar tissue. A game fighter in his day, I thought, but not a very good one. A guy who had never quite learned how to cover up against the big punches, the hammerblows that put you down and out.

"Sure, I been expectin' you," he said when I told him who I was. "Irv Feinberg, he said you'd be around. You findin' out anything the cops dint?"

"It's too soon to tell, Mr. Slattery."

"Charley," he said, "I hate that Mr. Slattery crap."

"All right, Charley."

"Well, I wish I could tell you somethin' would help you,

but I can't think of nothin'. I dint even see Nick for two-three days before he was murdered."

"Any idea who might have killed him?"

"Well, some punk off the street, I guess. Guy Nick was arguin' with that night—George Weaver, he told you about that, dint he? What he heard?"

"Yes. He also said he met you upstairs just afterward."

Slattery nodded. "I was headin' down the lobby for a Coke, they got a machine down there, and George, he come out of the elevator with his cane and this little radio unner his arm. He looked kind of funny and I ast him what's the matter and that's when he told me about the argument."

"What did you do then?"

"What'd I do? Went down to get my Coke."

"You didn't go to the basement?"

"Nah, damn it. George, he said it was just a argument Nick was havin' with somebody. I never figured it was nothin', you know, violent. If I had—Yeah, Eddie? You need somethin'?"

A muscular black man in his mid-thirties, naked except for a pair of silver-blue boxing trunks, had come up. He said, "Towel and some soap, Charley. No soap in the showers again."

"Goddamn. I catch the guy keeps swipin' it," Slattery said, "I'll kick his ass." He went and got a clean towel and a bar of soap, and the black man moved off with them to a back row of lockers. Slattery watched him go; then he said to me, "That's Eddie Jordan. Pretty fair welterweight once, but he never trained right, never had the right manager. He could of been good, that boy, if—" He broke off, frowning. "I shouldn't ought to call him that, I guess. 'Boy.' Blacks, they don't like to be called that nowadays."

"No," I said, "they don't."

159

"But I don't mean nothin' by it. I mean, we always called em 'boy,' it was just somethin' we called 'em. 'Nigger,' too, same thing. It wasn't nothin' personal, you know?"

I knew, all right, but it was not something I wanted to or ever could explain to Charley Slattery. Race relations, the whole question of race, was too complex an issue. In his simple world, "nigger" and "boy" were just words, meaningless words without a couple of centuries of hatred and malice behind them, and it really wasn't anything personal.

"Let's get back to Nick," I said. "You liked him, didn't you, Charley?"

"Sure I did. He was goofy, him and his skeletons, but he worked hard and he never bothered nobody."

"I had a talk with Wesley Thane a while ago. He told me you had some trouble with Nick not long ago."

Slattery's eroded face arranged itself into a scowl. "That damn actor, he don't know what he's talkin' about. Why don't he mind his own damn business? I never had no trouble with Nick."

"Not even a little? A disagreement of some kind, maybe?"

He hesitated. Then he shrugged and said, "Well, yeah, I guess we had that. A kind of disagreement."

"When was this?"

"I dunno. Couple of weeks ago."

"What was it about?"

"Garbage," Slattery said.

"Garbage?"

"Nick, he dint like nobody touchin' the cans in the basement. But hell, I was in there one night and the cans unner the chutes was full, so I switched 'em for empties. Well, Nick come around and yelled at me, and I wasn't feelin' too good so I yelled back at him. Next thing, I got sore and kicked over one of the cans and spilled out some garbage. Dan Cady, he heard the noise clear up in the lobby and come down and that son of a bitch Wes Thane was with him. Dan, he got Nick and me calmed down. That's all there was to it."

"How were things between you and Nick after that?"

"Okay. He forgot it and so did I. It dint mean nothin'. Just one of them things."

"Did Nick have problems with any other people in the hotel?" I asked.

"Nah. I don't think so."

"What about Wes Thane? He admitted he and Nick didn't get along very well."

"I never heard about them havin' no fight or anythin' like that."

"How about trouble Nick might have had with somebody outside the Medford?"

"Nah," Slattery said. "Nick, he got along with everybody, you know? Everybody liked Nick, even if he was goofy."

Yeah, I thought, everybody liked Nick, even if he was goofy. Then why is he dead?

I went back to the Medford and talked with three more residents, none of whom could offer any new information or any possible answers to that question of motive. It was almost five when I gave it up for the day and went next door to the office.

Eberhardt was there, but I didn't see him at first because he was on his hands and knees behind his desk. He poked his head up as I came inside and shut the door.

"Fine thing," I said, "you down on your knees like that. What if I'd been a prospective client?"

"So? I wouldn't let somebody like you hire me."

"What're you doing down there anyway?"

"I was cleaning my pipe and I dropped the damn bit." He

161

disappeared again for a few seconds, muttered, "Here it is," reappeared, and hoisted himself to his feet.

There were pipe ashes all over the front of his tie and his white shirt; he'd even managed to get a smear of ash across his jowly chin. He was something of a slob, Eberhardt was, which gave us one of several common bonds: I was something of a slob myself. We had been friends for more than thirty years, and we'd been through some hard times together—some very hard times in the recent past. I hadn't been sure at first that taking him in as a partner after his retirement was a good idea, for a variety of reasons; but it had worked out so far.

He sat down and began brushing pipe dottle off his desk—he must have dropped a bowlful on it as well as on himself. He said as I hung up my coat, "How goes the Nick Damiano investigation?"

"Not too good. Did you manage to get a copy of the police report?"

"On your desk. But I don't think it'll tell you much."

The report was in an unmarked manila envelope; I read it standing up. Eberhardt was right that it didn't enlighten me much. Nick Damiano had been struck on the head at least three times by a heavy blunt instrument and had died of a brain hemorrhage, probably within seconds of the first blow. The wounds were "consistent with" a length of three-quarter-inch steel pipe, but the weapon hadn't been positively identified because no trace of it had been found. As for Nick's background, nothing had been found there either. No items of personal history among his effects, no hint of relatives or even of his city of origin. They'd run a check on his fingerprints through the FBI computer, with negative results: he had never been arrested on a felony charge, never been in military service or applied for a civil

162

service job, never been fingerprinted at all.

When I put the report down Eberhardt said, "Anything?"

"Doesn't look like it." I sat in my chair and looked out the window for a time, at heavy rainclouds massing above the Federal Building down the hill. "There's just nothing to go on in this thing, Eb—no real leads or suspects, no apparent motive."

"So maybe it's random. A street-killing, drug-related, like the report says."

"Maybe."

"You don't think so?"

"Our client doesn't think so."

"You want to talk over the details?"

"Sure. But let's do it over a couple of beers and some food."

"I thought you were on a diet."

"I am. Whenever Kerry's around. But she's working late tonight—new ad campaign she's writing. A couple of beers won't hurt me. And we'll have something non-fattening to eat."

"Sure we will," Eberhardt said.

We went to an Italian place out on Clement and had four beers apiece and plates of fettucine alfredo and half a loaf of garlic bread. But the talking we did got us nowhere. If one of the residents of the Medford had killed Nick Damiano, what was the damn motive? A broken-down old actor's petulant jealousy? A mindless dispute over garbage cans? Just what was the argument all about that George Weaver had over-heard?

Eberhardt and I split up early and I drove home to my flat in Pacific Heights. The place had a lonely feel; after spending most of the day in and around the Medford, I needed something to cheer me up—I needed Kerry. I thought about calling her at Bates and Carpenter, her ad agency, but she didn't like to be disturbed while she was working. And she'd said she expected to be there most of the evening.

I settled instead for cuddling up to my collection of pulp magazines—browsing here and there, finding something to read. On nights like this the pulps weren't much of a substitute for human companionship in general and Kerry in particular, but at least they kept my mind occupied. I found a 1943 issue of *Dime Detective* that looked interesting, took it into the bathtub, and lingered there reading until I got drowsy. Then I went to bed, went right to sleep for a change—

—and woke up at three a.m. by the luminous dial of the nightstand clock, because the clouds had finally opened up and unleashed a wailing torrent of wind-blown rain; the sound of it on the roof and on the rainspouts outside the window was loud enough to wake up a deaf man. I lay there half groggy, listening to the storm and thinking about how the weather had gone all screwy lately.

And then all of a sudden I was thinking about something else, and I wasn't groggy anymore. I sat up in bed, wide awake. And inside of five minutes, without much effort now that I had been primed, I knew what it was the police had overlooked and I was reasonably sure I knew who had murdered Nick Damiano.

But I still didn't know why. I didn't have an inkling of *why*.

The Medford's front door was still on its night security lock when I got there at a quarter to eight. Dan Cady let me in. I asked him a couple of questions about Nick's janitorial habits, and the answers he gave me pretty much confirmed my suspicions. To make absolutely sure, I went down to the basement and spent ten minutes poking around in its hot and noisy gloom.

Now the hard part, the part I never liked. I took the elevator to the third floor and knocked on the door to Room 304. He was there; not more than five seconds passed before he called out, "Door's not locked." I opened it and stepped inside.

He was sitting in a faded armchair near the window, staring out at the rain and the wet streets below. He turned his head briefly to look at me, then turned it back again to the window. The stubby little pipe was between his teeth and the overheated air smelled of his tobacco, a kind of dry, sweet scent, like withered roses.

"More questions?" he said.

"Not exactly, Mr. Weaver. You mind if I sit down?"

"Bed's all there is."

I sat on the bottom edge of the bed, a few feet away from him. The room was small, neat—not much furniture, not much of anything; old patterned wallpaper and a threadbare carpet, both of which had a patina of gray. Maybe it was my mood and the rain-dull day outside, but the entire room seemed gray, full of that aura of age and hopelessness.

"Hot in here," I said. "Furnace is going full blast down in the basement."

"I don't mind it hot."

"Nick Damiano did a better job of regulating the heat, I understand. He'd turn it on for a few hours in the morning, leave it off most of the day, turn it back on in the evenings, and then shut it down again by midnight. The night he died, though, he didn't have time to shut it down."

Weaver didn't say anything.

"It's pretty noisy in the basement when that furnace is on," I said. "You can hardly hold a normal conversation with somebody standing right next to you. It'd be almost impossible to hear anything, even raised voices, from a distance. So you couldn't have heard an argument inside Nick's room, not from back by the storage lockers. And probably not even if you stood right next to the door, because the door's thick and made of metal."

He still didn't stir, didn't speak.

"You made up the argument because you ran into Charley Slattery. He might have told the police he saw you come out of the elevator around the time Nick was killed, and that you seemed upset; so you had to protect yourself. Just like you protected yourself by unlocking the alley door after the murder."

More silence.

"You murdered Nick, all right. Beat him to death with your cane—hickory like that is as thick and hard as three-quarter-inch steel pipe. Charley told me you had it under your arm when you got off the elevator. Why under your arm? Why weren't you walking with it like you usually do? Has to be that you didn't want your fingers around the handle, the part you clubbed Nick with, even if you did wipe off most of the blood and gore."

He was looking at me now, without expression—just a dull, steady, waiting look.

"How'd you clean the cane once you were here in your room? Soap and water? Cleaning fluid of some kind? It doesn't matter, you know. There'll still be minute traces of blood on it that the forensics lab can match up to Nick's."

He put an end to his silence then; by saying in a clear, toneless voice, "All right. I done it," and that made it a little easier on both of us. The truth is always easier, no matter how painful it might be.

I said, "Do you want to tell me about it, Mr. Weaver?"

"Not much to tell," he said. "I went to the basement to get

166

my other radio, like I told you before. He was fixing the door to one of the storage bins near mine. I looked at him up close, and I knew he was the one. I'd had a feeling he was ever since I moved in, but that night, up close like that, I knew it for sure."

He paused to take the pipe out of his mouth and lay it carefully on the table next to his chair. Then he said, "I accused him point blank. He put his hands over his ears like a woman, like he couldn't stand to hear it, and ran to his room. I went after him. Got inside before he could shut the door. He started babbling, crazy things about skeletons, and I saw that skeleton of his grinning across the room, and I . . . I don't know, I don't remember that part too good. He pushed me, I think, and I hit him with my cane, I kept hitting him . . ."

His voice trailed off and he sat there stiffly, with his big gnarled hands clenched in his lap.

"Why, Mr. Weaver? You said he was the one, that you accused him. Accused him of what?"

He didn't seem to hear me. He said, "After I come to my senses, I couldn't breathe. Thought I was having a heart attack. God, it was hot in there . . . hot as hell. I opened the alley door to get some air and I guess I must have left it unlocked. I never did that on purpose. Only the story about the argument."

"Why did you kill Nick Damiano?"

No answer for a few seconds; I thought he still wasn't listening and I was about to ask the question again. But then he said, "My Bible's over on the desk. Look inside the front cover."

The Bible was a well-used Gideon and inside the front cover was a yellowed newspaper clipping. I opened the clipping. It was from the *Chicago Sun-Times*, dated June 23, 1957—a news story, with an accompanying photograph, that bore the headline: FLOWER SHOP BOMBER IDENTIFIED.

I took it back to the bed and sat again to read it. It said that the person responsible for a homemade bomb that had exploded in a crowded florist shop the day before, killing seven people, was a handyman named Nicholas Donato. One of the dead was Marjorie Donato, the bomber's estranged wife and an employee of the shop; another victim was the shop's owner, Arthur Cullen, with whom Mrs. Donato had apparently been having an affair. According to friends, Nicholas Donato had been despondent over the estrangement and the affair, had taken to drinking heavily, and had threatened "to do something drastic" if his wife didn't move back in with him. He had disappeared the morning of the explosion and had not been apprehended at the time the news story was printed. His evident intention had been to blow up only his wife and her lover; but Mrs. Donato had opened the package containing the bomb immediately after it was brought by messenger, in the presence of several customers, and the result had been mass slaughter.

I studied the photograph of Nicholas Donato. It was a head-and-shoulders shot, of not very good quality, and I had to look at it closely for a time to see the likeness. But it was there: Nicholas Donato and Nick Damiano had been the same man.

Weaver had been watching me read. When I looked up from the clipping he said, "They never caught him. Traced him to Indianapolis, but then he disappeared for good. All these years, twenty-seven years, and I come across him here in San Francisco. Coincidence. Or maybe it was supposed to happen that way. The hand of the Lord guides us all, and we don't always understand the whys and wherefores."

"Mr. Weaver, what did that bombing have to do with you?"

"One of the people he blew up was my youngest daughter. Twenty-two that year. Went to that flower shop to pick out an arrangement for her wedding. I saw her after it happened, I saw what his bomb did to her . . ."

He broke off again; his strong voice trembled a little now. But his eyes were dry. He'd cried once, he'd cried many times, but that had been long ago. There were no tears left any more.

I got slowly to my feet. The heat and the sweetish tobacco scent were making me feel sick to my stomach. And the grayness, the aura of age and hopelessness and tragedy, were like an oppressive weight.

I said, "I'll be going now."

"Going?" he said. "Telephone's right over there."

"I won't be calling the police, Mr. Weaver. From here or from anywhere else."

"What's that? But . . . you know I killed him . . ."

"I don't know anything," I said. "I don't even remember coming here today."

I left him quickly, before he could say anything else, and went downstairs and out to O'Farrell Street. Wind-hurled rain buffeted me, icy and stinging, but the feel and smell of it was a relief. I pulled up the collar on my overcoat and hurried next door.

Upstairs in the office I took Irv Feinberg's two hundred dollars out of the lock-box in the desk and slipped the envelope into my coat pocket. He wouldn't like getting it back; he wouldn't like my calling it quits on the investigation, just as the police had done. But that didn't matter. Let the dead lie still, and the dying find what little peace they had left. The judgment was out of human hands anyway.

I tried not to think about Nick Damiano any more, but it was too soon and I couldn't blot him out yet. Harmless old Nick, the happy whack. Jesus Christ. Seven people—he had slaughtered seven people that day in 1957. And for what? For a lost woman; for a lost love. No wonder he'd gone batty and developed an obsession for skeletons. He had lived with them, seven of them, all those years, heard them clattering and clacking all those thousands of nights. And now, pretty soon, he would be one himself.

Skeleton rattle your mouldy leg.

All men's lovers come to this.

Incident in a Neighborhood Tavern

When the holdup went down I was sitting at the near end of the Foghorn Tavern's scarred mahogany bar talking to the owner, Matt Candiotti.

It was a little before seven of a midweek evening, lull-time in working-class neighborhood saloons like this one. Blue-collar locals would jam the place from four until about six-thirty, when the last of them headed home for dinner; the hard-core drinkers wouldn't begin filtering back in until about seven-thirty or eight. Right now there were only two customers, and the jukebox and computer hockey games were quiet. The TV over the back bar was on, but with the sound turned down to a tolerable level. One of the customers, a porky guy in his fifties, drinking Anchor Steam out of the bottle, was watching the last of the NBC national news. The other customer, an equally porky and middle-aged female barfly, half in the bag on red wine, was trying to convince him to pay attention to her instead of Tom Brokaw.

I had a draft beer in front of me, but that wasn't the reason I was there. I'd come to ask Candiotti, as I had asked two dozen other merchants here in the Outer Mission, if he could offer any leads on the rash of burglaries that were plaguing small businesses in the neighborhood. The police hadn't come up with anything positive after six weeks, so a couple of the victims had gotten up a fund and hired me to see what I could find out. They'd picked me because I had been born and raised in the Outer Mission, I still had friends and shirt-tail relatives living here, and I understood the neighborhood a good deal better than any other private detective in San Francisco.

But so far I wasn't having any more luck than the SFPD. None of the merchants I'd spoken with today had given me any new ideas. And Candiotti was proving to be no exception. He stood slicing limes into wedges as we talked. They might have been onions the way his long, mournful face was screwed up, like a man trying to hold back tears. His gray-stubbled jowls wobbled every time he shook his head. He reminded me of a tired old hound, friendly and sad, as if life had dealt him a few kicks but not quite enough to rob him of his good nature.

"Wish I could help," he said. "But hell, I don't hear nothing. Must be pros from Hunters Point or the Fillmore, hah?"

Hunters Point and the Fillmore were black sections of the city, which was a pretty good indicator of where his head was at. I said, "Some of the others figure it for local talent."

"Out of this neighborhood, you mean?"

I nodded, drank some of my draft.

"Nah, I doubt it," he said. "Guys that organized, they don't shit where they eat. Too smart, you know?"

"Maybe. Any break-ins or attempted break-ins here?"

"Not so far. I got bars on all the windows, double dead-bolt locks on the storeroom door off the alley. Besides, what's for them to steal besides a few cases of whiskey?"

"You don't keep cash on the premises overnight?"

"Fifty bucks in the till," Candiotti said, "that's all; that's my limit. Everything else goes out of here when I close up, down to the night deposit at the B of A on Mission. My mama didn't raise no airheads." He scraped the lime wedges off his board into a plastic container, and racked the serrated knife he'd been using. "One thing I did hear," he said. "I heard some of the loot turned up down in San Jose. You know about that?"

"Not much of a lead there. Secondhand dealer named Pitman had a few pieces of stereo equipment stolen from the factory outlet store on Geneva. Said he bought it from a guy at the San Jose flea market, somebody he didn't know, never saw before."

"Yeah, sure," Candiotti said wryly. "What do the cops think?"

"That Pitman bought it off a fence."

"Makes sense. So maybe the boosters are from San Jose, hah?"

"Could be," I said, and that was when the kid walked in.

He brought bad air in with him; I sensed it right away and so did Candiotti. We both glanced at the door when it opened, the way you do, but we didn't look away again once we saw him. He was in his early twenties, dark-skinned, dressed in chinos, a cotton windbreaker, sharp-toed shoes polished to a high gloss. But it was his eyes that put the chill on my neck, the sudden clutch of tension down low in my belly. They were bright, jumpy, on the wild side, and in the dim light of the Foghorn's interior, the pupils were so small they seemed nonexistent. He had one hand in his jacket pocket and I knew it was clamped around a gun even before he took it out and showed it to us.

He came up to the bar a few feet on my left, the gun jabbing the air in front of him. He couldn't hold it steady; it kept jerking up and down, from side to side, as if it had a kind of spasmodic life of its own. Behind me, at the other end of the bar, I heard Anchor Steam suck in his breath, the barfly make a sound like a stifled moan. I eased back a little on the stool, watching the gun and the kid's eyes flick from Candiotti to

me to the two customers and back around again. Candiotti
didn't move at all, just stood there staring with his hound's
face screwed up in that holding-back-tears way.

"All right all right," the kid said. His voice was high
pitched, excited, and there was drool at one corner of his
mouth. You couldn't get much more stoned than he was and
still function. Coke, crack, speed—maybe a combination.
The gun that kept flicking this way and that had to be a goddamn Saturday night special. "Listen good, man, everybody
listen good. I don't want to kill none of you, man, but I will if
I got to, you better believe it."

None of us said anything. None of us moved.

The kid had a folded-up paper sack in one pocket; he
dragged it out with his free hand, dropped it, broke quickly
at the middle to pick it up without lowering his gaze. When
he straightened again there was sweat on his forehead, more
drool coming out of his mouth. He threw the sack on the
bar.

"Put the money in there Mr. Cyclone Man," he said to
Candiotti. "All the money in the register but not the coins, I
don't want the fuckin' coins, you hear me?"

Candiotti nodded; reached out slowly, caught up the sack,
turned toward the back bar with his shoulders hunched up
against his neck. When he punched No Sale on the register,
the ringing thump of the cash drawer sliding open seemed
overloud in the electric hush. For a few seconds the kid
watched him scoop bills into the paper sack; then his eyes and
the gun skittered my way again. I had looked into the muzzle
of a handgun before and it was the same feeling each time:
dull fear, helplessness, a kind of naked vulnerability.

"Your wallet on the bar, man, all your cash." The gun
barrel and the wild eyes flicked away again, down the length
of the plank, before I could move to comply. "You down

there, dude, you and fat mama put your money on the bar. All of it, hurry up."

Each of us did as we were told. While I was getting my wallet out I managed to slide my right foot off the stool, onto the brass rail, and to get my right hand pressed tight against the beveled edge of the bar. If I had to make any sudden moves, I would need the leverage.

Candiotti finished loading the sack, turned from the register. There was a grayish cast to his face now—the wet gray color of fear. The kid said to him, "Pick up their money, put it in the sack with the rest. Come on come on come on!"

Candiotti went to the far end of the plank, scooped up the wallets belonging to Anchor Steam and the woman; then he came back my way, added my wallet to the contents of the paper sack, put the sack down carefully in front of the kid.

"Okay," the kid said, "okay all right." He glanced over his shoulder at the street door, as if he'd heard something there; but it stayed closed. He jerked his head around again. In his sweaty agitation the Saturday night special almost slipped free of his fingers; he fumbled a tighter grip on it, and when it didn't go off I let the breath I had been holding come out thin and slow between my teeth. The muscles in my shoulders and back were drawn so tight I was afraid they might cramp.

The kid reached out for the sack, dragged it in against his body. But he made no move to leave with it. Instead he said, "Now we go get the big pile, man."

Candiotti opened his mouth, closed it again. His eyes were almost as big and starey as the kid's.

"Come on Mr. Cyclone Man, the safe, the safe in your office. We goin' back there now."

"No money in that safe," Candiotti said in a thin, scratchy voice. "Nothing valuable."

"Oh man I'll kill you man I'll blow your fuckin' head off! I ain't playin' no games I want that money!"

He took two steps forward, jabbing with the gun up close to Candiotti's gray face. Candiotti backed off a step, brought his hands up, took a tremulous breath.

"All right," he said, "but I got to get the key to the office. It's in the register."

"Hurry up hurry up!"

Candiotti turned back to the register, rang it open, rummaged inside with his left hand. But with his right hand, shielded from the kid by his body, he eased up the top on a large wooden cigar box adjacent. The hand disappeared inside; came out again with metal in it, glinting in the back bar lights. I saw it and I wanted to yell at him, but it wouldn't have done any good, would only have warned the kid . . . and he was already turning with it, bringing it up with both hands now—the damn gun of his own he'd had hidden inside the cigar box. There was no time for me to do anything but shove away from the bar and sideways off the stool just as Candiotti opened fire.

The state he was in, the kid didn't realize what was happening until it was too late for him to react; he never even got a shot off. Candiotti's first slug knocked him halfway around, and one of the three others that followed it opened up his face like a piece of ripe fruit smacked by a hammer. He was dead before his body, driven backward, slammed into the cigarette machine near the door, slid down it to the floor.

The half-drunk woman was yelling in broken shrieks, as if she couldn't get enough air for a sustained scream. When I came up out of my crouch I saw that Anchor Steam had hold of her, clinging to her as much for support as in an effort to calm her down. Candiotti stood flat-footed, his arms down at his sides, the gun out of sight below the bar, staring at the bloody remains of the kid as if he couldn't believe what he was seeing, couldn't believe what he'd done.

Some of the tension in me eased as I went to the door, found the lock on its security gate, fastened it before anybody could come in off the street. The Saturday night special was still clutched in the kid's hand; I bent, pulled it free with my thumb and forefinger, and broke the cylinder. It was loaded, all right—five cartridges. I dropped it into my jacket pocket, thought about checking the kid's clothing for identification, didn't do it. It wasn't any of my business, now, who he'd been. And I did not want to touch him or any part of him. There was a queasiness in my stomach, a fluttery weakness behind my knees—the same delayed reaction I always had to violence and death—and touching him would only make it worse.

To keep from looking at the red ruin of the kid's face, I pivoted back to the bar. Candiotti hadn't moved. Anchor Steam had gotten the woman to stop screeching and had coaxed her over to one of the handful of tables near the jukebox; now she was sobbing, "I've got to go home, I'm gonna be sick if I don't go home." But she didn't make any move to get up and neither did Anchor Steam.

I walked over near Candiotti and pushed hard words at him in an undertone. "That was a damn fool thing to do. You could have got us all killed."

"I know," he said. "I know."

"Why'd you do it?"

"I thought . . . hell, you saw the way he was waving that piece of his . . ."

"Yeah," I said. "Call the police. Nine-eleven."

"Nine-eleven. Okay."

"Put that gun of yours down first. On the bar."

He did that. There was a phone on the back bar; he went away to it in shaky strides. While he was talking to the Emergency operator I picked up his weapon, saw that it was a .32 Charter Arms revolver. I held it in my hand until Candiotti finished with the call, then set it down again as he came back to where I stood.

"They'll have somebody here in five minutes," he said.

I said, "You know that kid?"

"Christ, no."

"Ever see him before? Here or anywhere else?"

"No."

"So how did he know about your safe?"

Candiotti blinked at me. "What?"

"The safe in your office. Street kid like that . . . how'd he know about it?"

"How should I know? What difference does it make?"

"He seemed to think you keep big money in that safe."

"Well, I don't. There's nothing in it."

"That's right, you told me you don't keep more than fifty bucks on the premises overnight. In the till."

"Yeah."

"Then why have you got a safe, if it's empty?"

Candiotti's eyes narrowed. "I used to keep my receipts in it, all right? Before all these burglaries started. Then I figured I'd be smarter to take the money to the bank every night."

"Sure, that explains it," I said. "Still, a kid like that, looking for a big score to feed his habit, he wasn't just after what was in the till and our wallets. No, it was as if he'd gotten wind of a heavy stash—a few grand or more."

Nothing from Candiotti.

I watched him for a time. Then I said, "Big risk you took, using that thirty-two of yours. How come you didn't make your play the first time you went to the register? How come you waited until the kid mentioned your office safe?"

"I didn't like the way he was acting, like he might start

shooting any second. I figured it was our only chance. Listen, what're you getting at, hah?"

"Another funny thing," I said, "is the way he called you 'Mr. Cyclone Man.' Now why would a hopped-up kid use a term like that to a bar owner he didn't know?"

"How the hell should I know?"

"Cyclone," I said. "What's a cyclone but a big destructive wind? Only one other thing I can think of."

"Yeah? What's that?"

"A fence. A cyclone fence."

Candiotti made a fidgety movement. Some of the wet gray pallor was beginning to spread across his cheeks again, like a fungus.

I said, "And a fence is somebody who receives and distributes stolen goods. A Mr. Fence Man. But then you know that, don't you, Candiotti? We were talking about that kind of fence before the kid came in . . . how Pitman, down in San Jose, bought some hot stereo equipment off of one. That fence could just as easily be operating here in San Francisco, though. Right here in this neighborhood, in fact. Hell, suppose the stuff taken in all those burglaries never left the neighborhood. Suppose it was brought to a place nearby and stored until it could be trucked out to other cities—a tavern storeroom, for instance. Might even be some of it is still in that storeroom. And the money he got for the rest he'd keep locked up in his safe, right? Who'd figure it? Except maybe a poor junkie who picked up a whisper on the street somewhere—"

Candiotti made a sudden grab for the .32, caught it and backed up a step with it leveled at my chest. "You smart son of a bitch," he said. "I ought to kill you too."

"In front of witnesses? With the police due any minute?"

He glanced over at the two customers. The woman was

still sobbing, lost in a bleak outpouring of self-pity; but Anchor Steam was staring our way, and from the expression on his face he'd heard every word of my exchange with Candiotti.

"There's still enough time for me to get clear," Candiotti said grimly. He was talking to himself, not to me. Sweat had plastered his lank hair to his forehead; the revolver was not quite steady in his hand. "Lock you up in my office, you and those two back there . . ."

"I don't think so," I said.

"Goddamn you, you think I won't use this gun again?"

"I know you won't use it. I emptied out the last two cartridges while you were on the phone."

I took the two shells from my left-hand jacket pocket and held them up where he could see them. At the same time I got the kid's Saturday night special out of the other pocket, held it loosely pointed in his direction. "You want to put your piece down now, Candiotti? You're not going anywhere, not for a long time."

He put it down—dropped it clattering onto the bartop. And as he did, his sad hound's face screwed up again, only this time he didn't even try to keep the wetness from leaking out of his eyes. He was leaning against the bar, crying like the woman, submerged in his own outpouring of self-pity, when the cops showed up a few minutes later.

Stakeout

Four o'clock in the morning. And I was sitting huddled and ass-numb in my car in a freezing rainstorm, waiting for a guy I had never seen in person to get out of a nice warm bed and drive off in his Mercedes, thus enabling me to follow him so I could find out where he lived.

Thrilling work if you can get it. The kind that makes any self-respecting detective wonder why he didn't become a plumber instead.

Rain hammered against the car's metal surfaces, sluiced so thickly down the windshield that it transformed the glass into an opaque screen; all I could see were smeary blobs of light that marked the street lamps along this block of Forty-Seventh Avenue. Wind buffeted the car in forty-mile-an-hour gusts off the ocean nearby. Condensation had formed again on the driver's door window, even though I had rolled it down half an inch; I rubbed some of the mist away and took another bleary-eyed look across the street.

This was one of San Francisco's older middle-class residential neighborhoods, desirable as long as you didn't mind fog-belt living because Sutro Heights Park was just a block away and you were also within walking distance of Ocean Beach, the Cliff House, and Land's End. Most of the houses had been built in the thirties and stood shoulder-to-shoulder with their neighbors, but they seemed to have more individuality than the bland row houses dominating the avenues farther inland; out here, California Spanish was the dominant

181

style. Asians had bought up much of the city's west side housing in recent years, but fewer of those close to the ocean than anywhere else. A lot of homes in pockets such as this were still owned by older-generation, blue-collar San Franciscans.

The house I had under surveillance, number 9279, was one of the Spanish stucco jobs, painted white with a red tile roof. Yucca palms, one large and three small, dominated its tiny front yard. The three-year-old Mercedes with the Washington state license plates was still parked, illegally, across the driveway. Above it, the house's front windows remained dark. If anybody was up yet I couldn't tell it from where I was sitting.

I shifted position for the hundredth time, wincing as my stiffened joints protested with creaks and twinges. I had been here four and a half hours now, with nothing to do except to sit and wait and try not to fall asleep; to listen to the rain and the rattle and stutter of my thoughts. I was weary and irritable and I wanted some hot coffee and my own warm bed. It would be well past dawn, I thought bleakly, before I got either one.

Stakeouts. God, how I hated them. The passive waiting, the boredom, the slow, slow passage of dead time. How many did this make over the past thirty-odd years? How many empty, wasted, lost hours? Too damn many, whatever the actual figure. The physical discomfort was also becoming less tolerable, especially on nights like this, when not even a heavy overcoat and gloves kept the chill from penetrating bone deep. I had lived fifty-eight years; fifty-eight is too old to sit all-night stakeouts on the best of cases, much less on a lousy split-fee skip-trace.

I was starting to hate Randolph Hixley, too, sight unseen. He was the owner of the Mercedes across the street and my reason for being here. To his various and sundry employers, past and no doubt present, he was a highly paid freelance computer consultant. To his ex-wife and two kids, he was a probable deadbeat who currently owed some twenty-four thousand in back alimony and child support. To me and Puget Sound Investigations of Seattle, he was what should have been a small but adequate fee for routine work. Instead, he had developed into a minor pain in the ass. Mine.

Hixley had quit Seattle for parts unknown some four months ago, shortly after his wife divorced him for what she referred to as "sexual misconduct," and had yet to make a single alimony or child support payment. For reasons of her own, the wife had let the first two barren months go by without doing anything about it. On the occasion of the third due date, she had received a brief letter from Hixley informing her in tear-jerk language that he was so despondent over the breakup of their marriage he hadn't worked since leaving Seattle and was on the verge of becoming one of the homeless. He had every intention of fulfilling his obligations, though, the letter said; he would send money as soon as he got back on his feet. So would she bear with him for a while and please not sic the law on him? The letter was postmarked San Francisco, but with no return address.

The ex-wife, who was no dummy, smelled a rat. But because she still harbored some feelings for him, she had gone to Puget Sound Investigations rather than to the authorities, the object being to locate Hixley and determine if he really was broke and despondent. If so, then she would show the poor dear compassion and understanding. If not, then she would obtain a judgment against the son of a bitch and force him to pay up or get thrown in the slammer.

Puget Sound had taken the job, done some preliminary work, and then called a San Francisco detective—me—and farmed out the tough part for half the fee. That kind of cooperative thing is done all the time when the client isn't wealthy enough and the fee isn't large enough for the primary agency to send one of its own operatives to another state. No private detective likes to split fees, particularly when he's the one doing most of the work, but ours is sometimes a back-scratching business. Puget Sound had done a favor for me once; now it was my turn.

Skip-tracing can be easy or it can be difficult, depending on the individual you're trying to find. At first I figured Randolph Hixley, broke or not, might be one of the difficult ones. He had no known relatives or friends in the Bay Area. He had stopped using his credit cards after the divorce, and had not applied for new ones, which meant that if he was working and had money, he was paying his bills in cash. In Seattle, he'd provided consultancy services to a variety of different companies, large and small, doing most of the work at home by computer link. If he'd hired out to one or more outfits in the Bay Area, Puget Sound had not been able to turn up a lead as to which they might be, so I probably wouldn't be able to either. There is no easy way to track down that information, not without some kind of insider pull with the IRS.

And yet despite all of that, I got lucky right away—so lucky I revised my thinking and decided, prematurely and falsely, that Hixley was going to be one of the easy traces after all. The third call I made was to a contact in the San Francisco City Clerk's office, and it netted me the information that the 1987 Mercedes 560 SL registered in Hixley's name had received two parking tickets on successive Thursday mornings, the most recent of which was the previous week. The tickets were for identical violations: illegal parking across a private driveway and illegal parking during posted street-cleaning hours. Both citations had been issued between seven and seven-thirty a.m. And in both instances, the address was the same: 9279 Forty-Seventh Avenue.

I looked up the address in my copy of the reverse city directory; 9279 Forty-Seventh Avenue was a private house occupied by one Anne Carswell, a commercial artist, and two other Carswells, Bonnie and Margo, whose ages were given as eighteen and nineteen, respectively, and who I presumed were her daughters. The Carswells didn't own the house; they had been renting it for a little over two years.

Since there had been no change of registration on the Mercedes—I checked on that with the DMV—I assumed that the car still belonged to Randolph Hixley. And I figured things this way: Hixley, who was no more broke and despondent than I was, had met and established a relationship with Anne Carswell, and taken to spending Wednesday nights at her house. Why only Wednesdays? For all I knew, once a week was as much passion as Randy and Anne could muster up. Or it could be the two daughters slept elsewhere that night. In any case, Wednesday was Hixley's night to howl.

So the next Wednesday evening I drove out there, looking for his Mercedes. No Mercedes. I made my last check at midnight, went home to bed, got up at six a.m., and drove back to Forty-Seventh Avenue for another look. Still no Mercedes.

Well, I thought, they skipped a week. Or for some reason they'd altered their routine. I went back on Thursday night. And Friday night and Saturday night. I made spot checks during the day. On one occasion I saw a tall, willowy redhead in her late thirties—Anne Carswell, no doubt—driving out of the garage. On another occasion I saw the two daughters, one blond, one brunette, both attractive, having a conversation with a couple of sly college types. But that was all I saw. Still no Mercedes, still no Randolph Hixley.

I considered bracing one of the Carswell women on a ruse,

trying to find out that way where Hixley was living. But I didn't do it. He might have put them wise to his background and the money he owed, and asked them to keep mum if anyone ever approached them. Or I might slip somehow in my questioning and make her suspicious enough to call Hixley. I did not want to take the chance of warning him off.

Last Wednesday had been another bust. So had early Thursday—I drove out there at five a.m. that time. And so had the rest of the week. I was wasting time and gas and sleep, but it was the only lead I had. All the other skip-trace avenues I'd explored had led me nowhere near my elusive quarry.

Patience and perseverance are a detective's best assets; hang in there long enough and as often as not you find what you're looking for.

Tonight I'd finally found Hixley and his Mercedes, back at the Carswell house after a two-week absence.

The car hadn't been there the first two times I drove by, but when I made what would have been my last pass, at twenty of twelve, there it was, once again illegally parked across the driveway. Maybe he didn't give a damn about parking tickets because he had no intention of paying them. Or maybe he disliked walking fifty feet or so, which was how far away the nearest legal curb space was. Or, hell, maybe he was just an arrogant bastard who thumbed his nose at the law any time it inconvenienced him. Whatever his reason for blocking Anne Carswell's driveway, it was his big mistake.

The only choice I had, spotting his car so late, was to stake it out and wait for him to show. I would have liked to go home and catch a couple of hours' sleep, but for all I knew he wouldn't spend the entire night this time. If I left and came back and he was gone, I'd have to go through this whole rigmarole yet again.

So I parked and settled in. The lights in the Carswell

house had gone off at twelve-fifteen and hadn't come back on since. It had rained off and on all evening, but the first hard rain started a little past one. The storm had steadily worsened until, now, it was a full-fledged howling, ripping blow. And still I sat and still I waited . . .

A blurred set of headlights came boring up Forty-Seventh toward Geary, the first car to pass in close to an hour. When it went swishing by I held my watch up close to my eyes: 4:07. Suppose he stays in there until eight or nine? I thought. Four or five more hours of this and I'd be too stiff to move. It was meatlocker cold in the car. I couldn't start the engine and put the heater on because the exhaust, if not the idle, would call attention to my presence. I'd wrapped my legs and feet in the car blanket, which provided some relief; even so, I could no longer feel my toes when I tried to wiggle them.

The hard drumming beat of the rain seemed to be easing a little. Not the wind, though; a pair of back-to-back gusts shook the car, as if it were a toy in the hands of a destructive child. I shifted position again, pulled the blanket more tightly around my ankles.

A light went on in the Carswell house.

I scrubbed mist off the driver's door window, peered through the wet glass. The big front window was alight over there, behind drawn curtains. That was a good sign: People don't usually put their living room lights on at four a.m. unless somebody plans to be leaving soon.

Five minutes passed while I sat chafing my gloved hands together and moving my feet up and down to improve circulation. Then another light went on—the front porch light this time. And a few seconds after that, the door opened and somebody came out onto the stoop.

It wasn't Randolph Hixley; it was a young blond woman wearing a trenchcoat over what looked to be a lacy nightgown. One of the Carswell daughters. She stood still for a moment, looking out over the empty street. Then she drew the trenchcoat collar up around her throat and ran down the stairs and over to Hixley's Mercedes.

For a few seconds she stood hunched on the sidewalk on the passenger side, apparently unlocking the front door with a set of keys. She pulled the door open, as if making sure it was unlocked, then slammed it shut again. She turned and ran back up the stairs and vanished into the house.

I thought: Now what was that all about?

The porch light stayed on. So did the light in the front room. Another three minutes dribbled away. The rain slackened a little more, so that it was no longer sheeting; the wind continued to wail and moan. And then things got even stranger over there.

First the porch light went off. Then the door opened and somebody exited onto the stoop, followed a few seconds later by a cluster of shadow—shapes moving in an awkward, confused fashion. I couldn't identify them or tell what they were doing while they were all grouped on the porch; the tallest yucca palm cast too much shadow and I was too far away. But when they started down the stairs, there was just enough extension of light from the front window to individuate the shapes for me.

There were four of them, by God—three in an uneven line on the same step, the fourth backing down in front of them as though guiding the way. Three women, one man. The man— several inches taller, wearing an overcoat and hat, head lolling forward as if he were drunk or unconscious—was being supported by two of the women.

They all managed to make it down the slippery stairs without any of them suffering a misstep. When they reached the sidewalk, the one who had been guiding ran ahead to the

Mercedes and dragged the front passenger door open. In the faint outspill from the dome light, I watched the other two women, with the third one's help, push and prod the man inside. Once they had the door shut again, they didn't waste any time catching their breaths. Two of them went running back to the house; the third hurried around to the driver's door, bent to unlock it. She was the only one of the three, I realized then, who was fully dressed: raincoat, rainhat, slacks, boots. When she slid in under the wheel I had a dome-lit glimpse of reddish hair and a white, late-thirties face under the rainhat. Anne Carswell.

She fired up the Mercedes, let the engine warm for all of five seconds, switched on the headlights, and eased away from the curb at a crawl, the way you'd drive over a surface of broken glass. The two daughters were already back inside the house, with the door shut behind them.

I had long since unwrapped the blanket from around my legs; I didn't hesitate in starting my car. Or in trying to start it: The engine was cold and it took three whiffing tries before it caught and held. If Anne Carswell had been driving fast, I might have lost her. As it was, with her creeping along, she was only halfway along the next block behind me when I swung out into a tight U-turn.

I ran dark through the rain until she completed a slow turn west on Point Lobos and passed out of sight. Then I put on my lights and accelerated across Geary to the Point Lobos intersection. I got there in time to pick up the Mercedes' taillights as it went through the flashing yellow traffic signal at Forty-Eighth Avenue. I let it travel another fifty yards downhill before I turned onto Point Lobos in pursuit.

Five seconds later, Anne Carswell had another surprise for me.

I expected her to continue down past the Cliff House and

around onto the Great Highway; there is no other through direction once you pass Forty-Eighth. But she seemed not to be leaving the general area after all. The Mercedes' brake lights came on and she slow-turned into the Merrie Way parking area above the ruins of the old Sutro Baths. The combination lot and overlook had only the one entrance/exit; it was surrounded on its other three sides by cliffs and clusters of wind-shaped cypress trees and a rocky nature trail that led out beyond the ruins to Land's End.

Without slowing, I drove on past. She was crawling straight down the center of the unpaved, potholed lot, toward the trees at the far end. Except for the Mercedes, the rain-drenched expanse appeared deserted.

Below Merrie Way, on the other side of Point Lobos, there is a newer, paved parking area carved out of Sutro Heights Park for sightseers and patrons of Louis' Restaurant opposite and the Cliff House bars and eateries farther down. It, too, was deserted at this hour. From the overlook above, you can't see this curving downhill section of Point Lobos; I swung across into the paved lot, cut my lights, looped around to where I had a clear view of the Merrie Way entrance. Then I parked, shut off the engine, and waited.

For a few seconds I could see a haze of slowly moving light up there, but not the Mercedes itself. Then the light winked out and there was nothing to see except wind-whipped rain and dark. Five minutes went by. Still nothing to see. She must have parked, I thought, but to do what?

Six minutes, seven. At seven and a half, a shape materialized out of the gloom above the entrance—somebody on foot, walking fast, bent against the lashing wind. Anne Carswell. She was moving at an uphill angle out of the overlook, climbing to Forty-Eighth Avenue.

When she reached the sidewalk, a car came through the

flashing yellow at the intersection and its headlight beams swept over her; she turned away from them, as if to make sure her face wasn't seen. The car swished down past where I was, disappeared beyond the Cliff House. I watched Anne Carswell cross Point Lobos and hurry into Forty-Eighth at the upper edge of the park.

Going home, I thought. Abandoned Hixley and his Mercedes on the overlook and now she's hoofing it back to her daughters.

What the hell?

I started the car and drove up to Forty-Eighth and turned there. Anne Carswell was now on the opposite side of the street, near where Geary dead-ends at the park; when my lights caught her she turned her head away as she had a couple of minutes ago. I drove two blocks, circled around onto Forty-Seventh, came back a block, and then parked and shut down again within fifty yards of the Carswell house. Its porch light was back on, which indicated that the daughters were anticipating her imminent return. Two minutes later she came fast-walking out of Geary onto Forty-Seventh. One minute after that, she climbed the stairs to her house and let herself in. The porch light went out immediately, followed fifteen seconds later by the light in the front room.

I got the car moving again and made my way back down to the Merrie Way overlook.

The Mercedes was still the only vehicle on the lot, parked at an angle just beyond the long terraced staircase that leads down the cliffside to the pitlike bottom of the ruins. I pulled in alongside, snuffed my lights. Before I got out, I armed myself with the flashlight I keep clipped under the dash.

Icy wind and rain slashed at me as I crossed to the Mercedes. Even above the racket made by the storm, I could hear the barking of sea lions on the offshore rocks beyond the

Cliff House. Surf boiled frothing over those rocks, up along the cliffs and among the concrete foundations that are all that's left of the old bathhouse. Nasty night, and a nasty business here to go with it. I was sure of that now.

I put the flashlight up against the Mercedes' passenger window, flicked it on briefly. He was in there, all right; she'd shoved him over so that he lay half sprawled under the wheel, his head tipped back against the driver's door. The passenger door was unlocked. I opened it and got in and shut the door again to extinguish the dome light. I put the flash beam on his face, shielding it with my hand.

Randolph Hixley, no doubt of that; the photograph Puget Sound Investigations had sent me was a good one. No doubt, either, that he was dead. I checked for a pulse, just to make sure. Then I moved the light over him, slowly, to see if I could find out what had killed him.

There weren't any discernible wounds or bruises or other marks on his body; no holes or tears or bloodstains on his damp clothing. Poison? Not that, either. Most any deadly poison produces convulsions, vomiting, rictus; his facial muscles were smooth and when I sniffed at his mouth I smelled nothing except Listerine.

Natural causes, then? Heart attack, stroke, aneurysm? Sure, maybe. But if he'd died of natural causes, why would Anne Carswell and her daughters have gone to all the trouble of moving his body and car down here? Why not just call Emergency Services?

On impulse I probed Hixley's clothing and found his wallet. It was empty—no cash, no credit cards, nothing except some old photos. Odd. He'd quit using credit cards after his divorce; he should have been carrying at least a few dollars. I took a close look at his hands and wrists. He was wearing a watch, a fairly new and fairly expensive one. No rings or other jewelry but there was a white mark on his other-wise tanned left pinkie, as if a ring had been recently re-moved.

They rolled him, I thought. All the cash in his wallet and a ring off his finger. Not the watch because it isn't made of gold or platinum and you can't get much for a watch, anyway, these days.

But why? Why would they kill a man for a few hundred bucks? Or rob a dead man and then try to dump the body? In either case, the actions of those three women made no damn sense . . .

Or did they?

I was beginning to get a notion.

I backed out of the Mercedes and went to sit and think in my own car. I remembered some things, and added them to-gether with some other things, and did a little speculating, and the notion wasn't a notion anymore—it was the answer.

Hell, I thought then, I'm getting old. Old and slow on the uptake. I should have seen this part of it as soon as they brought the body out. And I should have tumbled to the other part a week ago, if not sooner.

I sat there for another minute, feeling my age and a little sorry for myself because it was going to be quite a while yet before I got any sleep. Then, dutifully, I hauled up my mobile phone and called in the law.

They arrested the three women a few minutes past seven a.m. at the house on Forty-Seventh Avenue. I was present for identification purposes. Anne Carswell put up a blustery pro-test of innocence until the inspector in charge, a veteran named Ginzberg, tossed the words "foul play" into the con-versation; then the two girls broke down simultaneously and soon there were loud squawks of denial from all three: "We

didn't hurt him! He had a heart attack, he died of a heart attack!" The girls, it turned out, were not named Carswell and
were not Anne Carswell's daughters. The blonde was Bonnie
Harper; the brunette was Margo LaFond. They were both
former runaways from southern California.

The charges against the trio included failure to report a
death, unlawful removal of a corpse, and felony theft. But the
main charge was something else entirely.

The main charge was operating a house of prostitution.

Later that day, after I had gone home for a few hours'
sleep, I laid the whole thing out for my partner, Eberhardt.

"I should have known they were hookers and Hixley was a
customer," I said. "There were enough signs. His wife divorced him for 'sexual misconduct;' that was one. Another
was how unalike those three women were—different hair
colors, which isn't typical in a mother and her daughters.
Then there were those sly young guys I saw with the two girls.
They weren't boyfriends, they were customers too."

"Hixley really did die of a heart attack?" Eberhardt asked.

"Yeah. Carswell couldn't risk notifying Emergency Services; she didn't know much about Hixley and she was afraid
somebody would come around asking questions. She had a
nice discreet operation going there, with a small but high-
paying clientele, and she didn't want a dead man to rock the
boat. So she and the girls dressed the corpse and hustled it
out of there. First, though, they emptied Hixley's wallet and
she stripped a valuable garnet ring off his pinkie. She figured
it was safe to do that; if anybody questioned the empty wallet
and missing ring, it would look like the body had been rolled
on the Merrie Way overlook, after he'd driven in there himself and had his fatal heart attack. As far as she knew, there
was nothing to tie Hixley to her and her girls—no direct link,

anyhow. He hadn't told her about the two parking tickets."

"Uh-huh. And he was in bed with all three of them when he croaked?"

"So they said. Right in the middle of a round of fun and games. That was what he paid them for each of the times he went there—seven hundred and fifty bucks for all three, all night."

"Jeez, three women at one time." Eberhardt paused, thinking about it. Then he shook his head. "How?" he said.

I shrugged. "Where there's a will, there's a way."

"Kinky sex—I never did understand it. I guess I'm old fashioned."

"Me too. But Hixley's brand is pretty tame, really, compared to some of the things that go on nowadays."

"Seems like the whole damn world gets a little kinkier every day," Eberhardt said. "A little crazier every day, too. You know what I mean?"

"Yeah," I said, "I know what you mean."

La Bellezza delle Bellezze

1

That Sunday, the day before she died, I went down to Aquatic Park to watch the old men play bocce. I do that sometimes on weekends when I'm not working, when Kerry and I have nothing planned. More often than I used to, out of nostalgia and compassion and maybe just a touch of guilt, because in San Francisco bocce is a dying sport.

Only one of the courts was in use. Time was, all six were packed throughout the day and there were spectators and waiting players lined two and three deep at courtside and up along the fence on Van Ness. No more. Most of the city's older Italians, to whom bocce was more a religion than a sport, have died off. The once large and closeknit North Beach Italian community has been steadily losing its identity since the fifties—families moving to the suburbs, the expansion of Chinatown, and the gobbling up of North Beach real estate by wealthy Chinese—and even though there has been a small new wave of immigrants from Italy in recent years, they're mostly young and upscale. Young, upscale Italians don't play bocce much, if at all; their interests lie in soccer, in the American sports where money and fame and power have replaced a love of the game itself. The Di Massimo bocce courts at the North Beach Playground are mostly closed now; the only place you can find a game every Saturday and Sunday is on the one Aquatic Park court. And the players get older, and sadder, and fewer each year.

197

There were maybe fifteen players and watchers on this Sunday, almost all of them older than my fifty-eight. The two courts nearest the street are covered by a high, pillar-supported roof, so that contests can be held even in wet weather; and there are wooden benches set between the pillars. I parked myself on one of the benches midway along. The only other seated spectator was Pietro Lombardi, in a patch of warm May sunlight at the far end, and this surprised me. Even though Pietro was in his seventies, he was one of the best and spryest of the regulars, and also one of the most social. To see him sitting alone, shoulders slumped and head bowed, was puzzling.

Pining away for the old days, maybe, I thought—as I had just been doing. And a phrase popped into my head, a line from Dante that one of my uncles was fond of quoting when I was growing up in the Outer Mission: *Nessun maggior dolore che ricordarsi del tempo felice nella miseria.* The bitterest of woes is to remember old happy days.

Pietro and his woes didn't occupy my attention for long. The game in progress was spirited and voluable, as only a game of bocce played by elderly *paesanos* can be, and I was soon caught up in it.

Bocce is simple—deceptively simple. You play it on a long narrow packed-earth pit with low wooden sides. A wooden marker ball the size of a walnut is rolled to one end; the players stand at the opposite end and in turn roll eight larger, heavier balls, grapefruit-sized, in the direction of the marker, the object being to see who can put his bocce ball closest to it. One of the required skills is slow-rolling the ball, usually in a curving trajectory, so that it kisses the marker and then lies up against it—the perfect shot—or else stops an inch or two away. The other required skill is knocking an opponent's ball away from any such close lie without disturbing the marker.

The best players, like Pietro Lombardi, can do this two out of three times on the fly—no mean feat from a distance of fifty feet. They can also do it by caroming the ball off the pit walls, with topspin or reverse spin after the fashion of pool-shooters.

Nobody paid much attention to me until after the game in progress had been decided. Then I was acknowledged with hand gestures and a few words—the tolerant acceptance accorded to known spectators and occasional players. Unknowns got no greeting at all; these men still clung to the old ways, and one of the old ways was clannishness.

Only one of the group, Dominick Marra, came over to where I was sitting. And that was because he had something on his mind. He was in his mid-seventies, white-haired, white-mustached; a bantamweight in baggy trousers held up by galluses. He and Pietro Lombardi had been close friends for most of their lives. Born in the same town—Agropoli, a village on the Gulf of Salerno not far from Naples; moved to San Francisco with their families a year apart, in the late twenties; married cousins, raised large families, were widowered at almost the same time a few years ago. The kind of friendship that is almost a blood tie. Dominick had been a baker; Pietro had owned a North Beach trattoria that now belonged to one of his daughters.

What Dominick had on his mind was Pietro. "You see how he sits over there, hah? He's got trouble—*la miseria*."

"What kind of trouble?"

"His granddaughter. Gianna Fornessi."

"Something happen to her?"

"She's maybe go to jail," Dominick said.

"What for?"

"Stealing money."

199

"I'm sorry to hear it. How much money?"

"Two thousand dollars."

"Who did she steal it from?"

"Che?"

"Who did she steal the money from?"

Dominick gave me a disgusted look. "She don't steal it. Why you think Pietro he's got *la miseria,* hah?"

I knew what was coming now; I should have known it the instant Dominick started confiding to me about Pietro's problem. I said, "You want me to help him and his grand-daughter."

"Sure. You a detective."

"A busy detective."

"You got no time for old man and young girl? *Compaesani?"*

I sighed, but not so he could hear me do it. "All right, I'll talk to Pietro. See if he wants my help, if there's anything I can do."

"Sure he wants your help. He just don't know it yet."

We went to where Pietro was sitting alone in the sun. He was taller than Dominick, heavier, balder. And he had a fondness for Toscanas, those little twisted black Italian cigars; one protruded now from a corner of his mouth. He didn't want to talk at first, but Dominick launched into a monologue in Italian that changed his mind and put a glimmer of hope in his sad eyes. Even though I've lost a lot of the language over the years, I can understand enough to follow most conversations. The gist of Dominick's monologue was that I was not just a detective but a miracle worker, a cross between Sherlock Holmes and the Messiah. Italians are given to hyperbole in times of excitement or stress, and there isn't much you can do to counteract it—especially when you're one of the *compaesani* yourself.

"My Gianna, she's good girl," Pietro said. "Never give

trouble, even when she's little one. *La bellezza delle bellezze,* you understand?"

The beauty of beauties. His favorite grandchild, probably. I said, "I understand. Tell me about the money, Pietro."

"She don't steal it," he said. "*Una ladra,* my Gianna? No, no, it's all big lie."

"Did the police arrest her?"

"They got no evidence to arrest her."

"But somebody filed charges, is that it?"

"Charges," Pietro said. "Bah," he said and spat.

"Who made the complaint?"

Dominick said, "Ferry," as if the name were an obscenity.

"Who's Ferry?"

He tapped his skull. "*Caga di testa,* this man."

"That doesn't answer my question."

"He live where she live. Same apartment building."

"And he says Gianna stole two thousand dollars from him."

"Liar," Pietro said. "He lies."

"Stole it how? Broke in or what?"

"She don't break in nowhere, not my Gianna. This Ferry, this *bastardo,* he says she take the money when she's come to pay rent and he's talk on telephone. But how she knows where he keep his money? Hah? How she knows he have two thousand dollars in his desk?"

"Maybe he told her."

"Sure, that's what he says to police," Dominick said. "Maybe he told her, he says. He don't tell her nothing."

"Is that what Gianna claims?"

Pietro nodded. Threw down what was left of his Toscana and ground in into the dirt with his shoe—a gesture of anger and frustration. "She don't steal that money," he said. "What she need to steal money for? She got good job, she live good, she don't have to steal."

"What kind of job does she have?"

"She sell drapes, curtains. In . . . what you call that business, Dominick?"

"Interior decorating business," Dominick said.

"*Si*. In interior decorating business."

"Where does she live?" I asked.

"Chestnut Street."

"Where on Chestnut Street? What number?"

"Seventy-two fifty."

"You make that Ferry tell the truth, hah?" Dominick said to me. "You fix it up for Gianna and her goombah?"

"I'll do what I can."

"*Va bene*. Then you come tell Pietro right away."

"If Pietro will tell me where he lives—"

There was a sharp whacking sound as one of the bocce balls caromed off the side wall near us, then a softer clicking of ball meeting ball, and a shout went up from the players at the far end: another game won and lost. When I looked back at Dominick and Pietro they were both on their feet. Dominick said, "You find Pietro okay, good detective like you," and Pietro said, *"Grazie, mi amico,"* and before I could say anything else the two of them were off arm in arm to join the others.

Now I was the one sitting alone in the sun, holding up a burden. Primed and ready to do a job I didn't want to do, probably couldn't do, and would not be paid well for if at all. Maybe this man Ferry wasn't the only one involved who had *caga di testa*—shit for brains. Maybe I did too.

2

The building at 7250 Chestnut Street was an old three-story, brown-shingled job, set high in the shadow of Coit Tower and across from the retaining wall where Telegraph Hill falls off steeply toward the Embarcadero. From each of the apartments, especially the ones on the third floor, you'd have quite a view of the bay, the East Bay, and both bridges. Prime North Beach address, this. The rent would be well in excess of two thousand a month.

A man in a tan trenchcoat was coming out of the building as I started up the steps to the vestibule. I called out to him to hold the door for me—it's easier to get apartment dwellers to talk to you once you're inside the building—but either he didn't hear me or he chose to ignore me. He came hurrying down without a glance my way as he passed. City-bred paranoia, I thought. It was everywhere these days, rich and poor neighborhoods both, like a nasty strain of social disease. Bumpersticker for the nineties: Fear Lives.

There were six mailboxes in the foyer, each with Dymo-Label stickers identifying the tenants. Gianna Fornessi's name was under box #4, along with a second name: Ashley Hansen. It figured that she'd have a roommate; salespersons working in the interior design trade are well but not extravagantly paid. Box #1 bore the name George Ferry and that was the bell I pushed. He was the one I wanted to talk to first.

A minute died away, while I listened to the wind that was savaging the trees on the hillside below. Out on the bay hundreds of sailboats formed a mosaic of white on blue. Somewhere among them a ship's horn sounded—to me, a sad false note. Shipping was all but dead on this side of the bay, thanks to wholesale mismanagement of the port over the past few decades.

The intercom crackled finally and a male voice said, "Who is it?" in wary tones.

I asked if he was George Ferry, and he admitted it, even more guardedly. I gave him my name, said that I was there to ask him a few questions about his complaint against Gianna Fornessi. He said, "Oh Christ." There was a pause, and then, "I called you people yesterday, I told Inspector Cullen I was dropping the charges. Isn't that enough?"

He thought I was a cop. I could have told him I wasn't; I could have let the whole thing drop right there, since what he'd just said was a perfect escape clause from my commitment to Pietro Lombardi. But I have too much curiosity to let go of something, once I've got a piece of it, without knowing the particulars. So I said, "I won't keep you long, Mr. Ferry. Just a few questions."

Another pause. "Is it really necessary?"

"I think it is, yes."

An even longer pause. But then he didn't argue, didn't say anything else—just buzzed me in.

His apartment was on the left, beyond a carpeted, dark-wood staircase. He opened the door as I approached it. Mid-forties, short, rotund, with a nose like a blob of putty and a Friar Tuck fringe of reddish hair. And a bruise on his left cheekbone, a cut along the right corner of his mouth. The marks weren't fresh, but then they weren't very old either. Twenty-four hours, maybe less.

He didn't ask to see a police ID; if he had, I would have told him immediately that I was a private detective, because nothing can lose you a California investigator's license faster than impersonating a police officer. On the other hand, you can't be held accountable for somebody's false assumption. Ferry gave me a nervous once-over, holding his head tilted downward as if that would keep me from seeing his bruise and cut, then stood aside to let me come in.

The front room was neat, furnished in a self-consciously masculine fashion: dark woods, leather, expensive sporting prints. It reeked of leather, dust, and his lime-scented cologne.

As soon as he shut the door, Ferry went straight to a li-quor cabinet and poured himself three fingers of Jack Daniels, no water or mix, no ice. Just holding the drink seemed to give him courage. He said, "So. What is it you want to know?"

"Why you dropped your complaint against Gianna Fornessi."

"I explained to Inspector Cullen."

"Explain to me, if you don't mind."

He had some of the sour mash. "Well, it was all a mis-take . . . just a silly mistake. She didn't take the money after all."

"You know who did take it, then?"

"Nobody took it. I . . . misplaced it."

"Misplaced it. Uh-huh."

"I thought it was in my desk," Ferry said. "That's where I usually keep the cash I bring home. But I'd put it in my safe deposit box along with some other papers, without realizing it. It was in an envelope, you see, and the envelope got mixed up with the other papers."

"Two thousand dollars is a lot of cash to keep at home. You make a habit of that sort of thing?"

"In my business . . ." The rest of the sentence seemed to hang up in his throat; he oiled the route with the rest of his drink. "In my business I need to keep a certain amount of cash on hand, both here and at the office. The amount I keep here isn't usually as large as two thousand dollars, but I—"

"What business are you in, Mr. Ferry?"

"I run a temp employment agency for domestics."

"Temp?"

"Short for temporary," he said. "I supply domestics for part-time work in offices and private homes. A lot of them are poor, don't have checking accounts, so they prefer to be paid in cash. Most come to the office, but a few—"

"Why did you think Gianna Fornessi had stolen the two thousand dollars?"

"... What?"

"Why Gianna Fornessi? Why not somebody else?"

"She's the only one who was here. Before I thought the money was missing, I mean. I had no other visitors for two days and there wasn't any evidence of a break-in."

"You and she are good friends, then?"

"Well ... no, not really. She's a lot younger ..."

"Then why was she here?"

"The rent," Ferry said. "She was paying her rent for the month. I'm the building manager, I collect for the owner. Before I could write out a receipt I had a call, I was on the phone for quite a while and she ... I didn't pay any attention to her and I thought she must have ... you see why I thought she'd taken the money?"

I was silent.

He looked at me, looked at his empty glass, licked his lips, and went to commune with Jack Daniels again.

While he was pouring I asked him, "What happened to your face, Mr. Ferry?"

His hand twitched enough to clink bottle against glass. He had himself another taste before he turned back to me. "Clumsy," he said, "I'm clumsy as hell. I fell down the stairs, the front stairs, yesterday morning." He tried a laugh that didn't come off. "Fog makes the steps slippery. I just wasn't watching where I was going."

"Looks to me like somebody hit you."

"Hit me? No, I told you ... I fell down the stairs."

"You're sure about that?"

"Of course I'm sure. Why would I lie about it?"

That was a good question. Why would he lie about that,

and about all the rest of it too? There was about as much truth in what he'd told me as there is value in a chunk of fool's gold.

3

The young woman who opened the door of apartment #4 was not Gianna Fornessi. She was blonde, with the kind of fresh-faced Nordic features you see on models for Norwegian ski wear. Tall and slender in a pair of green silk lounging pajamas; arms decorated with hammered gold bracelets, ears with dangly gold triangles. Judging from the expression in her pale eyes, there wasn't much going on behind them. But then, with her physical attributes, not many men would care if her entire brain had been surgically removed.

"Well," she said, "hello."

"Ashley Hansen?"

"That's me. Who're you?"

When I told her my name her smile brightened, as if I'd said something amusing or clever. Or maybe she just liked the sound of it.

"I knew right away you were Italian," she said. "Are you a friend of Jack's?"

"Jack?"

"Jack Bisconte." The smile dulled a little. "You are, aren't you?"

"No," I said, "I'm a friend of Pietro Lombardi."

"Who?"

"Your roommate's grandfather. I'd like to talk to Gianna, if she's home."

Ashley Hansen's smile was gone now; her whole demeanor had changed, become less self-assured. She nibbled at a corner of her lower lip, ran a hand through her hair, fiddled with one of her bracelets. Finally she said, "Gianna isn't here."

"When will she be back?"

"She didn't say."

"You know where I can find her?"

"No. What do you want to talk to her about?"

"The complaint George Ferry filed against her."

"Oh, that," she said. "That's all been taken care of."

"I know. I just talked to Ferry."

"He's a creepy little prick, isn't he?"

"That's one way of putting it."

"Gianna didn't take his money. He was just trying to hassle her, that's all."

"Why would he do that?"

"Well, why do you think?"

I shrugged. "Suppose you tell me."

"He wanted her to do things."

"You mean go to bed with him?"

"Things," she said. "Kinky crap, *real* kinky."

"And she wouldn't have anything to do with him."

"No way, Jose. What a creep."

"So he made up the story about the stolen money to get back at her, is that it?"

"That's it."

"What made him change his mind, drop the charges?"

"He didn't tell you?"

"No."

"Who knows?" She laughed. "Maybe he got religion."

"Or a couple of smacks in the face."

"Huh?"

"Somebody worked him over yesterday," I said. "Bruised his cheek and cut his mouth. You have any idea who?"

"Not me, mister. How come you're so interested, anyway?"

"I told you, I'm a friend of Gianna's grandfather."

"Yeah, well . . ."

"Gianna have a boyfriend, does she?"

". . . Why do you want to know that?"

"Jack Bisconte, maybe? Or is he yours?"

"He's just somebody I know." She nibbled at her lip again, did some more fiddling with her bracelets. "Look, I've got to go. You want me to tell Gianna you were here?"

"Yes." I handed her one of my business cards. "Give her this and ask her to call me."

She looked at the card; blinked at it and then blinked at me.

"You . . . you're a detective?"

"That's right."

"My God," she said, and backed off, and shut the door in my face.

I stood there for a few seconds, remembering her eyes—the sudden fear in her eyes when she'd realized she had been talking to a detective.

What the hell?

4

North Beach used to be the place you went when you wanted pasta fino, espresso and biscotti, conversation about *la dolce vita* and *il patria d'Italia*. Not anymore. There are still plenty of Italians in North Beach, and you can still get the good food and some of the good conversation; but their turf continues to shrink a little more each year, and despite the best efforts of the entreprenurial new immigrants, the vitality and most of the Old World atmosphere are just memories.

The Chinese are partly responsible, not that you can blame them for buying available North Beach real estate when Chinatown, to the west, began to burst its boundaries. Another culprit is the Bohemian element that took over upper Grant Avenue in the fifties, paving the way for the hippies and the introduction of hard drugs in the sixties, which in turn paved the way for the jolly current mix of motorcycle toughs, aging hippies, coke and crack dealers, and the pimps and smalltime crooks who work the flesh palaces along lower Broadway. Those "Silicone Alley" nightclubs, made famous by Carol Doda in the late sixties, also share responsibility: they added a smutty leer to the gaiety of North Beach, turned the heart of it into a ghetto.

Parts of the neighborhood, particularly those up around Coit Tower where Gianna Fornessi lived, are still prime city real estate, and the area around Washington Square Park, *il giardino* to the original immigrants, is where the city's literati now congregates. Here and there, too, you can still get a sense of what it was like in the old days. But most of the landmarks are gone—Enrico's, Vanessi's, The Bocce Ball where you could hear mustachioed waiters in gondolier costumes singing arias from operas by Verdi and Puccini—and so is most of the flavor. North Beach is oddly tasteless now, like a week-old mostaccioli made without good spices or garlic. And that is another thing that is all but gone: twenty-five years ago you could not get within a thousand yards of North Beach without picking up the fine, rich fragrance of garlic. Nowadays you're much more likely to smell fried egg roll and the sour stench of somebody's garbage.

Parking in the Beach is the worst in the city; on weekends you can drive around its hilly streets for hours without finding a legal parking space. So today, in the perverse way of things, I found a spot waiting for me when I came down Stockton.

In a public telephone booth near Washington Square Park

I discovered a second minor miracle: a directory that had yet to be either stolen or mutilated. The only Bisconte listed was Bisconte Florist Shop, with an address on upper Grant a few blocks away. I took myself off in that direction, through the usual good-weather Sunday crowds of locals and gawking sightseers and drifting homeless.

Upper Grant, like the rest of the area, has changed drastically over the past few decades. Once a rock-ribbed Little Italy, it has become an ethnic mixed bag: Italian markets, trattorias, pizza parlors, bakeries cheek by jowl with Chinese sewing-machine sweat shops, food and herb vendors, and fortune-cookie companies. But most of the faces on the streets are Asian and most of the apartments in the vicinity are occupied by Chinese.

The Bisconte Florist Shop was a hole-in-the-wall near Filbert, sandwiched between an Italian saloon and the Sip Hing Herb Company. It was open for business, not surprisingly on a Sunday in this neighborhood: tourists buy flowers too, given the opportunity.

The front part of the shop was cramped and jungly with cut flowers, ferns, plants in pots and hanging baskets. A small glass-fronted cooler contained a variety of roses and orchids. There was nobody in sight, but a bell had gone off when I entered and a male voice from beyond a rear doorway called, "Be right with you." I shut the door, went up near the counter. Some people like florist shops; I don't. All of them have the same damp, cloyingly sweet smell that reminds me of funeral parlors; of my mother in her casket at the Figlia Brothers Mortuary in Daly City nearly forty years ago. That day, with all its smells, all its painful images, is as clear to me now as if it were yesterday.

I had been waiting about a minute when the voice's owner came out of the back room. Late thirties, dark, on the beefy side; wearing a professional smile and a floral-patterned apron that should have been ludicrous on a man of his size and coloring but wasn't. We had a good look at each other before he said, "Sorry to keep you waiting—I was putting up an arrangement. What can I do for you?"

"Mr. Bisconte? Jack Bisconte?"

"That's me. Something for the wife, maybe?"

"I'm not here for flowers. I'd like to ask you a few questions."

The smile didn't waver. "Oh? What about?"

"Gianna Fornessi."

"Who?"

"You don't know her?"

"Name's not familiar, no."

"She lives up on Chestnut with Ashley Hansen."

"Ashley Hansen . . . I don't know that name either."

"She knows you. Young, blonde, looks Norwegian."

"Well, I know a lot of young blondes," Bisconte said. He winked at me. "I'm a bachelor and I get around pretty good, you know?"

"Uh-huh."

"Lot of bars and clubs in North Beach, lot of women to pick and choose from." He shrugged. "So how come you're asking about these two?"

"Not both of them. Just Gianna Fornessi."

"That so? You a friend of hers?"

"Of her grandfather's. She's had a little trouble."

"What kind of trouble?"

"Manager of her building accused her of stealing some money. But somebody convinced him to drop the charges."

"That so?" Bisconte said again, but not as if he cared.

"Leaned on him to do it. Scared the hell out of him."

"You don't think it was me, do you? I told you, I don't

know anybody named Gianna Fornessi."

"So you did."

"What's the big deal anyway?" he said. "I mean, if the guy dropped the charges, then this Gianna is off the hook, right?"

"Right."

"Then why all the questions?"

"Curiosity," I said. "Mine and her grandfather's."

Another shrug. "I'd like to help you, pal, but like I said, I don't know the lady. Sorry."

"Sure."

"Come back any time you need flowers," Bisconte said. He gave me a little salute, waited for me to turn, and then did the same himself. He was hidden away again in the back room when I let myself out.

Today was my day for liars. Liars and puzzles.

He hadn't asked me who I was or what I did for a living; that was because he already knew. And the way he knew, I thought, was that Ashley Hansen had gotten on the horn after I left and told him about me. He knew Gianna Fornessi pretty well too, and exactly where the two women lived.

He was the man in the tan trenchcoat I'd seen earlier, the one who wouldn't hold the door for me at 7250 Chestnut.

5

I treated myself to a plate of linguine and fresh clams at a ristorante off Washington Square and then drove back over to Aquatic Park. Now, in mid-afternoon, with fog seeping in through the Gate and the temperature dropping sharply, the number of bocce players and kibitzers had thinned by half. Pietro Lombardi was one of those remaining; Dominick Marra was another. Bocce may be dying easy in the city but not in men like them. They cling to it and to the other old ways as tenaciously as they cling to life itself.

I told Pietro—and Dominick, who wasn't about to let us talk in private—what I'd learned so far. He was relieved that Ferry had dropped his complaint, but just as curious as I was about the Jack Bisconte connection.

"Do you know Bisconte?" I asked him.

"No. I see his shop but I never go inside."

"Know anything about him?"

"Niente."

"How about you, Dominick?"

He shook his head. "He's too old for Gianna, hah? Almost forty, you say—that's too old for girl twenty-three."

"If that's their relationship," I said.

"Men almost forty they go after young woman, they only got one reason. *Fatto 'na bella chiavata.* You remember, eh, Pietro?"

"Pazzo! You think I forget *'na bella chiavata?"*

I asked Pietro, "You know anything about Gianna's room-mate?"

"Only once I meet her," he said. "Pretty, but not so pretty like my Gianna, *la bellezza delle bellezze.* I don't like her too much."

"Why not?"

"She don't have respect like she should."

"What does she do for a living, do you know?"'

"No. She don't say and Gianna don't tell me."

"How long have they been sharing the apartment?"

"Eight, nine months."

"Did they know each other long before they moved in to-gether?"

He shrugged. "Gianna and me, we don't talk much like when she's little girl," he said sadly. "Young people now, they got no time for *la famiglia.*" Another shrug, a sigh. *"Ognuno* pensa per *sè*," he said. Everybody thinks only of himself.

Dominick gripped his shoulder. Then he said to me, "You find out what's happen with Bisconte and Ferry and those girls. Then you see they don't bother them no more. Hah?"

"If I can, Dominick. If I can."

The fog was coming in thickly now and the other players were making noises about ending the day's tournament. Dominick got into an argument with one of them; he wanted to play another game or two. He was outvoted, but he was still pleading his case when I left. Their Sunday was almost over. So was mine.

I went home to my flat in Pacific Heights. And Kerry came over later on and we had dinner and listened to some jazz. I thought maybe Gianna Fornessi might call but she didn't. No one called. Good thing, too. I would not have been pleased to hear the phone ring after eight o'clock; I was busy then.

Men in their late fifties are just as interested in *'na bella chiavata*. Women in their early forties, too.

6

At the office in the morning I called TRW for credit checks on Jack Bisconte, George Ferry, Gianna Fornessi, and Ashley Hansen. I also asked my partner, Eberhardt, who has been off the cops just a few years and who still has plenty of cronies sprinkled throughout the SFPD, to find out what Inspector Cullen and the Robbery Detail had on Ferry's theft complaint, and to have the four names run through R&I for any local arrest record.

The report out of Robbery told me nothing much. Ferry's complaint had been filed on Friday morning; Cullen had gone to investigate, talked to the two principals, and determined that there wasn't enough evidence to take Gianna Fornessi into custody. Thirty hours later Ferry had called in and withdrawn the complaint, giving the same flimsy reason he'd handed me. As far as Cullen and the department were concerned, it was all very minor and routine.

The TRW and R&I checks took a little longer to come through, but I had the information by noon. It went like this:

Jack Bisconte. Good credit rating. Owner and sole operator, Bisconte Florist Shop, since 1978; lived on upper Greenwich Street, in a rented apartment, same length of time. No listing of previous jobs held or previous local addresses. No felony or misdemeanor arrests.

George Ferry. Excellent credit rating. Owner and principal operator, Ferry Temporary Employment Agency, since 1972. Resident of 7250 Chestnut since 1980. No felony arrests; one DWI arrest and conviction following a minor traffic accident in May 1981, sentenced to ninety days in jail (suspended), driver's license revoked for six months.

Gianna Fornessi. Fair to good credit rating. Employed by Home Draperies, Showplace Square, as a sales representative since 1988. Resident of 7250 Chestnut for eight months; address prior to that, her parents' home in Daly City. No felony or misdemeanor arrests.

Ashley Hansen. No credit rating. No felony or misdemeanor arrests.

There wasn't much in any of that, either, except for the fact that TRW had no listing on Ashley Hansen. Almost everybody uses credit cards these days, establishes some kind of credit—especially a young woman whose income is substantial enough to afford an apartment in one of the city's best neighborhoods. Why not Ashley Hansen?

She was one person who could tell me; another was Gianna Fornessi. I had yet to talk to Pietro's granddaughter and I thought it was high time. I left the office in Eberhardt's care, picked up my car, and drove south of Market to Showplace Square.

The Square is a newish complex of manufacturers' showrooms for the interior decorating trade—carpets, draperies, lighting fixtures, and other types of home furnishings. It's not open to the public, but I showed the photostat of my license to one of the security men at the door and talked him into calling the Home Draperies showroom and asking them to send Gianna Fornessi out to talk to me.

They sent somebody out but it wasn't Gianna Fornessi. It was a fluffy looking little man in his forties named Lundquist, who said, "I'm sorry, Ms. Fornessi is no longer employed by us."

"Oh? When did she leave?"

"Eight months ago."

"Eight months?"

"At the end of September."

"Quit or terminated?"

"Quit. Rather abruptly, too."

"To take another job?"

"I don't know. She gave no adequate reason."

"No one called afterward for a reference?"

"No one," Lundquist said.

"She worked for you two years, is that right?"

"About two years, yes."

"As a sales representative?"

"That's correct."

"May I ask her salary?"

"I really couldn't tell you that."

"Just this, then: Was hers a high-salaried position? In excess of thirty thousand a year, say?"

Lundquist smiled a faint, fluffy smile. "Hardly," he said.

"Were her skills such that she could have taken another,

better paying job in the industry?"

Another fluffy smile. And another "Hardly."

So why had she quit Home Draperies so suddenly eight months ago, at just about the same time she moved into the Chestnut Street apartment with Ashley Hansen? And what was she doing to pay her share of the rent?

7

There was an appliance store delivery truck double-parked in front of 7250 Chestnut, and when I went up the stairs I found the entrance door wedged wide open. Nobody was in the vestibule or lobby, but the murmur of voices filtered down from the third floor. If I'd been a burglar I would have rubbed my hands together in glee. As it was, I walked in as if I belonged there and climbed the inside staircase to the second floor.

When I swung off the stairs I came face to face with Jack Bisconte.

He was hurrying toward me from the direction of apartment #4, something small and red and rectangular clutched in the fingers of his left hand. He broke stride when he saw me; and then recognition made him do a jerky double-take and he came to a halt. I stopped, too, with maybe fifteen feet separating us. That was close enough, and the hallway was well-lighted enough, for me to get a good look at his face. It was pinched, sweat-slicked, the eyes wide and shiny—the face of a man on the cutting edge of panic.

Frozen time, maybe five seconds of it, while we stood staring at each other. There was nobody else in the hall; no audible sounds on this floor except for the quick rasp of Bisconte's breathing. Then we both moved at the same time— Bisconte in the same jerky fashion of his double-take, shoving the red object into his coat pocket as he came forward. And then, when we had closed the gap between us by half, we both stopped again as if on cue. It might have been a mildly amusing little pantomime if you'd been a disinterested observer. It wasn't amusing to me. Or to Bisconte, from the look of him.

I said, "Fancy meeting you here. I thought you didn't know Gianna Fornessi or Ashley Hansen."

"Get out of my way."

"What's your hurry?"

"Get out of my way. I mean it." The edge of panic had cut into his voice; it was thick, liquidy, as if it were bleeding.

"What did you put in your pocket, the red thing?"

He said, "Christ!" and tried to lunge past me.

I blocked his way, getting my hands up between us to push him back. He made a noise in his throat and swung at me. It was a clumsy shot; I ducked away from it without much effort, so that his knuckles just grazed my neck. But then the son of a bitch kicked me, hard, on the left shinbone. I yelled and went down. He kicked out again, this time at my head; didn't connect because I was already rolling away. I fetched up tight against the wall and by the time I got myself twisted back around he was pelting toward the stairs.

I shoved up the wall to my feet, almost fell again when I put weight on the leg he'd kicked. Hobbling, wiping pain-wet out of my eyes, I went after him. People were piling down from the third floor; the one in the lead was George Ferry. He called something that I didn't listen to as I started to descend. Bisconte, damn him, had already crossed the lobby and was running out through the open front door.

Hop, hop, hop down the stairs like a contestant in a one-legged race, using the railing for support. By the time I reached the lobby, some of the sting had gone out of my shinbone and I could put more weight on the leg. Out into the vestibule, half running and half hobbling now, looking for him. He was across the street and down a ways, fumbling with a set of keys at the driver's door of a new silver Mercedes.

But he didn't stay there long. He was too wrought up to get the right key into the lock, and when he saw me pounding across the street in his direction, the panic goosed him and he ran again. Around behind the Mercedes, onto the sidewalk, up and over the concrete retaining wall. And gone.

I heard him go sliding or tumbling through the undergrowth below. I staggered up to the wall, leaned over it. The slope down there was steep, covered with trees and brush, strewn with the leavings of semi-humans who had used it for a dumping ground. Bisconte was on his buttocks, digging hands and heels into the ground to slow his momentum. For a few seconds I thought he was going to turn into a one-man avalanche and plummet over the edge where the slope ended in a sheer bluff face. But then he managed to catch hold of one of the tree trunks and swing himself away from the bluff, in among a tangle of bushes where I couldn't see him anymore. I could hear him—and then I couldn't. He'd found purchase, I thought, and was easing himself down to where the backside of another apartment building leaned in against the cliff.

There was no way I was going down there after him. I turned and went to the Mercedes.

It had a vanity plate, the kind that makes you wonder why somebody would pay twenty-five dollars extra to the DMV to put it on his car: BISFLWR. If the Mercedes had had an external hood release, I would have popped it and disabled the engine; but it didn't, and all four doors were locked. All right. Chances were, he wouldn't risk coming back soon—and even if he ran the risk, it would take him a good long while to get here.

I limped back to 7250. Four people were clustered in the vestibule, staring at me—Ferry and a couple of uniformed deliverymen and a fat woman in her forties. Ferry said as I came up the steps, "What happened, what's going on?" I didn't answer him. There was a bad feeling in me now; or maybe it had been there since I'd first seen the look on Bisconte's face. I pushed through the cluster—none of them tried to stop me—and crossed the lobby and went up to the second floor.

Nobody answered the bell at apartment #4. I tried the door, and it was unlocked, and I opened it and walked in and shut it again and locked it behind me.

She was lying on the floor in the living room, sprawled and bent on her back near a heavy teak coffee table, peach-colored dressing gown hiked up over her knees; head twisted at an off-angle, blood and a deep triangular puncture wound on her left temple. The blood was still wet and clotting. She hadn't been dead much more than an hour.

In the sunlight that spilled in through the undraped windows, the blood had a kind of shimmery radiance. So did her hair—her long gold-blond hair.

Goodbye Ashley Hansen.

8

I called the Hall of Justice and talked to a Homicide inspector I knew slightly named Craddock. I told him what I'd found, and about my little skirmish with Jack Bisconte, and said that yes, I would wait right here and no, I wouldn't touch anything. He didn't tell me not to look around and I didn't say that I wouldn't.

Somebody had started banging on the door. Ferry, probably. I went the other way, into one of the bedrooms. Ashley

Hansen's: there was a photograph of her prominently displayed on the dresser, and lots of mirrors to give her a live image of herself. A narcissist, among other things. On one nightstand was a telephone and an answering machine. On the unmade bed, tipped on its side with some of the contents spilled out, was a fancy leather purse. I used the backs of my two index fingers to stir around among the spilled items and the stuff inside. Everything you'd expect to find in a woman's purse and one thing that should have been there and wasn't.

Gianna Fornessi's bedroom was across the hall. She also had a telephone and an answering machine; the number on the telephone dial was different from her roommate's. I hesitated for maybe five seconds, then I went to the answering machine and pushed the button marked "playback calls" and listened to two old messages before I stopped the tape and rewound it. One message would have been enough.

Back into the living room. The knocking was still going on. I started over there; stopped after a few feet and stood sniffing the air. I thought I smelled something—a faint lingering acrid odor. Or maybe I was just imagining it . . .

Bang, bang, bang. And Ferry's voice: "What's going on in there?"

I moved ahead to the door, threw the bolt lock, yanked the door open. "Quit making so damned much noise."

Ferry blinked and backed off a step; he didn't know whether to be afraid of me or not. Behind and to one side of him, the two deliverymen and the fat woman looked on with hungry eyes. They would have liked seeing what lay inside; blood attracts some people, the gawkers, the insensitive ones, the same way it attracts flies.

"What's happened?" Ferry asked nervously.

"Come in and see for yourself. Just you."

I opened up a little wider and he came in past me, showing

reluctance. I shut and locked the door again behind him. And when I turned he said, "Oh my God," in a sickened voice. He was staring at the body on the floor, one hand pressed up under his breastbone. "Is she . . . ?"

"Very."

"Gianna . . . is she here?"

"No."

"Somebody did that to Ashley? It wasn't an accident?"

"What do you think?"

"Who? Who did it?"

"You know who, Ferry. You saw me chase him out of here."

"I . . . don't know who he is. I never saw him before."

"The hell you never saw him. He's the one put those cuts and bruises on your face."

"No," Ferry said, "that's not true." He looked and sounded even sicker now. "I told you how that happened . . ."

"You told me lies. Bisconte roughed you up so you'd drop your complaint against Gianna. He did it because Gianna and Ashley Hansen have been working as call girls and he's their pimp and he didn't want the cops digging into her background and finding out the truth."

Ferry leaned unsteadily against the wall, facing away from what was left of the Hansen woman. He didn't speak.

"Nice quiet little operation they had," I said, "until you got wind of it. That's how it was, wasn't it? You found out and you wanted some of what Gianna's been selling."

Nothing for ten seconds. Then, softly, "It wasn't like that, not at first. I . . . loved her."

"Sure you did."

"I did. But she wouldn't have anything to do with me."

"So then you offered to pay her."

". . .Yes. Whatever she charged."

"Only you wanted kinky sex and she wouldn't play."

"No! I never asked for anything except a night with her . . . one night. She pretended to be insulted; she denied that she's been selling herself to men. She . . . she said she'd never go to bed with a man as . . . ugly . . ." He moved against the wall—a writhing movement, as if he were in pain.

"That was when you decided to get even with her."

"I wanted to hurt her, the way she'd hurt me. It was stupid, I know that, but I wasn't thinking clearly. I just wanted to hurt her . . ."

"Well, you succeeded," I said. "But the one you really hurt is Ashley Hansen. If it hadn't been for you, she'd still be alive."

He started to say something but the words were lost in the sudden summons of the doorbell.

"That'll be the police," I said.

"The police? But . . . I thought you were . . ."

"I know you did. I never told you I was, did I?"

I left him holding up the wall and went to buzz them in.

9

I spent more than two hours in the company of the law, alternately answering questions and waiting around. I told Inspector Craddock how I happened to be there. I told him how I'd come to realize that Gianna Fornessi and Ashley Hansen were call girls, and how George Ferry and Jack Bisconte figured into it. I told him about the small red rectangular object I'd seen Bisconte shove into his pocket—an address book, no doubt, with the names of some of Hansen's johns. That was the common item that was missing from her purse.

Craddock seemed satisfied. I wished I was.

When he finally let me go I drove back to the office. But I

didn't stay long; it was late afternoon, Eberhardt had already gone for the day, and I felt too restless to tackle the stack of routine paperwork on my desk. I went out to Ocean Beach and walked on the sand, as I sometimes do when an edginess is on me. It helped a little—not much.

I ate an early dinner out, and when I got home I put in a call to the Hall of Justice to ask if Jack Bisconte had been picked up yet. But Craddock was off duty and the inspector I spoke to wouldn't tell me anything.

The edginess stayed with me all evening, and kept me awake past midnight. I knew what was causing it, all right; and I knew what to do to get rid of it. Only I wasn't ready to do it yet.

In the morning, after eight, I called the Hall again. Craddock came on duty at eight, I'd been told. He was there and willing to talk, but what he had to tell me was not what I wanted to hear. Bisconte was in custody but not because he'd been apprehended. At eight-thirty Monday night he'd walked into the North Beach precinct station with his lawyer in tow and given himself up. He'd confessed to being a pimp for the two women; he'd confessed to working over George Ferry; he'd confessed to being in the women's apartment just prior to his tussle with me. But he swore up and down that he hadn't killed Ashley Hansen. He'd never had any trouble with her, he said; in fact he'd been half in love with her. The cops had Gianna Fornessi in custody too by this time, and she'd confirmed that there had never been any rough stuff or bad feelings between her roommate and Bisconte.

Hansen had been dead when he got to the apartment, Bisconte said. Fear that he'd be blamed had pushed him into a panic. He'd taken the address book out of her purse—he hadn't thought about the answering machine tapes or he'd have erased the messages left by eager johns—and when he'd encountered me in the hallway he'd lost his head completely. Later, after he'd had time to calm down, he'd gone to the lawyer, who had advised him to turn himself in.

Craddock wasn't so sure Bisconte was telling the truth, but I was. I knew who had been responsible for Ashley Hansen's death; I'd known it a few minutes after I found her body. I just hadn't wanted it to be that way.

I didn't tell Craddock any of this. When he heard the truth it would not be over the phone. And it would not be from me.

10

It did not take me long to track him down. He wasn't home but a woman in his building said that in nice weather he liked to sit in Washington Square Park with his cronies. That was where I found him, in the park. Not in the company of anyone; just sitting alone on a bench across from the Saints Peter and Paul Catholic Church, in the same slumped, bowed-head posture as when I'd first seen him on Sunday—the posture of *la miseria*.

I sat down beside him. He didn't look at me, not even when I said, "*Buon giorno*, Pietro."

He took out one of his twisted black cigars and lit it carefully with a kitchen match. Its odor was acrid on the warm morning air—the same odor that had been in his granddaughter's apartment, that I'd pretended to myself I was imagining. Nothing smells like a Toscana; nothing. And only old men like Pietro smoke Toscanas these days. They don't even have to smoke one in a closed room for the smell to linger after them; it gets into and comes off the heavy user's clothing.

"It's time for us to talk," I said.

"*Che sopra?*"

"Ashley Hansen. How she died."

A little silence. Then he sighed and said, "You already know, hah, good detective like you? How you find out?"

"Does it matter?"

"It don't matter. You tell police yet?"

"It'll be better if you tell them."

More silence, while he smoked his little cigar.

I said, "But first tell me. Exactly what happened."

He shut his eyes; he didn't want to relive what had happened.

"It was me telling you about Bisconte that started it," I said to prod him. "After you got home Sunday night you called Gianna and asked her about him. Or she called you."

". . . I call her," he said. "She's angry, she tell me mind my own business. Never before she talks to her goombah this way."

"Because of me. Because she was afraid of what I'd find out about her and Ashley Hansen and Bisconte."

"Bisconte." He spat the name, as if ridding his mouth of something foul.

"So this morning you asked around the neighborhood about him. And somebody told you he wasn't just a florist, about his little sideline. Then you got on a bus and went to see your granddaughter."

"I don't believe it, not about Gianna. I want her tell me it's not true. But she's not there. Only the other one, the *bionda*."

"And then?"

"She don't want to let me in, that one. I go in anyway. I ask if she and Gianna are . . . if they sell themselves for money. She laugh. In my face she laugh, this girl what have no respect. She says what difference it make? She says I am old man—dinosaur, she says. But she pat my cheek like I am little boy or big joke. Then she . . . ah, *Cristo,* she come up close to me and she say you want some, old man, I give you some. To me she says this. Me." Pietro shook his head; there were tears in his eyes now. "I push her away. I feel . . . *feroce*, like when I am young man and somebody he make trouble with me. I push her too hard and she fall, her head hit the table and I see blood and she don't move . . . ah, *mio Dio!* She was wicked, that one, but I don't mean to hurt her . . ."

"I know you didn't, Pietro."

"I think, call doctor quick. But she is dead. And I hurt here, inside"—he tapped his chest—"and I think, what if Gianna she come home? I don't want to see Gianna. You understand? Never again I want to see her."

"I understand," I said. And I thought: Funny—I've never laid eyes on her, not even a photograph of her. I don't know what she looks like; now I don't want to know. I never want to see her.

Pietro finished his cigar. Then he straightened on the bench, seemed to compose himself. His eyes had dried; they were clear and sad. He looked past me, across at the looming Romanesque pile of the church. "I make confession to priest," he said, "little while before you come. Now we go to police and I make confession to them."

"Yes."

"You think they put me in gas chamber?"

"I doubt they'll put you in prison at all. It was an accident. Just a bad accident."

Another silence. On Pietro's face was an expression of the deepest pain. "This thing, this accident, she shouldn't have happen. Once . . . ah, once . . ." Pause. *"Morto,"* he said.

He didn't mean the death of Ashley Hansen. He meant the death of the old days, the days when families were tightly knit and there was respect for elders, the days when bocce was king of his world and that world was a far simpler and better place. The bitterest of woes is to remember old happy days . . .

We sat there in the pale sun. And pretty soon he said, in a voice so low I barely heard the words, *"La bellezza delle bellezze."* Twice before he had used that phrase in my presence and both times he had been referring to his granddaughter. This time I knew he was not.

"Si, 'paesano," I said. *"La bellezza delle bellezze."*

Souls Burning

Hotel Majestic, Sixth Street, downtown San Francisco. A hell of an address—a hell of a place for an ex-con not long out of Folsom to set up housekeeping. Sixth Street, south of Market—South of the Slot, it used to be called—is the heart of the city's Skid Road and has been for more than half a century.

Eddie Quinlan. A name and a voice out of the past, neither of which I'd recognized when he called that morning. Close to seven years since I had seen or spoken to him, six years since I'd even thought of him. Eddie Quinlan. Edgewalker, shadow-man with no real substance or purpose, drifting along the narrow catwalk that separates conventional society from the underworld. Information seller, gofer, small-time bagman, doer of any insignificant job, legitimate or otherwise, that would help keep him in food and shelter, liquor and cigarettes. The kind of man you looked at but never really saw: a modern-day Yehudi, the little man who wasn't there. Eddie Quinlan. Nobody, loser—fall guy. Drug bust in the Tenderloin one night six and a half years ago; one dealer setting up another, and Eddie Quinlan, small-time bagman, caught in the middle; hard-assed judge, five years in Folsom, goodbye Eddie Quinlan. And the drug dealers? They walked, of course. Both of them.

And now Eddie was out, had been out for six months. And after six months of freedom, he'd called me. Would I come to his room at the Hotel Majestic tonight around eight? He'd tell me why when he saw me. It was real important—would I come? All right, Eddie. But I couldn't figure it. I had bought information from him in the old days, bits and pieces for five or ten dollars; maybe he had something to sell now. Only I wasn't looking for anything and I hadn't put the word out, so why pick me to call?

If you're smart you don't park your car on the street at night South of the Slot. I put mine in the Fifth and Mission Garage at seven forty-five and walked over to Sixth. It had rained most of the day and the streets were still wet, but now the sky was cold and clear. The kind of night that is as hard as black glass, so that light seems to bounce off the dark instead of shining through it; lights and their colors so bright and sharp reflecting off the night and the wet surfaces that the glare is like splinters against your eyes.

Friday night, and Sixth Street was teeming. Sidewalks jammed—old men, young men, bag ladies, painted ladies, blacks, whites, Asians, addicts, pushers, muttering mental cases, drunks leaning against walls in tight little clusters while they shared paper-bagged bottles of sweet wine and cans of malt liquor; men and women in filthy rags, in smart new outfits topped off with sunglasses, carrying ghetto blasters and red-and-white canes, some of the canes in the hands of individuals who could see as well as I could, carrying a hidden array of guns and knives and other lethal instruments. Cheap hotels, greasy spoons, seedy taverns, and liquor stores complete with barred windows and cynical proprietors that stayed open well past midnight. Laughter, shouts, curses, threats; bickering and dickering. The stenches of urine and vomit and unwashed bodies and rotgut liquor, and over those like an umbrella, the subtle effluvium of despair. Predators and prey, half hidden in shadow, half revealed in the bright, sharp dazzle of fluorescent lights and bloody neon.

Souls Burning

It was a mean street, Sixth, one of the meanest, and I walked it warily. I may be fifty-eight but I'm a big man and I walk hard too; and I look like what I am. Two winos tried to panhandle me and a fat hooker in an orange wig tried to sell me a piece of her tired body, but no one gave me any trouble.

The Majestic was five stories of old wood and plaster and dirty brick, just off Howard Street. In front of its narrow entrance, a crack dealer and one of his customers were haggling over the price of a baggie of rock cocaine; neither of them paid any attention to me as I moved past them. Drug deals go down in the open here, day and night. It's not that the cops don't care, or that they don't patrol Sixth regularly; it's just that the dealers outnumber them ten to one. On Skid Road any crime less severe than aggravated assault is strictly low priority.

Small, barren lobby: no furniture of any kind. The smell of ammonia hung in the air like swamp gas. Behind the cubbyhole desk was an old man with dead eyes that would never see anything they didn't want to see. I said, "Eddie Quinlan," and he said, "Two-oh-two" without moving his lips. There was an elevator but it had an Out of Order sign on it; dust speckled the sign. I went up the adjacent stairs.

The disinfectant smell permeated the second floor hallway as well. Room 202 was just off the stairs, fronting on Sixth; one of the metal 2s on the door had lost a screw and was hanging upside down. I used my knuckles just below it. Scraping noise inside, and a voice said, "Yeah?"

I identified myself. A lock clicked, a chain rattled, the door wobbled and for the first time in nearly seven years I was looking at Eddie Quinlan.

He hadn't changed much. Little guy, about five-eight, and

past forty now. Thin, nondescript features, pale eyes, hair the color of sand. The hair was thinner and the lines in his face were longer and deeper, almost like incisions where they bracketed his nose. Otherwise he was the same Eddie Quinlan.

"Hey," he said, "thanks for coming. I mean it, thanks."

"Sure, Eddie."

"Come on in."

The room made me think of a box—the inside of a huge rotting packing crate. Four bare walls with the scaly remnants of paper on them like psoriatic skin, bare uncarpeted floor, unshaded bulb hanging from the center of a bare ceiling. The bulb was dark; what light there was came from a low-wattage reading lamp and a wash of red-and-green neon from the hotel's sign that spilled in through a single window. Old iron-framed bed, unpainted nightstand, scarred dresser, straight-backed chair next to the bed and in front of the window, alcove with a sink and toilet and no door, closet that wouldn't be much larger than a coffin.

"Not much, is it," Eddie said.

I didn't say anything.

He shut the hall door, locked it. "Only place to sit is that chair there. Unless you want to sit on the bed? Sheets are clean. I try to keep things clean as I can."

"Chair's fine."

I went across to it; Eddie put himself on the bed. A room with a view, he'd said on the phone. Some view. Sitting here you could look down past Howard and up across Mission—almost two full blocks of the worst street in the city. It was so close you could hear the beat of its pulse, the ugly sounds of its living and its dying.

"So why did you ask me here, Eddie? If it's information for sale, I'm not buying right now."

"No, no, nothing like that, I ain't in the business anymore."

"Is that right?"

"Prison taught me a lesson. I got rehabilitated." There was no sarcasm or irony in the words; he said them matter-of-factly.

"I'm glad to hear it."

"I been a good citizen ever since I got out. No lie. I haven't had a drink, ain't even been in a bar."

"What are you doing for money?"

"I got a job," he said. "Shipping department at a wholesale sporting goods outfit on Brannan. It don't pay much but it's honest work."

I nodded. "What is it you want, Eddie?"

"Somebody I can talk to, somebody who'll understand—that's all I want. You always treated me decent. Most of 'em, no matter who they were, they treated me like I wasn't even human. Like I was a turd or something."

"Understand what?"

"About what's happening down there."

"Where? Sixth Street?"

"Look at it," he said. He reached over and tapped the window; stared through it. "Look at the people . . . there, you see that guy in the wheelchair and the one pushing him? Across the street there?"

I leaned closer to the glass. The man in the wheelchair wore a military camouflage jacket, had a heavy wool blanket across his lap; the black man manipulating him along the crowded sidewalk was thick-bodied, with a shiny bald head. "I see them."

"White guy's name is Baxter," Eddie said. "Grenade blew up under him in 'Nam and now he's a paraplegic. Lives right here in the Majestic, on this floor down at the end. Deals crack and smack out of his room. Elroy, the black dude, is his bodyguard and roommate. Mean, both of 'em. Couple of months ago, Elroy killed a guy over on Minna that tried to stiff them. Busted his head with a brick. You believe it?"

"I believe it."

"And they ain't the worst on the street. Not the worst."

"I believe that too."

"Before I went to prison I lived and worked with people like that and I never saw what they were. I mean I just never saw it. Now I do, I see it clear—every day walking back and forth to work, every night from up here. It makes you sick after a while, the things you see when you see 'em clear."

"Why don't you move?"

"Where to? I can't afford no place better than this."

"No better room, maybe, but why not another neighborhood? You don't have to live on Sixth Street."

"Wouldn't be much better, any other neighborhood I could buy into. They're all over the city now, the ones like Baxter and Elroy. Used to be it was just Skid Road and the Tenderloin and the ghettos. Now they're everywhere, more and more every day. You know?"

"I know."

"Why? It don't have to be this way, does it?"

Hard times, bad times: alienation, poverty, corruption, too much government, not enough government, lack of social services, lack of caring, drugs like a cancer destroying society. Simplistic explanations that were no explanations at all and as dehumanizing as the ills they described. I was tired of hearing them and I didn't want to repeat them, to Eddie Quinlan or anybody else. So I said nothing.

He shook his head. "Souls burning everywhere you go," he said, and it was as if the words hurt his mouth coming out.

Souls burning. "You find religion at Folsom, Eddie?"

"Religion? I don't know, maybe a little. Chaplain we had there, I talked to him sometimes. He used to say that about the hardtimers, that their souls were burning and there wasn't nothing he could do to put out the fire. They were doomed, he said, and they'd doom others to burn with 'em."

I had nothing to say to that either. In the small silence a voice from outside said distinctly, "Dirty bastard, what you doin' with my pipe?" It was cold in there, with the hard bright night pressing against the window. Next to the door was a rusty steam radiator but it was cold too; the heat would not be on more than a few hours a day, even in the dead of winter, in the Hotel Majestic.

"That's the way it is in the city," Eddie said. "Souls burning. All day long, all night long, souls on fire."

"Don't let it get to you."

"Don't it get to you?"

". . . Yes. Sometimes."

He bobbed his head up and down. "You want to do something, you know? You want to try to fix it somehow, put out the fires. There has to be a way."

"I can't tell you what it is," I said.

He said, "If we all just did something. It ain't too late. You don't think it's too late?"

"No."

"Me neither. There's still hope."

"Hope, faith, blind optimism—sure."

"You got to believe," he said, nodding. "That's all, you just got to believe."

Angry voices rose suddenly from outside; a woman screamed, thin and brittle. Eddie came off the bed, hauled up the window sash. Chill, damp air and street noises came pouring in: shouts, cries, horns honking, cars whispering on the wet pavement, a Muni bus clattering along Mission; more shrieks. He leaned out, peering downward.

"Look," he said, "look."

I stretched forward and looked. On the sidewalk below, a hooker in a leopard-skin coat was running wildly toward Howard; she was the one doing the yelling. Chasing behind her, tight black skirt hiked up over the tops of net stockings and hairy thighs, was a hideously rouged transvestite waving a pocket knife. A group of winos began laughing and chanting, "Rape! Rape!" as the hooker and the transvestite ran zigzagging out of sight on Howard.

Eddie pulled his head back in. The flickery neon wash made his face seem surreal, like a hallucinogenic vision. "That's the way it is," he said sadly. "Night after night, day after day."

With the window open, the cold was intense; it penetrated my clothing and crawled on my skin. I'd had enough of it, and of this room and Eddie Quinlan and Sixth Street.

"Eddie, just what is it you want from me?"

"I already told you. Talk to somebody who understands how it is down there."

"Is that the only reason you asked me here?"

"Ain't it enough?"

"For you, maybe." I got to my feet. "I'll be going now."

He didn't argue. "Sure, you go ahead."

"Nothing else you want to say?"

"Nothing else." He walked to the door with me, unlocked it, and then put out his hand. "Thanks for coming. I appreciate it, I really do."

"Yeah. Good luck, Eddie."

"You too," he said. "Keep the faith."

I went out into the hall, and the door shut gently and the lock clicked behind me.

Downstairs, out of the Majestic, along the mean street and

back to the garage where I'd left my car. And all the way I kept thinking: There's something else, something more he wanted from me . . . and I gave it to him by going there and listening to him. But what? What did he really want?

I found out later that night. It was all over the TV—special bulletins and then the eleven o'clock news.

Twenty minutes after I left him, Eddie Quinlan stood at the window of his room-with-a-view, and in less than a minute, using a high-powered semiautomatic rifle he'd taken from the sporting goods outfit where he worked, he shot down fourteen people on the street below. Nine dead, five wounded, one of the wounded in critical condition and not expected to live. Six of the victims were known drug dealers; all of the others also had arrest records, for crimes ranging from prostitution to burglary. Two of the dead were Baxter, the paraplegic ex-Vietnam vet, and his bodyguard, Elroy.

By the time the cops showed up, Sixth Street was empty except for the dead and the dying. No more targets, and up in his room, Eddie Quinlan had sat on the bed and put the rifle's muzzle in his mouth and used his big toe to pull the trigger.

My first reaction was to blame myself. But how could I have known or even guessed? Eddie Quinlan. Nobody, loser, shadow-man without substance or purpose. How could anyone have figured him for a thing like that?

Somebody I can talk to, somebody who'll understand—that's all I want.

No. What he'd wanted was somebody to help him justify to himself what he was about to do. Somebody to record his verbal suicide note. Somebody he could trust to pass it on af-terward, tell it right and true to the world.

You want to do something, you know? You want to try to fix it somehow, put out the fires. There has to be a way.

239

Nine dead, five wounded, one of the wounded in critical condition and not expected to live. Not that way.

Souls burning. All day long, all night long, souls on fire.

The soul that had burned tonight was Eddie Quinlan's.

Bomb Scare

He was a hypertensive little man with overlarge ears and buck teeth—Brer Rabbit dressed up in a threadbare brown suit and sunglasses. In his left hand he carried a briefcase with a broken catch; it was held closed by a frayed strap that looked as though it might pop loose at any second. And inside the briefcase . . .

"A bomb," he kept announcing in a shrill voice. "I've got a remote-controlled bomb in here. Do what I tell you, don't come near me, or I'll blow us all up."

Nobody in the branch office of the San Francisco Trust Bank was anywhere near him. Lawrence Metaxa, the manager, and the other bank employees were frozen behind the row of tellers' cages. The four customers, me included, stood in a cluster out front. None of us was doing anything except waiting tensely for the little rabbit to quit hopping around and get down to business.

It took him another few seconds. Then, with his free hand, he dragged a cloth sack from his coat and threw it at one of the tellers. "Put all the money in there. Stay away from the silent alarm or I'll set off the bomb. I mean it."

Metaxa assured him in a shaky voice that they would do whatever he asked.

"Hurry up, then." The rabbit waved his empty right hand in the air, jerkily, as if he were directing some sort of mad symphony. "Hurry up, hurry up!"

The tellers got busy. While they hurriedly emptied cash

drawers, the little man produced a second cloth sack and moved in my direction. The other customers shrank back. I stayed where I was, so he pitched the sack to me.

"Put your wallet in there," he said in a voice like glass cracking. "All your valuables. Then get everybody else's."

I said, "I don't think so."

"What? What?" He hopped on one foot, then the other, making the briefcase dance. "What's the matter with you? Do what I told you!"

When he'd first come in and started yelling about his bomb, I'd thought that I couldn't have picked a worse time to take care of my bank deposits. Now I was thinking that I couldn't have picked a better time. I took a measured step toward him. Somebody behind me gasped. I took another step.

"Stay back!" the little guy shouted. "I'll push the button, I'll blow us up."

I said, "No, you won't," and rushed him and yanked the briefcase out of his hand.

More gasps, a cry, the sounds of customers and employees scrambling for cover. But nothing happened, except that the little guy tried to run away. I caught him by the collar and dragged him back. His struggles were brief and half-hearted; he'd gambled and lost and he knew when he was licked.

Scared faces peered over counters and around corners. I held the briefcase up so they could all see it. "No bomb in here, folks. You can relax now, it's all over."

It took a couple of minutes to restore order, during which time I marched the little man around to Metaxa's desk and pushed him into a chair. He sat slumped, twitching and muttering. "Lost my job, so many debts . . . must've been crazy to do a thing like this . . . I'm sorry, I'm sorry." Poor little rabbit. He wasn't half as sorry now as he was going to be later.

I opened the case while Metaxa called the police. The only

thing inside was a city telephone directory for weight.

When Metaxa hung up he said to me, "You took a crazy risk, grabbing the briefcase like that. If he really had had a bomb in there . . ."

"I knew he didn't."

"*Knew* he didn't? How could you?"

"I'm a detective, remember? Three reasons. One: Bombs are delicate mechanisms and people who build them are cautious by necessity. They don't put explosives in a cheap case with a busted catch and just a frayed strap holding it together, not unless they're suicidal. Two: He claimed it was remote-controlled. But the hand he kept waving was empty and all he had in the other one was the case. Where was the remote control? In one of his pockets, where he couldn't get at it easily? No. A real bomber would've had it out in plain sight to back up his threat."

"Still," Metaxa said, "you could've been wrong on both counts. Neither is an absolute certainty."

"No, but the third reason is as close to one as you can get."

"Yes?"

"It takes more than just skill to make a bomb. It takes nerve, coolness, patience, and a very steady hand. Look at our friend here. He doesn't have any of those attributes; he's the chronically nervous type, as jumpy as six cats. He could no more manufacture an explosive device than you or I could fly. If he'd ever tried, he'd have blown himself up in two minutes flat."

The Big Bite

I laid a red queen on a black king, glanced up at Jay Cohalan through the open door of his office. He was pacing again, back and forth in front of his desk, his hands in constant restless motion at his sides. The office was carpeted: his footfalls made no sound. There was no discernible sound anywhere except for the faint snap and slap when I turned over a card and put it down. An office building at night is one of the quietest places there is. Eerily so, if you spend enough time listening to the silence.

Trey. Nine of diamonds. Deuce. Jack of spades. I was marrying the jack to the red queen when Cohalan quit pacing and came over to stand in the doorway. He watched me for a time, his hands still doing scoop-shovel maneuvers—a big man in his late thirties, handsome except for a weak chin, a little sweaty and disheveled now.

"How can you just sit there playing cards?" he said.

There were several answers to that. Years of stakeouts and dull routine. We'd been waiting only about two hours. The money, fifty thousand in fifties and hundreds, didn't belong to me. I wasn't worried, upset, or afraid that something might go wrong. I passed on all of those and settled instead for a neutral response: "Solitaire's good for waiting. Keeps your mind off the clock."

"It's after seven. Why the hell doesn't he call?"

"You know the answer to that. He wants you to sweat."

"Sadistic bastard."

245

"Blackmail's that kind of game," I said. "Torture the victim, bend his will to yours."

"Game. My God." Cohalan came out into the anteroom and began to pace in front of his secretary's desk, where I was sitting. "It's driving me crazy, trying to figure out who he is, how he found out about my past. Not a hint, any of the times I talked to him. But he knows everything, every damn detail."

"You'll have the answers before long."

"Yeah." He stopped abruptly, leaned toward me. "Listen, this has to be the end of it. You've got to stay with him, see to it he's arrested. I can't take any more."

"I'll do my job. Mr. Cohalan, don't worry."

"Fifty thousand dollars. I almost had a heart attack when he told me that was how much he wanted this time. The last payment, he said. What a crock. He'll come back for more someday. I know it, Carolyn knows it, you know it." Pacing again. "Poor Carolyn. Highstrung, emotional . . . it's been even harder on her. She wanted me to go to the police this time, did I tell you that?"

"You told me."

"I should have, I guess. Now I've got to pay a middleman for what I could've had for nothing . . . no offense."

"None taken."

"I just couldn't bring myself to do it, walk into the Hall of Justice and confess everything to a cop. It was hard enough letting Carolyn talk me into hiring a private detective. That trouble when I was a kid . . . it's a criminal offense, I could still be prosecuted for it. And it's liable to cost me my job if it comes out. I went through hell telling Carolyn in the beginning, and I didn't go into all the sordid details. With you, either. The police . . . no. I know that bastard will probably spill the whole story when he's arrested, try to drag me down with him, but still . . . I keep hoping he won't. You understand?"

"I understand," I said.

"I shouldn't've paid him when he crawled out of the woodwork eight months ago. I know that now. But back then it seemed like the only way to keep from ruining my life. Carolyn thought so, too. If I hadn't started paying him, half of her inheritance wouldn't already be gone . . ." He let the rest of it trail off, paced in bitter silence for a time, and started up again. "I hated taking money from her—hated it, no matter how much she insisted it belongs to both of us. And I hate myself for doing it, almost as much as I hate him. Blackmail's the worst goddamn crime there is short of murder."

"Not the worst," I said, "but bad enough."

"This has to be the end of it. The fifty thousand in there . . . it's the last of her inheritance, our savings. If that son of a bitch gets away with it, we'll be wiped out. You can't let that happen."

I didn't say anything. We'd been through all this before, more than once.

Cohalan let the silence resettle. Then, as I shuffled the cards for a new hand, "This job of mine, you'd think it pays pretty well, wouldn't you? My own office, secretary, executive title, expense account . . . looks good and sounds good, but it's a frigging dead end. Junior account executive stuck in corporate middle management—that's all I am or ever will be. Sixty thousand a year gross. And Carolyn makes twenty-five teaching. Eighty-five thousand for two people, no kids, that seems like plenty but it's not, not these days. Taxes, high cost of living, you have to scrimp to put anything away. And then some stupid mistake you made when you were a kid comes back to haunt you, drains your future along with your bank account, preys on your mind so you can't sleep, can barely do your work . . . you see what I mean? But I didn't think I had a choice at first, I was afraid of losing this crappy job, going to prison. Caught between a rock and a hard place. I still feel that way, but now I don't care, I just want that scum to get what's coming to him . . ."

Repetitious babbling caused by his anxiety. His mouth had a wet look and his eyes kept jumping from me to other points in the room.

I said, "Why don't you sit down?"

"I can't sit. My nerves are shot."

"Take a few deep breaths before you start to hyperventilate."

"Listen, don't tell me what—"

The telephone on his desk went off.

The sudden clamor jerked him half around, as if with an electric shock. In the quiet that followed the first ring I could hear the harsh rasp of his breathing. He looked back at me as the bell sounded again. I was on my feet, too, by then.

I said, "Go ahead, answer it. Keep your head."

He went into his office, picked up just after the third ring. I timed the lifting of the extension to coincide so there wouldn't be a second click on the open line.

"Yes," he said, "Cohalan."

"You know who this is." The voice was harsh, muffled, indistinctively male. "You got the fifty thousand?"

"I told you I would. The last payment, you promised me."

"Yeah, the last one."

"Where this time?"

"Golden Gate Park. Kennedy Drive, in front of the buffalo pen. Put it in the trash barrel beside the bench there."

Cohalan was watching me through the open doorway. I shook my head at him. He said into the phone, "Can't we make it someplace else? There might be people around . . ."

"Not at nine p.m."

"Nine? But it's only a little after seven now—"

"Nine sharp. Be there with the cash."

The line went dead.

I cradled the extension. Cohalan was still standing along-side his desk, hanging onto the receiver the way a drowning man might hang onto a lifeline, when I went into his office. I said, "Put it down, Mr. Cohalan."

"What? Oh, yes." He lowered the receiver. "Christ," he said then.

"You all right?"

His head bobbed up and down a couple of times. He ran a hand over his face and then swung away to where his brief-case lay. The fifty thousand was in there; he'd shown it to me when I first arrived. He picked the case up, set it down again. Rubbed his face another time.

"Maybe I shouldn't risk the money," he said.

He wasn't talking to me so I didn't answer.

"I could leave it right here where it'll be safe. Put a phone book or something in for weight." He sank into his desk chair, popped up again like a jack-in-the-box. He was wired so tight I could almost hear him humming. "No, what's the matter with me? That won't work. I'm not thinking straight. He might open the case in the park. There's no telling what he'd do if the money's not there. And he's got to have it in his pos-session when the police come."

"That's why I insisted we mark some of the bills."

"Yes, right, I remember. Proof of extortion. All right, but for God's sake don't let him get away with it."

"He won't get away with it."

Another jerky nod. "When're you leaving?"

"Right now. You stay put until at least eight-thirty. It won't take you more than twenty minutes to get out to the park."

"I'm not sure I can get through another hour of waiting around here."

"Keep telling yourself it'll be over soon. Calm down. The state you're in now, you shouldn't even be behind the wheel."

"I'll be okay."

"Come straight back here after you make the drop. You'll hear from me as soon as I have anything to report."

"Just don't make me wait too long," Cohalan said. And then, again and to himself, "I'll be okay."

Cohalan's office building was on Kearney, not far from where Kerry works at the Bates and Carpenter ad agency on lower Geary. She was on my mind as I drove down to Geary and turned west toward the park: my thoughts prompted me to lift the car phone and call the condo. No answer. Like me, she puts in a lot of overtime night work. A wonder we manage to spend as much time together as we do.

I tried her private number at B & C and got her voice mail. In transit probably, the same as I was. Headlights crossing the dark city. Urban night riders. Except that she was going home and I was on my way to nail a shakedown artist for a paying client.

That started me thinking about the kind of work I do. One of the downsides of urban night riding is that it gives vent to sometimes broody self-analysis. Skip traces, insurance claim investigations, employee background checks—they're the meat of my business. There used to be some challenge to jobs like that, some creative maneuvering required, but nowadays it's little more than routine legwork (mine) and a lot of computer time (Tamara Corbin, my techno-whiz assistant). I don't get to use my head as much as I once did. My problem, in Tamara's Generation X opinion, was that I was a "retro dick" pining away for the old days and old ways. True enough; I never have adapted well to change. The detective racket just isn't as satisfying or stimulating after thirty-plus years and with a new set of rules.

Every now and then, though, a case comes along that stirs the juices—one with some spark and sizzle and a much higher satisfaction level than the run-of-the-mill stuff. I live for cases like that; they're what keep me from packing it in, taking an early retirement. They usually involve a felony of some sort, and sometimes a whisper if not a shout of danger, and allow me to use my full complement of functional brain cells. This Cohalan case, for instance. This one I liked, because shake-down artists are high on my list of worthless lowlifes and I enjoy hell out of taking one down.

Yeah, this one I liked a whole lot.

Golden Gate Park has plenty of daytime attractions—museums, tiny lakes, rolling lawns, windmills, an arboretum—but on a foggy November night it's a mostly empty dark place to pass through on your way to somewhere else. Mostly empty because it does have its night denizens: homeless squatters, not all of whom are harmless or drug-free, and predators on the prowl in its sprawling acres of shadows and nightshapes. On a night like this it also has an atmosphere of lonely isolation, the fog hiding the city lights and turning street lamps and passing headlights into surreal blurs.

The buffalo enclosure is at the westward end, less than a mile from the ocean—the least-traveled section of the park at night. There were no cars in the vicinity, moving or parked, when I came down Kennedy Drive. My lights picked out the fence on the north side, the rolling pastureland beyond; the trash barrel and bench were about halfway along, at the edge of the bicycle path that parallels the road. I drove past there, looking for a place to park and wait. I didn't want to sit on

Kennedy; a lone car close to the drop point would be too conspicuous. I had to do this right. If anything did not seem ko-
sher, the whole thing might fail to go off the way it was
supposed to.

The perfect spot came up fifty yards or so from the trash
barrel, opposite the buffalo feeding corral—a narrow road
that leads to Anglers Lodge, where the city maintains casting
pools for fly fishermen to practice on. Nobody was likely to go
up there at night, and trees and shrubbery bordered one side,
the shadows in close to them thick and clotted. Kennedy
Drive was still empty in both directions; I cut in past the Anglers Lodge sign and drove up the road until I found a place
where I could turn around. Then I shut off my lights, made
the U-turn, and coasted back down into the heavy shadows.
From there I could see the drop point clearly enough, even
with the low-riding fog. I shut off the engine, slumped down
on the seat with my back against the door.

No detective, public or private, likes stakeouts. Dull,
boring, dead time that can be a literal pain in the ass if it goes
on long enough. This one wasn't too bad because it was
short, only about an hour, but time lagged and crawled just
the same. Now and then a car drifted by, its lights reflecting
off rather than boring through the wall of mist. The ones
heading west might have been able to see my car briefly in
dark silhouette as they passed, but none of them happened to
be a police patrol and nobody else was curious enough or
venal enough to stop and investigate.

The luminous dial on my watch showed five minutes to
nine when Cohalan arrived. Predictably early because he was
so anxious to get it over with. He came down Kennedy too
fast for the conditions; I heard the squeal of brakes as he
swung over and rocked to a stop near the trash barrel. I
watched the shape of him get out and run across the path to

make the drop and then run back. Ten seconds later his car hissed past where I was hidden, again going too fast, and was gone.

Nine o'clock.

Nine oh five.

Nine oh eight.

Headlights probed past, this set heading east, the car low-slung and smallish. It rolled along slowly until it was opposite the barrel, then veered sharply across the road and slid to a crooked stop with its brake lights flashing blood red. I sat up straighter, put my hand on the ignition key. The door opened without a light coming on inside, and the driver jumped out in a hurry, bulky and indistinct in a heavy coat and some kind of head covering; ran to the barrel, scooped out the briefcase, raced back and hurled it inside; hopped in after it and took off. Fast, even faster than Cohalan had been driving, the car's rear end fishtailing a little as the tires fought for traction on the slick pavement.

I was out on Kennedy and in pursuit within seconds. No way I could drive in the fog-laden darkness without putting on my lights, and in the far reach of the beams I could see the other car a hundred yards or so ahead. But even when I accelerated I couldn't get close enough to read the license plate.

Where the drive forks on the east end of the buffalo enclosure, the sports job made a tight-angle left turn, brake lights flashing again, headlights yawing as the driver fought for control. Looping around Spreckels Lake to quit the park on Thirty-Sixth Avenue. I took the turn at about half the speed, but I still had it in sight when it made a sliding right through a red light on Fulton, narrowly missing an oncoming car, and disappeared to the east. I wasn't even trying to keep up any longer. If I continued pursuit, somebody—an innocent party—was liable to get hurt or killed. That was the last thing

I wanted to happen. High-speed car chases are for damn fools and the makers of trite Hollywood films.

I pulled over near the Fulton intersection, still inside the park, and used the car phone to call my client.

Cohalan threw a fit when I told him what had happened. He called me all kinds of names, the least offensive of which was "incompetent idiot." I just let him rant. There were no excuses to be made and no point in wasting my own breath.

He ran out of abuse finally and segued into lament. "What am I going to do now? What am I going to tell Carolyn? All our savings gone and I still don't have any idea who that blackmailing bastard is. What if he comes back for more? We couldn't even sell the house, there's hardly any equity . . ."

Pretty soon he ran down there, too. I waited through about five seconds of dead air. Then, "All right," followed by a heavy sigh. "But don't expect me to pay your bill. You can damn well sue me and you can't get blood out of a turnip." And he banged the receiver in my ear.

Some Cohalan. Some piece of work.

The apartment building was on Locust Street a half block off California, close to the Presidio. Built in the twenties, judging by its ornate facade, once somebody's modestly affluent private home, long ago cut up into three floors of studios and one-bedroom apartments. It had no garage, forcing its tenants—like most of those in the neighborhood buildings—into street parking. There wasn't a legal space to be had on that block, or in the next, or anywhere in the vicinity. Back on California, I slotted my car into a bus zone. If I got a ticket I got a ticket.

Not much chance I'd need a weapon for the rest of it, but sometimes trouble comes when you least expect it. So I unclipped the .38 Colt Bodyguard from under the dash, slipped it into my coat pocket before I got out for the walk down Locust.

The building had a tiny foyer with the usual bank of mailboxes. I found the button for 2-C, leaned on it. This was the ticklish part; I was banking on the fact that one voice sounds pretty much like another over an intercom. Turned out not to be an issue at all: the squawk box stayed silent and the door release buzzed instead, almost immediately. Confident. Arrogant. Or just plain stupid.

I pushed inside, smiling a little, cynically, and climbed the stairs to the second floor. The first apartment on the right was 2-C. The door opened just as I got to it, and Annette Byers put her head out and said with excitement in her voice, "You made really good—"

The rest of it snapped off when she got a look at me; the excitement gave way to confusion, froze her in the half-open doorway. I had time to move up on her, wedge my shoulder against the door before she could decide to jump back and slam it in my face. She let out a little bleat and tried to kick me as I crowded her inside. I caught her arms, gave her a shove to get clear of her. Then I nudged the door closed with my heel.

"I'll start screaming," she said. Shaky bravado, the kind without anything to back it up. Her eyes were frightened now. "These walls are paper thin, and I've got a neighbor who's a cop."

That last part was a lie. I said, "Go ahead. Be my guest."

"Who the hell do you think you are—"

"We both know who I am, Ms. Byers. And why I'm here. The reason's on the table over there."

In spite of herself she glanced to her left. The apartment was a studio, and the kitchenette and dining area were over that way. The briefcase sat on the dinette table, its lid raised.

I couldn't see inside from where I was, but then I didn't need to.

"I don't know what you're talking about," she said.

She hadn't been back long; she still wore the heavy coat and the head covering, a wool stocking cap that completely hid her blond hair. Her cheeks were flushed—the cold night, money lust, now fear. She was attractive enough in a too-ripe way, intelligent enough to hold down a job with a downtown travel service, and immoral enough to have been in trouble with the San Francisco police before this. She was twenty-three, divorced, and evidently a crankhead: she'd been arrested once for possession and once for trying to sell a small quantity of methamphetamine to an undercover cop.

"Counting the cash, right?" I said.

". . .What?"

"What you were doing when I rang the bell. Fifty thousand in fifties and hundreds. It's all there, according to plan."

"I don't know what you're talking about."

"You said that already."

I moved a little to get a better scan of the studio. Her phone was on a breakfast bar that separated the kitchenette from the living room, one of those cordless types with a built-in answering machine. The gadget beside it was clearly a portable cassette player. She hadn't bothered to put it away before she went out; there'd been no reason to, or so she'd have thought then. The tape would still be inside.

I looked at her again. "I've got to admit, you're a pretty good driver. Reckless as hell, though, the way you went flying out of the park on a red light. You came close to a collision with another car."

"I don't know what—" She broke off and backed away a couple of paces, her hand rubbing the side of her face, her tongue making little flicks between her lips. It was sinking in now, how it had all gone wrong, how much trouble she was in. "You couldn't have followed me. I *know* you didn't."

"That's right, I couldn't and I didn't."

"Then how—?"

"Think about it. You'll figure it out."

A little silence. And, "Oh God, you knew about me all along."

"About you, the plan, everything."

"How? How could you? I don't—"

The downstairs bell made a sudden racket.

Her gaze jerked past me toward the intercom unit next to the door. She sucked in her lower lip, began to gnaw on it.

"You know who it is," I said. "Don't use the intercom, just the door release."

She did what I told her, moving slowly. I went the other way, first to the breakfast bar, where I popped the tape out of the cassette player and slipped it into my pocket, then to the dinette table. I lowered the lid on the briefcase, snapped the catches. I had the case in my hand when she turned to face me again.

She said, "What're you going to do with the money?"

"Give it back to its rightful owner."

"Jay. It belongs to him."

I didn't say anything to that.

"You better not try to keep it for yourself," she said. "You don't have any right to that money . . ."

"You dumb kid," I said disgustedly, "neither do you."

She quit looking at me. When she started to open the door I told her no, wait for his knock. She stood with her back to me, shoulders hunched. She was no longer afraid; dull resignation had taken over. For her, I thought, the money was the only thing that had ever mattered.

Knuckles rapped on the door. She opened it without any

hesitation, and he blew in, talking fast the way he did when he was keyed up. "Oh, baby, baby, we did it, we pulled it off," and he grabbed her and started to pull her against him. That was when he saw me.

"Hello, Cohalan," I said.

He went rigid for three or four seconds, his eyes popped wide, then disentangled himself from the woman and stood gaping at me. His mouth worked but nothing came out. Manic as hell in his office, all nerves and talking a blue streak, but now he was speechless. Lies were easy for him; the truth would have to be dragged out.

I told him to close the door. He did it, automatically, and turned snarling on Annette Byers. "You let him follow you home!"

"I didn't," she said. "He already knew about me. He knows everything."

"No, you're lying . . ."

"You were so goddamn smart, you had it all figured out. You didn't fool him for a minute."

"Shut up." His eyes shifted to me. "Don't listen to her. She's the one who's been blackmailing me—"

"Knock it off, Cohalan," I said. "Nobody's been blackmailing you. You're the shakedown artist here, you and Annette—a fancy little scheme to get your wife's money. You couldn't just grab the whole bundle from her, and you couldn't get any of it by divorcing her—a spouse's inheritance isn't community property in this state. So you cooked up the phony blackmail scam. What were the two of you planning to do with the full hundred thousand? Run off somewhere together? Buy a load of crank for resale, try for an even bigger score?"

"You see?" Annette Byers said bitterly. "You see, smart guy? He knows everything."

Cohalan shook his head. He'd gotten over his initial shock; now he looked stricken, and his nerves were acting up again. His hands had begun repeating that scoop-shovel trick at his sides. "You believed me, I know you did."

'Wrong," I said. "I didn't believe you. I'm a better actor than you, is all. Your story didn't sound right from the first. Too elaborate, full of improbabilities. Fifty thousand is too big a blackmail bite for any crime short of homicide, and you swore to me—your wife, too—you weren't guilty of a major felony. Blackmailers seldom work in big bites anyway. They bleed their victims slow and steady, in small bites, to keep them from throwing the hook. We just didn't believe it, either of us."

"We? Jesus, you mean . . . you and Carolyn . . . ?"

"That's right. Your wife's my client, Cohalan, not you— that's why I never asked you for a retainer. She showed up at my office right after you did the first time; if she hadn't, I'd probably have gone to her. She'd been suspicious all along, but she gave you the benefit of the doubt until you hit her with the fifty-thousand-dollar bite. She figured you might be having an affair, too, and it didn't take me long to find out about Annette. You never had any idea you were being fol- lowed, did you? Once I knew about her, it was easy enough to put the rest of it together, including the funny business with the money drop tonight. And here we are."

"Damn you," he said, but there was no heat in the words. "You and that frigid bitch both."

He wasn't talking about Annette Byers, but she took the opportunity to dig into him again. "Smart guy. Big genius. I told you to just take the money and we'd run with it, didn't I?"

"Shut up."

"Don't tell me to shut up, you son of—"

259

"Don't say it. I'll slap you silly if you say it."

"You won't slap anybody," I said. "Not as long as I'm around."

He wiped his mouth on the sleeve of his jacket. "What're you going to do?"

"What do you think I'm going to do?"

"You can't go to the police. You don't have any proof. It's your word against ours."

"Wrong again." I showed him the voice-activated recorder I'd had hidden in my pocket all evening. High-tech, state-of-the-art equipment, courtesy of George Agonistes, fellow P.I. and electronics expert. "Everything that was said in your office and in this room tonight is on here. I've also got the cassette tape Annette played when she called earlier. Voice prints will prove the muffled voice on it is yours, that you were talking to yourself on the phone, giving yourself orders and directions. If your wife wants to press charges, she'll have more than enough evidence to put the two of you away."

"She won't press charges," he said. "Not Carolyn."

"Maybe not, if you return the rest of her money. What you and baby here haven't already blown."

He sleeved his mouth again. "I suppose you intend to take the briefcase straight to her."

"You suppose right."

"I could stop you," he said, as if he were trying to convince himself. "I'm as big as you, younger—I could take it away from you."

I repocketed the recorder. I could have showed him the .38, but I grinned at him instead. "Go ahead and try. Or else move away from the door. You've got five seconds to make up your mind."

He moved in three, as I started toward him. Sideways, clear of both me and the door. Annette Byers let out a sharp, scornful laugh, and he whirled on her—somebody his own size to face off against. "Shut your stupid mouth!" he yelled at her.

"Shut yours, big man. You and your brilliant ideas."

"Goddamn you . . ."

I went out and closed the door against their vicious, whining voices.

Outside, the fog had thickened to a near drizzle, slicking the pavement and turning the lines of parked cars along both curbs into two-dimensional black shapes. Parking was at such a premium in this neighborhood, there was now a car, dark and silent, double-parked across the street. I walked quickly to California. Nobody, police included, had bothered my wheels in the bus zone. I locked the briefcase in the trunk, let myself inside. A quick call to Carolyn Cohalan to let her know I was coming, a short ride out to her house by the zoo to deliver the fifty thousand, and I'd be finished for the night.

Only she didn't answer her phone.

Funny, when I'd called her earlier from the park, she'd said she would wait for my next call. No reason for her to leave the house in the interim. Unless—

Christ!

I heaved out of the car and ran back down Locust Street. The darkened vehicle was still double-parked across from Annette Byers' building. I swung into the foyer, jammed my finger against the bell button for 2-C and left it there. No response. I rattled the door—latched tight—and then began jabbing buttons on all the other mailboxes. The intercom crackled; somebody's voice said, "Who the hell is that?" I said, "Police emergency, buzz me in." Nothing, nothing, and then finally the door release sounded; I hit the door hard and lunged into the lobby.

I was at the foot of the stairs when the first shot echoed

from above. Two more in swift succession, a fourth as I was pounding up to the second-floor landing.

Querulous voices, the sound of a door banging open somewhere . . . and I was at 2-C. The door there was shut but not latched; I kicked it open, hanging back with the .38 in my hand for self-protection. But there was no need. It was over by then. Too late and all over.

All three of them were on the floor. Cohalan on his back next to the couch, blood obscuring his face, not moving. Annette Byers sprawled bloody and moaning by the dinette table. And Carolyn Cohalan sitting with her back against a wall, a long-barreled .22 on the carpet nearby, weeping in deep, broken sobs.

I leaned hard on the doorjamb, the stink of cordite in my nostrils, my throat full of bile. Telling myself it was not my fault, there was no way I could have known it wasn't the money but paying them back that mattered to her—the big payoff, the biggest bite there is. Telling myself I could've done nothing to prevent this, and remembering what I'd been thinking in the car earlier about how I lived for cases like this, how I liked this one a whole lot . . .

Season of Sharing
(with Marcia Muller)
McCONE

I stepped out of my office and looked over the garland-laden railing of the upstairs catwalk at the floor of Pier 24-1/2. Six o'clock, and the annual charity Christmas party for staff members of the various businesses housed there had just begun.

The cars that we customarily parked downstairs had been removed to the street; a buffet table and bar in the center of the huge space was already surrounded; the loving cup for the best decorations—nonecumenical, as many of us practiced Judaism, Buddhism, Islam, or no religion at all—sat on its pedestal, to be awarded at the end of the festivities. We called this event the Season of Sharing party, because we solicited cash and noncash donations for a designated charity, with one firm handling the collection and disbursement on a rotating basis. This year's cause was a group called Home for the Holidays, dedicated to housing and feeding homeless people during the season.

A party with a serious purpose, but that didn't mean we hadn't enjoyed preparing for it and wouldn't have a great time celebrating. The decorations this year were exceptional all around. My office manager, Ted Smalley, had opted for a galactic theme in this time of worldwide dissension, hanging from the garland silver stars, moons, planets, and crystal beads to represent the Milky Way. The architects on the opposite catwalk, Chandler & Santos, had fashioned a cityscape of colored lights and neon tubing; and their neighbors, a

263

group of certified public accountants, had suspended card-board cutouts of people of all races and genders holding hands. Below was a miniature Santa's Village, complete with electric tram (marketing consultants); a forest of small live fir trees dusted in realistic-looking snow, where replicas of various endangered animals took refuge (ecological nonprofit); swirls of rich, colorful cloth that a fan moved in a kaleido-scopic pattern (fashion designer); a Model T Ford with Santa at the wheel and presents in the rumbleseat (car leasing agency). One of these would win the big loving cup perched on the high pedestal for best of show.

I sighed with pleasure—both at the prospect of an enjoyable evening with good friends and at the knowledge that we would be bringing happy holidays to at least a few of the city's many homeless. Already the barrels of canned goods, new toys, and warm clothing were filled.

As I glanced at the one for cash offerings, I spotted my colleague and friend Wolf approaching with his wife Kerry. The party was limited to Pier 24-1/2 workers and their guests, but for the past month Wolf had been on my payroll, assisting on a complex fraud case that I hadn't had time to attend to myself, so I'd urged him to attend. It had taken a lot of urging. Wolf hated large gatherings, and I was certain he'd only agreed to come as a favor to me and his outgoing advertising-executive wife.

It wasn't the only way I was going to reward him for saving my butt, I thought with some anticipation. The job he'd done for me was an important one, for a client who threw a lot of business my agency's way. I'd been tied up on a long investigation into improprieties in the city's building-inspection department, that had revealed a senior official was taking kickbacks in exchange for speeding up the permit process.

Only half an hour ago Ted had given me a disc containing

my report, which I would deliver to the mayor's office on Monday—the only copy, as the deputy mayor who was my contact there had insisted on total confidentiality. It currently rested under a stack of files in my in-box, unimportant looking and labeled "Expenses, November, 2001," rather than in the office safe, which had been broken into a few days ago.

Wolf was already looking overwhelmed by the crowd down below. I donned my fuzzy Santa Claus hat and went to try to put him at ease.

"WOLF"

Kerry said, "Doesn't the pier look nice? So festive."

"Yeah," I said. "Festive."

"Look at all the different displays. Some are really clever."

I looked. "At least they don't have some poor jerk dressed up in a Santa Claus suit."

"I suppose that's a reference to the Christmas Charity Benefit. You're never going to let me forget that, are you?"

"Ho, ho, ho."

She poked me in the ribs. "Don't be grumpy."

"I'm not grumpy."

"If you're going to be grumpy . . ."

I said again, grumpily, that I wasn't grumpy. It was the truth. What I was was ill at ease. Parties of any kind have that effect on me. Large groups of people, no matter how festive the occasion, make me feel claustrophobic; I don't mix well, I'm not good at small talk even with people I know. Kerry keeps trying to socialize me and it keeps not working. The quiet of home and hearth is what I prefer, particularly during the Christmas season. The one other time I'd let her talk me into attending a Yuletide party, the infamous Gala Family

Christmas Charity Benefit a few years back, had been an un-mitigated disaster. And only partly because I'd allowed my-self to be stuffed into a Santa Claus suit, with little kiddies to make dents on my knees and share with me their innermost, toy-laden desires.

"Let's make a donation," Kerry said.

She'd hauled me into the midst of the Pier 24-1/2 party and we were now stopped in front of a red, white and blue barrel in the center of the concrete floor. Propped up in front was a sign: HOME FOR THE HOLIDAYS. *Season of Sharing Fund. Be Generous!*

Kerry put a folded twenty-dollar bill into the barrel. I took a five out of my wallet.

"For heaven's sake," she said, "don't be a Scrooge. Read the sign."

I said, "Be generous, Mr. Spade."

"What's that?"

"Never mind." I exchanged the five for two twenties and slotted them into the barrel.

"That's better. Oh, here's Sharon."

McCone came bustling up. The furred Santa Claus cap she wore over her black hair made my scalp itch. She hugged Kerry, waved some green plant stuff over my head, and then kissed me—on the mouth.

"Hey," I said, "I'm a married man. And you're young enough to be my daughter."

"Don't mind him," Kerry said. "He's in one of his grumpy moods."

"I am not grumpy!"

McCone said, "Well, whatever you are, I'm glad you're here. Both of you."

"Where's Ripinsky?" I asked her. Hy Ripinksy was her sig-nificant other and a fellow P.I.

"He had to fly down to RKI headquarters in San Diego. Urgent business. But he'll be back in time for us to spend Christmas together."

She and Kerry proceeded to jabber about how festive the pier looked, how innovative the displays were, particularly McCone Investigations' galactic theme, how all the businesses here were hoping to raise at least five thousand dollars for the homeless. It never ceases to amaze me how adaptable women are. Put two of them together, even a pair of strangers, into any social situation and they're not only immediately comfortable with each other and their surroundings, they never seem at a loss for words.

While they were chattering, I looked around some more. What galactic theme? I thought.

Pretty soon Kerry paused long enough to suggest I go and get us something to drink. "I'd like white wine," she said. "Sharon?"

"The same."

So I walked through the partygoers to the bar. The noise level in there, enhanced by a loud-speakered version of "Deck the Halls," was such that I had to raise my voice to a near-shout to put in my order. Two white wines, nothing more. My brain gets fuzzy enough at parties as it is.

Somebody came up and tapped my arm while I was waiting. McCone's office manager, Ted Smalley, and his bookseller partner, Neal Osborn, both of them wearing red stocking caps with tassels. Neal said, "Great party, isn't it? Didn't Ted do a terrific job of coordinating the decorations and displays?"

"Terrific," I said. "Great, uh, galactic theme, Ted."

He beamed at me. "Everyone cooperated beautifully."

Neal ordered for the two of them. When he was done he said to Ted, "Shall we tell him now or wait until later?"

"Now. I can't wait to see his face."

"Do you want to do the honors or shall I?"

"You go ahead. It was your idea."

"No, it was your idea. The surprise itself was mine. Mine and Sharon's."

I said, "What're you two talking about?"

"You'll find out," Neal said, "if you go upstairs to Sharon's office. There's something on her desk for you."

"A present? Why would you get me a present?"

"For all your help on the Patterson case," Ted said. "Do you still have the spare key Sharon gave you?"

I didn't know what to say, except "yes" and "thanks." I'm not used to getting presents from anyone other than Kerry and my assistant, Tamara Corbin.

"Don't open it up there," Neal said. "Bring it down so we can all watch."

Oh, boy. Being the center of attention is something I like about as much as parties. Even so, I felt touched and pleased.

I delivered the glasses of wine, told Kerry where I was going—Sharon grinned when I mentioned the present—and then went upstairs. As I approached McCone's private office, I had the spare key in my hand. But I didn't need it. The door was closed but not locked.

That in itself didn't make me suspicious, but what I saw when I opened the door and walked in set off alarm bells in my head. A man spun around from in front of Sharon's desk—a blond man who didn't work for McCone Investigations, who gave me a frightened-deer look and seemed to teeter briefly on the edge of panic. Then he got a grip on himself, put on a weak smile. He was familiar—I'd seen him around the pier before. An employee of one of the other firms, the architects on the opposite catwalk. His name was Kennett or Bennett.

268

"You startled me," he said. "What're you doing here?"

"I'll ask you the same question."

"Sharon asked me to get something for her. If you'll excuse me . . ."

He edged past where I stood, not making eye contact, one hand squeezed into the pocket of a pair of very tight leather pants. In other circumstances, or if he'd lingered a few more seconds, I would've restrained him; but I hesitated just long enough for him to get past me and out the door.

I followed as he hurried along the catwalk, close to the garland-festooned railing, his hand still in his pocket. Only fifty feet separated us when he reached the stairs; I had a clear look at him all the way down, but then the Model T Ford display cut off my view and the party swirl swallowed him.

I clambered down until I could once more see all of the pier floor. It was no more than fifteen seconds before I picked him out again. He stopped near some kind of trophy on a pedestal and joined a small group of people, making a gesture with the hand that had been in his pocket. Sharon McCone wasn't one of the group.

I spotted her nearby and made straight for her myself, keeping my eye on Leather Pants all the way.

McCONE

I was standing with Ted and Neal when Wolf came hurrying up, a frown darkening his rugged Italian features. He wasn't carrying his present.

"How could he not find the package?" Ted said. "It's right in the middle of your desk."

Something told me the frown had nothing to do with being unable to locate a package. Quickly I moved to meet him.

"Did you send somebody up to your office besides me?" He was looking past me at something or someone.

"No. Why?"

"Well, I just surprised a man inside. Five-ten or so, blond hair, dressed in black leather pants and a thin-ribbed black sweater. I think he works for the architects—Bennett? Kennett?"

Now it was my turn to frown. "Tony Kennett." He was a draftsman for Chandler & Santos, had taken to hanging around our offices lately, trying to persuade my newest hire, Julia Rafael, to go out with him. Julia, who at twenty-five had been through more bad relationships than most women experience in a lifetime, had so far resisted. "Did you talk with him? Ask him what he was doing there?"

"He claimed you'd sent him up to get something. But he had a guilty, scared look. He all but ran out, and came down here. He's over by that trophy."

I looked around, spotted Kennett. He was talking to some people, but even at a distance he looked nervous.

One of my operatives, Craig Morland, had just joined us. He said, "Kennett's been in Julia's and my office damn near every day this week, trying to put the moves on her."

"I don't like or trust him," Ted added.

"Ted, you and Craig keep an eye on him. Make sure he doesn't leave the pier."

They nodded, and Craig said to Neal, "Find Julia, Mick, and Charlotte. Just in case we need them."

A good man, the former FBI agent; he didn't waste time with unnecessary questions.

I turned to Wolf. "Let's go upstairs, see what Kennett might've been after." My voice was heavy with foreboding; I had a good suspicion what it was.

"Grandma Got Run Over by a Reindeer" was playing as we

climbed to the catwalk. The irreverent novelty song had always been a favorite of mine, but now I took no pleasure in it. We went along to my office. The door was slightly ajar, but Wolf had indicated he'd left it that way. We went in. The brightly wrapped package for Wolf still sat in the center of my desk, but the papers and files in my in-box had been disturbed.

"Dammit!" I exclaimed. I felt through the box's contents to where the disc containing the report on the building-inspection department should be.

Gone. My only copy.

"I knew it!"

"What's missing?" Wolf asked.

"Final report on that political case I've been working."

"The high-confidentiality one for City Hall?"

"Uh-huh. Kennett must've taken it. Unless we can get it back, it'll go straight into the wrong hands, and then there'll be a cover-up like this city's seldom seen."

"And we've seen some spectacular ones. How is Kennett involved?"

I didn't reply, because I'd spotted a key on the floor by my desk. Shiny new, as if it had just been cut by a machine at a hardware store. I picked it up, took my own office key out. They were a match.

"Now I'm sure it's Kennett," I said, holding up the key. "I run a pretty open shop here; the same key operates all the doors so staff members will have access to the other offices in case they need something. We trust each other, so we tend to trust the other tenants of the pier. Kennett's become something of a fixture here in the past week; simple enough for him to snag a key and have a copy made. And I think he's used it before, because three days ago our creaky old office safe was broken into."

"Anything taken?" Wolf asked.

I shook my head. "Not even my gun, which would be a natural for a common thief."

"You report it?"

"Ted did. There were no fingerprints on it except his and mine."

"Okay, but why was Kennett after the confidential report?"

I considered that, and then the answer came to me, filtered through a dim memory of an event nearly a year past. "Because he's a close friend of the city official I've been investigating—he was at the official's fortieth birthday party last January. Kennett's buddy must've found out there was an ongoing investigation and asked him to find out what I knew."

"Kennett must still have the disc on him."

"And we're going to get it back."

I led Wolf from my office, locking it after us like the proverbial barn door. We paused on the catwalk, surveying the crowd below. Kennett now stood near the bar, drink in hand, talking to someone else.

By the time we got down there, Kennett had moved to Santa's Village and was apparently admiring it. When he saw us he fidgeted and his eyes took on a flat, glassy look.

I said, "Where's the disc, Tony?"

"What disc?"

"The one you took from my office."

"I . . . don't know what you're talking about."

"Do you deny you were in my office around half an hour ago?"

"I certainly do."

I indicated Wolf. "Do you deny you told this man I'd asked you to go up there and get something?"

"I've never seen him before."

Beside me, I felt Wolf tense; a growly sound came from

deep in his throat. "You're a liar and a thief both, Kennett," he said.

Kennett gulped what liquor remained in his plastic cup, seemed fortified by it. He set the cup on the display table, extended his arms dramatically. "So search me," he said loudly. "Go ahead!"

People were looking at us now. I studied Kennett's clothing. The leather pants were skin tight; the outline of a disc would have shown clearly. The same with the sweater. Somehow he'd gotten rid of it—somewhere in this cavernous pier that was honeycombed with hiding places.

"That won't be necessary," I said. "Maybe we made a mistake. Enjoy the party."

When we were out of earshot of Kennett, Wolf grasped my elbow. "A mistake? Enjoy the party? What's that about?"

I said, "He's going to have to stay till the end—my people will see to that. In the meantime, we'll let him think he's getting away with the disc."

"Now all we have to do is find it before the party's over."

"That's all," I said grimly.

"WOLF"

McCone is as efficient an investigator as I've known in thirtysome years in the business. Doubly so in a crisis. She sought out and briefed the members of her staff, individually and in pairs, designating Craig Morland to stay close to Kennett, and her nephew, Mick, and Julia Rafael to watch the exits. The rest of us went upstairs to her office. Neal Osborn and Kerry included, Neal because we might need an extra hand and Kerry because she'd seen Kennett come downstairs with me in his wake.

When we were all settled, McCone behind her desk, the

rest of us sitting or standing, she said, "What we need to do is brainstorm this, see if we can get some idea of what Kennett did with the disc. Wolf and I will do most of the talking, but if anybody has anything to contribute, jump in any time."

The others nodded silently. That was another thing about Sharon: She ran a fairly loose ship, delegating a good deal of authority to her operatives, but when she took command she did it forcefully and got complete cooperation in return.

She asked me to go over again, in detail, what had happened earlier. When I was done, she said, "So Kennett didn't go around to the opposite catwalk before he went downstairs. That means he couldn't have hidden the disc in his own office."

"Right."

"And you had him in sight the whole time, except for those few seconds in the crowd. How many seconds, would you say?"

"No more than fifteen. That's probably when he got rid of the disc. First thing that occurs to me is that he passed it to someone else."

"Not likely. This feels like a one-man operation to me."

"Besides," Ted said, "I know all the other people at Chandler & Santos. He's the only one I wouldn't trust."

"Let's eliminate one other unlikely possibility," I said. "That Kennett hid the disc somewhere in here before I came in. The old purloined letter trick."

McCone shook her head. "He didn't expect to get caught and he'd be a fool to risk sneaking into my office another time. He had to've had it on him when he left."

"Okay. Next thing is whether he had any chance at all to hide it while I had him in sight. I'd say no, but I can't be a hundred percent certain. He did walk close to the railing all the way to the stairs. It's remotely possible he slipped the disc in among the decorations."

"I doubt it. All the ones on this side are ours, so again, he couldn't be sure of getting his hands on it later. Ted, go check and make sure."

As Ted went out, I said, "Something else I just remembered. Kennett had one hand in his pocket when I surprised him. It was still in his pocket on the catwalk, on the stairs, and when I lost sight of him. But when I picked him up again, the hand was out—he made a gesture with it when he joined the group by the trophy. That's another point in favor of a hiding place somewhere on the pier floor."

"Did he turn straight into the crowd when he came off the stairs?"

"Hard left turn, yeah."

"That means he passed right by the Model T Ford display."

"Good possibility. And right next to the Ford . . ."

Charlotte Keim said, "The ecological nonprofit display."

"Also possible. Among the branches of one of the fir trees."

"The only problem with that is, the way the little forest is set up, he'd have had to go into the display itself. That would be inviting attention."

"Have a look anyway."

Ted came in just then, shaking his head. "Nothing among the galactic decorations."

"Check the Model T next. Inside and out."

Neal said, "I'll go with him."

The three of them left together. I said to Kerry, "You also lost sight of Kennett for a time. Where was he when you spotted him again?"

"Over by Santa's Village, on his way toward the loving cup."

"The village is too small to hide anything," Sharon said, "even something as small as a computer disc."

"What about the cup? If it's hollow, he could've dropped it inside."

"It's hollow, but Kennett isn't very tall and the way the cup sits on the pedestal, he'd've had to stretch up on his toes. Too conspicuous. People would've noticed and wondered."

"Then it's got to be either the Model T or the fir trees."

But it was neither one. We waited restlessly until first Charlotte and then Ted and Neal returned empty-handed. Neal said, "I even got down on my hands and knees and checked underneath the car, just in case. You should've seen the looks I got."

I'd been ruminating. Now I said, "We've been going on the assumption that if I hadn't come in unexpectedly and caught him, Kennett would've kept the disc on his person until the party ended. But remember how he's dressed. If he'd had it in his pocket, as tight as those leather pants are, the outline would've showed."

"You're right," McCone said. "He wouldn't run that kind of risk. If he'd intended to keep it on him, he'd've worn looser clothing."

"Which means he planned to hide it all along. Someplace he'd picked out in advance, someplace he'd be sure to have easy access to later." I looked at Kerry. "You said Kennett was walking by Santa's Village. Straight past it toward the trophy?"

". . . Come to think of it, no. He was moving at an angle."

"From which direction, left or right?"

"Right. An angle from the right."

"So he didn't go more or less on a straight line through the crowd. He veered off to the right first, then veered back again."

"The bar and buffet are in the center, but farther back. What else is over that way?"

"Nothing, except—"

Mick said, "Home for the Holidays."

I said, "Be generous."

Ted said, "And this year it's Chandler & Santos' turn to disperse the donations."

McCone said, "That's it! That's where the disc has to be."

That was where, all right. Kennett's unfunny private joke, his own personal donation to the homeless. Right through that little slot into the Season of Sharing Fund barrel as he passed by.

McCONE

I wanted to go straight down and retrieve the disc, but Wolf persuaded me not to. This was a highly sensitive matter, and it wouldn't do to bring it to the attention of everyone in the pier. In the end I sent Ted, Charlotte and Neal out to keep an eye on Kennett, and Wolf, Kerry, and I settled down to wait till the end of the party.

The minutes, and then the hours, dragged by. Kerry went downstairs to fetch us food from the buffet, but after nibbling on a canape, I pushed my portion aside and let Wolf finish it off. He is one of the calmest men I know in tense situations, patiently waiting it out until the proper time to take action. He once told me how he chafes while on long surveillances, but from his manner that night I never would have guessed it. Of course, the current situation had given him the perfect excuse not to mingle with the crowd . . .

Neal stuck his head through the door at a few minutes

after eleven. "The pier's locked down and the clean-up crews're assembling."

Downstairs, party wreckage was everywhere: dirty plates and glasses, a sprinkling of confetti, balled up napkins, spills and splotches. The decorations—even Santa's Village, next to which the trophy sat—looked as tired as the people who had volunteered to remain to deal with the mess. I spotted Nat Chandler and Harvey Santos, partners in the architectural firm, hauling a barrel full of canned goods up the stairs to their offices. Tony Kennett wasn't in sight.

Mick was leaning casually on the cash-donations barrel— standing guard without being too obvious about it. I went over to him, asked, "Where's Kennett?"

"He went up to Chandler & Santos' offices about ten minutes ago. Probably waiting inside, planning to liberate the disc after the partners lock up and go home."

Nat and Harvey were coming back downstairs now. I signaled to them.

"I want you to witness this," I said when they came over.

Wolf lifted the slotted lid of the barrel. It was three-quarters full of cash, coins, and checks. I plunged my hand into the donations and felt around.

"What're you doing?" Harvey asked.

"You'll see."

My fingers touched a flat, round object encased in a thin plastic pouch. "Got it!" I said to Wolf and pulled it from the barrel.

As Nat and Harvey exchanged puzzled glances, I looked up at the catwalk in front of their offices. Kennett stood at the rail watching us. I held up the disc. Even at that distance I could see his shoulders sag and his face crumple.

"WOLF"

After the police had been summoned and Tony Kennett hauled off to jail, McCone invited her staff and Neal and Kerry and me back up to her office for a celebratory libation. I'd forgotten all about my Christmas present, which Sharon had slipped into a desk drawer during our earlier session. But she and the others hadn't forgotten. She brought the package out and handed it to me with a little flourish.

"With thanks and love from all of us," she said.

Embarrassed, I said, "I haven't gotten anything for any of you yet . . ."

"Never mind that. Open your present, Wolf."

I hefted it first. Not very heavy. I stripped off the paper, took the lid off the gift box—and inside was another, smaller box sealed with half a pound of Scotch tape. Ted's doing; I could tell from his expression. So I used my pocket knife to slice through the tape, opened the second box, rifled through a wad of tissue paper, and found . . .

Two plastic-bagged issues of *Black Mask*, and not just any two issues: rare, fine-condition copies of the September 1929 and February 1930 numbers, each containing an installment of the original six-part serial version of Hammett's *The Maltese Falcon*.

When I looked up, they were all grinning at me. I said, "How'd you know these were the only two *Falcon* issues I didn't have?" Funny, but my voice sounded a little choked up.

"I told them," Kerry said. "I checked your pulp collection to make sure."

"And I found the copies through one of my friends in the antiquarian book trade," Neal said.

"They must've cost a small fortune."

McCone waved that away. "What they cost doesn't matter. You not only helped close the Patterson case, and to get the disc back tonight, but you've been a good friend for a long time. It's the Season of Sharing with friends, too."

I just sat there.

Kerry said, "Aren't you going to say something?"

Only one thing came to mind. It didn't seem to be enough, but Kerry told me later that it was all that was needed.

"Happy holidays, everybody."

Wrong Place, Wrong Time

Sometimes it happens like this. No warning, no way to guard against it. And through no fault of your own. You're just in the wrong place at the wrong time.

Eleven p.m., drizzly, low ceiling and poor visibility. On my way back from four long days on a case in Fresno and eager to get home to San Francisco. Highway 152, the quickest route from 99 west through hills and valleys to 101. Roadside service station and convenience store, a lighted sign that said "Open Until Midnight." Older model car parked in the shadows alongside the restrooms, newish Buick drawn in at the gas pumps. People visible inside the store, indistinct images behind damp-streaked and sign-plastered glass.

I didn't need gas, but I did need some hot coffee to keep me awake. And something to fill the hollow under my breastbone: I hadn't taken the time to eat anything before leaving Fresno. So I swung off into the lot, parked next to the older car. Yawned and stretched and walked past the Buick to the store. Walked right into it.

Even before I saw the little guy with the gun, I knew something was wrong. It was in the air, a heaviness, a crackling quality, like the atmosphere before a big storm. The hair crawled on the back of my scalp. But I was two paces inside by then and it was too late to back out.

He was standing next to a rack of potato chips, holding the weapon in close to his body with both hands. The other two men stood ten feet away at the counter, one in front and one

281

behind. The gun, a long-barreled target pistol, was centered on the man in front; it stayed that way even though the little guy's head was half turned in my direction. I stopped and stayed still, with my arms down tight against my sides.

Time freeze. The four of us staring, nobody moving. Light rain on the roof, some kind of machine making thin wheezing noises—no other sound.

The one with the gun coughed suddenly, a dry, consumptive hacking that broke the silence but added to the tension. He was thin and runty, mid-thirties, going bald on top, his face drawn to a drum tautness. Close-set brown eyes burned with outrage and hatred. The clerk behind the counter, twenty-something, long hair tied in a ponytail, kept licking his lips and swallowing hard; his eyes flicked here and there, settled, flicked, settled like a pair of nervous flies. Scared, but in control of himself. The handsome, fortyish man in front was a different story. He couldn't take his eyes off the pistol, as if it had a hypnotic effect on him. Sweat slicked his bloodless face, rolled down off his chin in little drops. His fear was a tangible thing, sick and rank and consuming; you could see it moving under the sweat, under the skin, the way maggots move inside a slab of bad meat.

"Harry," he said in a voice that crawled and cringed. "Harry, for God's sake . . ."

"Shut up. Don't call me Harry."

"Listen . . . it wasn't me, it was Noreen . . ."

"Shut up shut up shut up." High-pitched, with a brittle, cracking edge. "You," he said to me. "Come over here where I can see you better."

I went closer to the counter, doing it slow. This wasn't what I'd first taken it to be. Not a hold-up—something personal between the little guy and the handsome one, something that had come to a lethal crisis point in here only a short time ago. Wrong place, wrong time for the young clerk, too.

I said, "What's this all about?"

"I'm going to kill this son of a bitch," the little guy said, "that's what it's all about."

"Why do you want to do that?"

"My wife and my savings, every cent I had in the world . . . he took them both away from me and now he's going to pay for it."

"Harry, please, you've got to—"

"Didn't I tell you to shut up? Didn't I tell you not to call me Harry?"

Handsome shook his head, a meaningless flopping like a broken bulb on a white stalk.

"Where is she, Barlow?" the little guy demanded.

"Noreen?"

"My bitch wife Noreen. Where is she?"

"I don't know . . ."

"She's not at your place. The house was dark when you left. Noreen wouldn't sit in a dark house alone. She doesn't like the dark."

"You . . . saw me at the house?"

"That's right. I saw you and I followed you twenty miles to this place. Did you think I just materialized out of thin air?"

"Spying on me? Looking through windows? Jesus . . ."

"I got there just as you were leaving," the little guy said. "Perfect timing. You didn't think I'd find out your name or where you lived, did you? You thought you were safe, didn't you? Stupid old Harry Chalfont, the cuckold, the sucker—no threat at all."

Another head flop. This one made beads of sweat fly off.

"But I did find out," the little guy said. "Took me two months, but I found you and now I'm going to kill you."

"Stop saying that! You won't, you can't . . ."

"Go ahead, beg. Beg me not to do it."

Barlow moaned and leaned back hard against the counter. Mortal terror unmans some people; he was as crippled by it as anybody I'd ever seen. Before long he would beg, down on his knees.

"Where's Noreen?"

"I swear I don't know, Harry . . . Mr. Chalfont. She . . . walked out on me . . . a few days ago. Took all the money with her."

"You mean there's still some of the ten thousand left? I figured it'd all be gone by now. But it doesn't matter. I don't care about the money anymore. All I care about is paying you back. You and then Noreen. Both of you getting just what you deserve."

Chalfont ached to pay them back, all right, yearned to see them dead. But wishing something and making it happen are two different things. He had the pistol cocked and ready and he'd worked himself into an overheated emotional state, but he wasn't really a killer. You can look into a man's eyes in a situation like this, as I had too many times, and tell whether or not he's capable of cold-blooded murder. There's a fire, a kind of deathlight, unmistakable and immutable, in the eyes of those who can, and it wasn't there in Harry Chalfont's eyes.

Not that its absence made him any less dangerous. He was wired to the max, and outraged and filled with hate, and his finger was close to white on the pistol's trigger. Reflex could jerk off a round, even two, at any time. And if that happened, the slugs could go anywhere—into Barlow, into the young clerk, into me.

"She was all I ever had," he said. "My job, my savings, my life . . . none of it meant anything until I met her. Little, ugly, lonely . . . that's all I was. But she loved me once, at least a little. Enough to marry me. And then you came along and destroyed it all."

"I didn't, I tell you, it was all her idea . . ."

"Shut up. It was *you*, Barlow, you turned her head, you corrupted her. Goddamn traveling salesman, goddamn cliché. You must've had other women. Why couldn't you leave her alone?"

Working himself up even more. Nerving himself to pull that trigger. I thought about jumping him, but that wasn't much of an option. Too much distance between us, too much risk of the pistol going off anyway. One other option. And I'd damn well better make it work.

I said quietly, evenly, "Give me the gun, Mr. Chalfont."

The words didn't register until I repeated them. Then he blinked, shifted his gaze to me without moving his head. "What did you say?"

"Give me the gun. Put an end to this before it's too late."

"No. Shut up."

"You don't want to kill anybody. You know it and I know it."

"He's going to pay. They're both going to pay."

"Fine, make them pay. Press theft charges against them. Send them to prison."

"That's not enough punishment for what they did."

"If you don't think so, then you've never seen the inside of a prison."

"What do you know about it? Who are you?"

A half-truth was more forceful than the whole truth. I said, "I'm a law officer."

Barlow and the clerk both jerked looks at me. The kid's had hope in it, but not Handsome's; his fear remained unchecked, undiluted.

"You're lying," Chalfont said.

"Why would I lie?"

He coughed again, hawked deep in his throat. "It doesn't make any difference. You can't stop me."

"That's right, I can't stop you from shooting Barlow. But I can stop you from shooting your wife. I'm off duty but I'm still armed." Calculated lie. "If you kill him, then I'll have to kill you. The instant your gun goes off, out comes mine and you're also a dead man. You don't want that."

". . . I don't care."

"You care, all right. I can see it your face. You don't want to die tonight, Mr. Chalfont."

That was right: He didn't. The deathlight wasn't there for himself, either.

"I have to make them pay," he said.

"You've already made Barlow pay. Just look at him—he's paying right now. Why put him out of his misery?"

For a little time Chalfont stood rigid, the pistol drawn in tight under his breastbone. Then his tongue poked out between his lips and stayed there, the way a cat's will. It made him look cross-eyed, and for the first time, uncertain.

"You don't want to die," I said again. "Admit it. You don't want to die."

"I don't want to die," he said.

"And you don't want the clerk or me to die, right? That could happen if shooting starts. Innocent blood on your hands."

"No," he said. "No, I don't want that."

I'd already taken two slow, careful steps toward him; I tried another, longer one. The pistol's muzzle stayed centered on Barlow's chest. I watched Chalfont's index finger. It seemed to have relaxed on the trigger. His two-handed grip on the weapon appeared looser, too.

"Let me have the gun, Mr. Chalfont."

He didn't say anything, didn't move.

Another step, slow, slow, with my hand extended.

"Give me the gun. You don't want to die tonight, nobody has to die tonight. Let me have the gun."

One more step. And all at once the outrage, the hate, the lust for revenge went out of his eyes, like a slate wiped suddenly clean, and he brought the pistol away from his chest one-handed and held it out without looking at me. I took it gently, dropped it into my coat pocket.

Situation diffused. Just like that.

The clerk let out an explosive breath, said, "Oh, man!" almost reverently. Barlow slumped against the counter, whimpered, and then called Chalfont a couple of obscene names. But he was too wrapped up in himself and his relief to work up much anger at the little guy. He wouldn't look at me either.

I took Chalfont's arm, steered him around behind the counter and sat him down on a stool back there. He wore a glazed look now, and his tongue was back out between his lips. Docile, disoriented. Broken.

"Call the law," I said to the clerk. "Local or county, whichever'll get here the quickest."

"County," he said. He picked up the phone.

"Tell them to bring a paramedic unit with them."

"Yessir." Then he said, "Hey! Hey, that other guy's leaving."

I swung around. Barlow had slipped over to the door; it was just closing behind him. I snapped at the kid to watch Chalfont and ran outside after Barlow.

He was getting into the Buick parked at the gas pumps. He slammed the door, but I got there fast enough to yank it open before he could lock it.

"You're not going anywhere, Barlow."

"You can't keep me here—"

"The hell I can't."

287

Bill Pronzini

I ducked my head and leaned inside. He tried to fight me. I jammed him back against the seat with my forearm, reached over with the other hand and pulled the keys out of the ignition. No more struggle then. I released him, backed clear.

"Get out of the car."

He came out in loose, shaky segments. Leaned against the open door, looking at me with fear-soaked eyes.

"Why the hurry to leave? Why so afraid of me?"

"I'm not afraid of you . . ."

"Sure you are. As much as you were of Chalfont and his gun. Maybe more. It was in your face when I said I was a cop; it's there now. And you're still sweating like a pig. Why?"

That floppy headshake again. He still wasn't making eye contact.

"Why'd you come here tonight? This particular place?"

"I needed gas . . ."

"Chalfont said he followed you for twenty miles. There must be an open service station closer to your house than this one. Late at night, rainy—why drive this far?"

Headshake.

"Has to be you didn't realize you were almost out of gas until you got on the road," I said. "Too distracted, maybe. Other things on your mind. Like something that happened tonight at your house, something you were afraid Chalfont might have seen if he'd been spying through windows."

I opened the Buick's back door. Seat and floor were both empty. Around to the rear, then, where I slid one of his keys into the trunk lock.

"No!" Barlow came stumbling back there, pawed at me, tried to push me away. I shouldered him aside instead, got the key turned and the trunk lid up.

The body stuffed inside was wrapped in a plastic sheet.

288

One pale arm lay exposed, the fingers bent and hooked. I pulled some of the sheet away, just enough for a brief look at the dead woman's face. Mottled, the tongue protruding and blackened. Strangled.

"Noreen Chalfont," I said. "Where were you taking her, Barlow? Some remote spot in the mountains for burial?"

He made a keening, hurt-animal sound. "Oh God, I didn't mean to kill her . . . we had an argument about the money and I lost my head, I didn't know what I was doing . . . I didn't mean to kill her . . ."

His legs quit supporting him; he sat down hard on the pavement with legs splayed out and head down. He didn't move after that, except for the heaving of his chest. His face was wetter than ever, a mingling now of sweat and drizzle and tears.

I looked over at the misted store window. That poor bastard in there, I thought. He wanted to make his wife pay for what she did, but he'll go to pieces when he finds out Barlow did the job for him.

I closed the trunk lid and stood there in the cold, waiting for the law.

Sometimes it happens like this, too.

You're in the wrong place at the wrong time, and still things work out all right. For some of the people involved, anyway.

About the Author

Shamus Award–winning author Bill Pronzini is the author of many mystery novels of true distinction, including *Blue Lonesome* and *A Wasteland of Strangers* among them. His "Nameless Detective" novels, popular now for more than three decades, are really chapters in the life of a working-class private investigator who lives in the spiritual epicenter of modern-day San Francisco, where Bill makes his home with his long-time partner, fellow mystery author Marcia Muller.